I Blame the Dimples

Jade Everhart

To Mara,

The girl who painstakingly read every update over 3 months.
You deserve so much more than the acknowledgement section.

CHAPTER 1

Lou

First days are the worst.

Take today for example: my first day of university.

Yup, you got it. I am that freshman carrying those boxes looking that awkward and feeling that out of place. And yes, I am aware that everyone is in the same boat as we embark on these so-called "best years of our lives," but trust me this isn't a boat anyone wants to be on. You know the famous scene where the titanic breaks in half and becomes a vertical death trap? That's it. That's the boat we are all on right now.

Rock meet bottom. Boat meet iceberg.

"Lou, quit dragging your feet and hurry up. We've got to get you unpacked in time for orientation," my mother huffs as she lugs two boxes through the narrow doorframe of my dorm room. Let's keep in mind the orientation she's referring to starts no sooner than four hours from now. My mother is nothing if not punctual.

As I step inside the room that will be my new home for the next eight months, one claustrophobic thought hits my mind: I hope the poor sucker who gets paid to sanitize these rooms gets paid well. On that note, please let someone get paid to sanitize these rooms. Because looking at the sad Styrofoam pad pressed tight against the far wall – am I supposed to *sleep* on that? – the random dents dotting the walls, and the discoloured splotches decorating the room from floor to ceiling, my faith in Taber University's health inspections is rapidly declining. If someone brought a blacklight in here, I have no doubt it would look like a crime scene.

Oh God, that mattress would probably glow entirely. *Ew.*

"Mom. I can't stay here. Think about how much DNA and germs are on that-

"You must be Lou! Hi, I'm your new roommate Stella." My pleas for a quick escape abruptly get cut off by a pretty blonde sticking her head through my doorway. My mother beams and shoves me forward.

"Nice to meet you Stella." Stumbling towards the stranger I'll soon be living with, I hold my hand out for a shake.

Stella maneuvers the rest of her body into the tight quarters and I take a second to survey my shockingly tiny new roommate. Barely coming up to my shoulder, Stella's height, or lack thereof, does nothing to lessen her dominant presence as she struts forward to take my hand. Rays of sunlight stream through the miniature corner window, and as the beams bounce of Stella's hair, I realize that my initial assumption of blonde was not totally correct. The shade is more of a pretty platinum with silver undertones, drawing a sharp contrast against the dark blue colour off Stella's eyes.

"Do you have to put up your hair to sit down?" I blurt out the question as Stella moves to shake my hand, her waist-length hair moving like a perfectly coiffed curtain behind her. You would think the length would be off putting but paired with her skin-tight black tank, camo joggers, and combat boots, this little G.I. Jane model somehow pulls it off.

She laughs, "No, although I'd be lying if I said I've never sat on it before. If you see me shifting in my seat in class, chances are I'm trying to release pieces stuck under my bum."

I smile in understanding. My own not-quite-curly yet not-quite-straight hair falls just below my shoulders but it still manages to get caught on every surface possible. So far, my trick to wear a ponytail most days has yet to fail me, but when it does, it will be 2007 Brittany all over again.

My description of Stella's small frame was accurate but only in terms of height. Tilting my head to get a better look at my roommate, who can't be more than five foot one in those combat boots, her frame isn't petite so much as lean with some seriously impressive arm definition. Picture a Malibu Barbie who decided to trade in her convertible sports car for a gym membership. Now, throw in some high-quality hair dye, a friendly smile, and eight months of living together and you've got my roommate.

When the silence stretches long enough to become uncomfortable, Stella finally wishes me luck with unpacking and heads back to her room. The door clicks gently behind her, and my mother turns to me, clapping her hands with glee.

"You've already made a friend! I told you university would be different from high school. And my goodness, isn't your roommate just adorable. I want to pack her up and take her home with me." My mother squeals and wraps me in a hug, already forgetting the fact Stella is one wall away and well within hearing distance.

"One conversation doesn't qualify as a friendship, mom." I sigh the words against her chest, the all-too familiar jaws of panic clamping around my neck.

"No, but it's a good start," my mother squeezes me tight and I will myself to grasp onto the shred of hope in the air.

University will be better than high school. It has to be.

Wes

First days are the best.

Fresh faces, new places, and an entire campus full of independent women who are ready to let loose? Say hello to the best year of my life.

Before you jump to conclusions, however, let me state for the record I am not your average playboy. Do I hookup with a different woman every week? Of course. I'm not a monk. But unlike some of my teammates, who undeniably fall into the hound dog territory, I respect women. Difficult to accept, I know, but let me put it to you this way: no matter what shape or size a woman is, her body deserves to be loved. And I, Wesley Williams, Taber Tigers' soon-to-be lacrosse rookie of the year, am more than happy to help her realize the pleasure waiting to be unlocked on the path to self-love.

So long as no emotions or promises are attached, I am like any other feminist devoted to positive body appreciation: give love and be loved. The only difference is my methods are a bit more hands on than your average spokesperson. But let me assure you, the same appreciation is achieved in the end.

I've been told my techniques are *very* satisfying.

Being signed to a varsity team means I moved in a couple weeks ago for pre-fall training camps. A benefit in my opinion, because now I've not only had the chance to explore campus and scout out the best hookup spots - hey, you can't play the field if you don't know all the field positions - but it also means I get to welcome the non-varsity students onto campus.

The first day jitters have long since worn off, but I've got to admit, watching the parking lot fill with students and parents jumping out to unload every box size possible gives me an unexpected thrill. Until now, I didn't notice how dormant the campus was with just the varsity teams in residence.

As I walk across Taber's impeccable lawns, the buzz of activity increases with every step closer to the freshmen dorms. The excitement in the air is so palpable I can't help but smile, absorbing some of the pulsing energy radiating from campus.

Taber University has woken once more.

Catching sight of someone struggling to carry three boxes stacked high, I quickly jog over.

"Hey there! Let me help you." I snatch the top two boxes off their load only to realize this person was balancing all three boxes on one hand because the other hand is preoccupied with a bag full of books and the handle of a suitcase.

I raise my eyebrows, meeting the startled grey eyes that appear from behind the stack of boxes I just removed.

"I hate doing more than one trip." The girl mumbles the words, shaking her golden-brown ponytail out of the way and ducking to pick up *another* bag with her almost-free hand. Jesus.

Remember when I mentioned that thing called strategy? Apparently this pack mule has never heard of it.

Shifting to tuck my own stack under one arm, I lean forward to pick up the bag the girl is struggling to get a grip on. Now, before we continue, let me just state for the record that what happens next is not from my lack of strategy, but from the evil genius of Sir Isaac Newton. Otherwise known as the force of gravity.

Intelligent science people would give you an equation for why my one-handed grab turns into a full-blown body slam due to boxes shifting, my momentum changing, etc. All I can tell you is one moment I'm saving a pretty freshman from a life of back pain, and the next I'm sprawled on top of Miss One Trip with cardboard boxes falling all around us.

CHAPTER 2

Lou

You have got to be kidding me.

When I told my mother I'd go get the rest of my stuff, and no I didn't need any help, I didn't realize how much was left to be carried in. An oversight on my part? Absolutely. But I had been managing just fine until some guy came along to "help" and now lies on top of me. Sure, it was nice of him to grab some of my boxes, and yes maybe I was struggling the teensiest bit before he came along, but at least I wasn't flat on my back with my underwear and God knows what else blowing around Taber's manicured lawns.

I try to squirm out from under this stranger, but my limbs won't move. He has successfully trapped me with his rock-hard body, which would be exciting except for the fact my lungs are slowly being crushed.

"Can you... get off?" Wheezing, I send up a prayer that the body-builder on top of me isn't unconscious. Based on the burning sensation in my chest, I've got two minutes, tops. Mind you, to suffocate under a muscular man is not the worst way to go. At least now I won't have to sleep on that dorm mattress.

The pros are starting to outweigh the cons here.

A breathless eternity goes by until finally the heavy-weight champion flops to the ground beside me with a groan. Now we look like two kids making snow angels with my fallen clothes on the front lawn of the residence building. For all my neighbours to see.

Killing it already, Lou.

Having successfully restored oxygen to my diaphragm, I scramble to my feet and begin wildly snatching the items closest to me. The good news is none of the boxes broke in the tackle, the bad news is my lacy thongs *and* granny panties are casually lying in a halo around the guy still on the ground. Not sure if his immobilization or his proximity to my cheek-covering knickers is more concerning.

Arguably the latter.

"Whoa." The stranger slowly sits up and looks around, blinking at my hasty clothing retrieval. Taking a quick look at him, I stifle a groan at his tussled midnight-coloured hair. Guys might be able to pull off the rumpled, just-took-a-quick-tumble-and-landed-flat-on-my-ass look, but there's no way I came out of this looking half as good. Especially considering I was the one plastered against the ground.

Consciously reaching up to touch what's left of my ponytail, I sigh when I feel half of it hanging loose. Oh, and now there's grass falling out.

Have I said how much I love first days?

"Do you think anyone got a video of that? We just ate shit."

My attention snaps back to the laughing stranger who'd nearly been the cause of my untimely asphyxiation and is currently the cause of my social destruction. Somewhere during my hasty snatch-and-grab system, Mr. Helpful got up from the ground and now stands directly in front of me, his shadow throwing shade over my face as I glare up at him.

"I was a little busy being tackled to the ground to notice." I huff, trying not to drop the bundle in my arms as I register the level of hotness standing before me. The darkness of his hair and thick eyebrows offset sparkling green eyes (nope, didn't know eyes could sparkle either), while the boyish grin taking up his face only gets cuter when dimples pop out on either side. Cursing my generation for its obsession with straight teeth, I also note the perfect, glistening white alignment of his smile.

From what I can tell, the only indication of our fall are the few strands of dark hair sticking a little too far out for the casual messy look. Otherwise, this six-foot bodybuilder looks untouched.

I'm annoyed at this walking toothpaste commercial already, and that's before he opens his mouth.

"I think the words you're looking for are thank you." He smirks in my direction before bending to grab the lacy thong that fell from my grasp.

I stare at him in disbelief, words spluttering out before I have a chance to think, "I'm supposed to thank you for... bodychecking me? Dumping all my clothes on the ground? No, wait. I got it. Thank you for the full body suffocation. I really appreciate it."

I snatch the thong from his hands and dump my bundle into a now-empty box.

"Hey, if you didn't decide to become the world's worst pack mule we could have easily made it to your dorm, which would have been entirely thanks to me swooping in to save the day. I can't remember, did I or didn't I grab two boxes off your initial load?" He taps his chin in mock consideration, then uses his finger to shoot me with an imaginary gun. "That's right, I did. Guess that means it's 1 point for me and none for Miss One Trip."

Logic has never been so lacking.

Pulling my brows into a scowl, I open my mouth to list all the ways that argument made no sense when a voice rings out over the crowd.

"Lou! There you are, I was starting to get worried. Did you have problems finding the car?" Saved from answering the idiot in front of me, I turn to see my mother heading our way. The guy follows my turn and lets out a low whistle.

"Now there's a woman who only gets better with age." Dimples flash at me as he hastily scoops the box from my arms and saunters over to introduce himself.

I would say I'm disgusted, but I really can't blame the guy. Even from a familial perspective, I am well aware my mother is an attractive woman. Her chestnut-coloured hair hangs in loose ringlets around a heart shaped face, and even though she's put on a few pounds over the years, she wears them well. I got a bit of my mother's curves, though not enough to hit the curvy status. And other than the average five-six height, my light grey eyes are the only thing I inherited from my bombshell of a mother. Not to say my father is any less attractive, the two of my parents make a striking pair for sure, but his towering six-two frame and pin straight blond hair leave me with genetic features that don't seem to fit any category.

Not blonde but not brunette either. Not tall but not short. Eyes that aren't blue, green, or brown.

The sad fact of the matter is I am the embodiment of an in-between line: the surface area that is always there but doesn't truly belong anywhere.

"You must be Lou's older sister. Wes Williams, at your service." I snap back to the present as Wes gives my mother a shit-eating grin and shakes the box he stole from me.

An attempt to prove his helpfulness, perhaps?

My mother laughs and slaps his box-carrying arms good-naturally, "Your charms won't work on me, young man. Thank you for helping my daughter with her things. She hates doing more than one trip to unload."

Wes shakes his head at the revelation.

"Well ma'am, I guess it was a good thing I happened to be walking by." He shoots me a wink and my scowl grows deeper.

***

I will never admit it out loud, but Wes ended up being a lot of help. The extra set of hands made it so the three of us emptied the car without difficulty. And as much as it pains me to admit, Wes distracting my mother with his charms definitely worked in my favour. He single-handily brought her stress levels down from a tense twelve to an easier eight.

Setting the last box down on my questionable sleeping arrangements, Wes gives me a nod and bends to kiss the back of my mother's hand with a flourish.

"It has been an honour making your acquaintance, Mrs. Mackenzie. Have a safe drive home and I'll make sure Lou settles in nicely here at Taber. Speaking of which..." He whirls around and thrusts his phone towards me, "Put your number in. The lacrosse team is throwing a party tonight, I'll text you the details."

Being careful not to accidentally brush his fingers, I gingerly take the phone from his hand and type my number in. After tucking it back into his pocket, Wes bids us a farewell, and with one last flash of his dimples, he heads out.

I exhale a breath I hadn't realized I'd been holding. My mother, meanwhile, cannot contain her excitement. She flits around the room, folding clothes and putting them in drawers while talking nonstop about her new best friend.

"Oh, Lou. Wasn't that boy lovely?! It was so sweet of him to help us carry in your boxes. My goodness, did you see those dimples? And to think he's also a varsity athlete. What a dedicated boy! Imagine trying to juggle all that training *and* classes..." I tune her out, turning my attention to unpacking and doing my best to ignore the knot growing in my stomach.

The discomfort isn't from the interaction with Wes, funny enough he made me feel comfortable for the first time today, but rather it's the knowledge that in a few short hours my mother will leave and I'll be left to fend for myself. Thanks to the confident rookie, I already feel more welcome at Taber than I ever did at Brooks Academy, but a sole acquaintance isn't enough to set the tone for my university experience. It's time to put myself out there, face my insecurities, and plunge into the deep end.

Let's hope this time I come up swimming.

CHAPTER 3

Wes

This party is *bumping*.

Gripping a red solo cup in each hand, I hold them high above my head as I weave through the throng of people milling around our team captain's living room. Besides the school's lacrosse legend, Maurice O'Brien aka Mighty Mo, Cody Ellsworth is the only sophomore ever to be nominated as team captain. Cody was lucky enough to play on the same field as Mo during his final varsity season last year, and just like the all-star forward player who broke the school's undefeated record with a fifth consecutive championship banner, Cody plans to lead the team to victory once again this season.

The rookie-of-the-year award is typically given to offensive players or goal keepers, but Cody's outstanding performance as a defenseman managed to win him the title last year. And as you probably guessed, it's the same trophy Mo won his freshman year. Two outstanding rookies, two sophomore team captains. A recipe for success and one I plan to see through.

Tucking the beers close to my chest, I duck past a groping session and arrive at my destination. I hand one of the beers to Taber's freshman goalie, otherwise known as Nico Montez, or as I like to think of him, best friend since second grade. He nods in the direction of the couple fumbling against the wall.

"I think we can check off Hunter's virginity after tonight."

I snort into my drink while Nico holds up his beer in cheer. Other than Nico and me, Hunter is the other newest addition to the team. An awkward but genuinely nice guy, Hunter never had a girlfriend during high school and claims the reason he's still holding his v-card is because he's not into hookups. So, unless he met that voluptuous redhead sometime before tonight, his attitude towards hookups has changed.

Ah, nothing like freshmen year to break people out of their comfort zones.

"Taber truly is an educational institution. The place where horny men and women come together to experiment, learn, and grow." I place the solo cup against my heart in prayer to the alcohol-infused laws of attraction.

Nico laughs and shakes his head, "Glad to see your afternoon tumble didn't affect your love of theatrics."

I grin, "Hey, someone's got to intimidate your boyfriend contenders. If they don't have my flair, they don't stand a chance."

Nico rolls his eyes, "That was one time. How was I to know Brad's ego wouldn't be able to stand being your understudy for the sixth-grade play?"

"The fact his name was Brad should have been the first clue." I chuckle at the memory.

Our school's sixth-grade spring drama production was a sad re-enactment of The Pirates of the Caribbean, and I wanted to be Jack

Sparrow. The casting roles for our middle school production was voted by our fellow students, so to increase my chances of winning, I started the rumour that I was the descendant of Blackbeard and had real pirate blood coursing through my veins. The funny part is I ended up winning the part thanks to my swash-buckling sword skills rather than fear of Blackbeard's revenge. The fact half the sixth form had a crush on me – Nico can confirm – probably helped as well.

Anyways, long story short, the infamous Bradley never forgave me for stealing his pre-pubescent spotlight, and Nico was cut off by association.

It was a true, tween tragedy. Shakespeare would have been proud.

"I sure hope Hunter isn't the only rookie getting action tonight." The man of the hour joins us with a mop and bucket in tow. Only coming up to my chin, what Cody lacks in height he more than makes up for in width. The guy is built like a brickhouse. It's no wonder the opposing teams can't get by his defence line.

"Aw Cap, the night is still young. Nico and I are just letting the other boys have a taste before we embark on the main course." I wiggle my eyebrows suggestively and Cody laughs.

"You're a confident one, Wes. I'll give you that."

"You know it. Need any help with clean up duty?" I gesture towards the mop, praying he won't take me up on the offer. Drunk people are the worst to clean up after.

"Nah, you boys have fun. I'm making the rounds and figured I'd best be prepared. Expect the unexpected and all that." Cody sighs, taking note of a shirtless Hunter and his partner who doesn't look far behind in the strip tease.

"I better send those two somewhere private. Enjoy the main course boys."

Nico and I raise our plastic cups in toast as our captain leaves to eliminate Hunter's pending lawsuit for public indecency.

"Hey, what happened to that girl you bulldozed this afternoon? I thought you'd have introduced me to your latest victim by now." Nico glances around the packed room, obviously forgetting he has no clue what this girl looks like.

I shrug, "I texted Lou the address but never heard back. She probably couldn't handle my dashing good looks twice in one day."

Nico snorts, "More like she's suffering from a mild concussion. You aren't exactly light my friend."

"Hey, I've never had any complaints from ladies before. I do my best work on top."

Cocking his head to the side, Nico smirks at me over his beer, "Not sure a body slam onto the front lawn is your best work, but I admire the effort."

I raise my cup in acknowledgment, shifting my gaze around the crowded room to see if Lou decided to make a late appearance.

Let's get one thing straight: I am not the type of guy who searches the crowd for a girl. Not that I'm against the romantic notion, it's just there are so many options that I've never understood how one person's absence could make such a difference. Especially if that person is attractive and of the opposite sex.

Here's my reasoning: why pine after one girl when there are plenty of other sexy, horny women who are more than happy to make my acquaintance? Exactly. It's a rhetorical question.

So, the fact that I am currently scanning the crowd for a particular grey-eyed freshman shows my integrity. I said I'd help the MILF's daughter settle in, and that's exactly what I plan to do.

Lou's absence is strangely... irritating. Could be I'm still butt-sore from being ghosted - first time ever - but I sensed the beginning of a friendship this afternoon. The fact she left me on read feels like a challenge. And when I set my mind to something, I achieve it. Whether it's winning the role of Jack Sparrow in sixth grade, making it on Taber's lacrosse team, or befriending the girl I tackled this afternoon, I always accomplish my goals.

Whether Miss One Trip knows it or not, she has set down a challenge. And it is not one I am about to lose.

Making eye contact with a gorgeous foreign exchange student, I immediately send dimples her way. The slanted eyes, sleek dark hair, and spectacular rack are all I need to follow her beckoning finger across the room.

Smiling coyly, all thoughts of Lou vanish from my mind as the Asian Goddess takes my hand and leads me to the nearest cloakroom. No names, no numbers, no promises.

Remember what I said about options?

Lou

I bailed on Wes' party.

I know, I know. Why would a girl who struggles to make friends turn down a perfectly good opportunity to make connections? The answer is pathetically simple.

The reason I struggle to make friends is because I am terrified of putting myself out there. And yes, I am aware that everyone is scared of wandering outside their comfort zone, but for me it's different. *I* am different.

No matter what group or club I try to join, I just never seem to... click with anyone. That sense of relief that comes with knowing you're among your people? I've never felt it. I've never even had people who I would consider to be my people.

In high school, I lost any connection I had with the few girls I grew up with when our lives split into the designated cliques. Some of them joined sport teams, others band assembly, and a couple even managed to hit the popular status. As for me, well, I had no clique. I was the loner of the loners. High school became three years of keeping my head down and making it through one day at a time.

Does any of this excuse my ghosting of Wes? No, it does not. But to be fair, he only texted me the address, so I'm guessing it was a copy-and-paste effort for all his contacts. I have no doubt my absence will go unnoticed.

To give myself some credit, I did *consider* going. For about two minutes until I realized Stella wasn't home and there was no way I was knocking on my neighbour's door to see if they wanted to be my calvary. Not exactly the first impression I wanted to make.

So that's how I end up spending my first evening of university alone in my room, breaking down the last few boxes, and playing the air guitar to Green Day. It's not so bad until the last piece of cardboard gets thrown away and suddenly it's just me and Billie's vocal cords. I sigh, flopping on my bed – heavily sanitized, don't worry – and stare at my new, patchy ceiling.

It's the down moments that are the worst. When you have places to go and moving boxes to break, your mind is occupied, you have a purpose and an activity that takes up your focus. But when that activity is finished, and you're left with just your thoughts for company, that's when the heaviness sinks in.

I contemplate calling my mother to kill time but immediately shoot down the idea. I don't want to her to be worried I'm calling five hours into my residence experience. Plus, I already know she would question my choice to stay home tonight, which for the record, I am perfectly content with.

American Idiot fades into Basket Case, and I smile, feeling relieved someone else is being the melodramatic fool.

I hear the exterior door bang open, and I scurry over to peek my head out. Mine and Stella's rooms are connected through the living room, so to get to the actual dorm door, we have to walk past two worn couches facing an ancient television set. There's a microwave across from the living area, which I'm assuming classifies itself as the kitchen, and our shared bathroom juts out next to our front door. The bathroom consists of one toilet and the tiniest shower ever made, so if I ever want to shave my legs again, I am going to have to increase my flexibility. Drastically.

My attention turns to my roommate, who is slumped against the closed door, eyes closed and looking utterly exhausted. I shuffle out of my room and awkwardly clear my throat.

"Uh, Stella? Are you okay?"

Startled, she lifts her head and looks around the room. Spotting me, a tired smile creeps along her face, "Don't mind me, Lou. How has your evening been?"

"It's been... good. Finished unpacking." I gesture towards my room, mentally bracing myself for Stella's questions as to why I'm not out partying my first night at university.

She smiles, "Well, I think this TV is older than my grandpa but I'm going to try and get some Netflix playing. Do you want to join me?"

Her response takes me by surprise. Where are the accusations of not putting myself out there? Of being lame for staying home instead of going out?

"I would love to." I hesitantly sit down on one of the couches – should probably sanitize these too – as Stella crouches in front of the dinosaur technology. After a few minutes of tinkering, she pumps her fist in victory, and tosses me the remote.

"Go ahead, pick our movie. I have a feeling there will be a lot of movie nights this year, so we can take turns choosing." She throws me a wink and jogs to her room.

I slowly scroll through the streaming options, second guessing each one I stop on. I can't remember the last time I had a movie night with a non-family member, and suddenly choosing the right movie has never felt so important.

Stella rejoins me in sweats and a sweatshirt, her small frame all but disappearing under the baggy clothes.

"Ooh, excellent choice! This is one of my favourites." I look at the screen and smile despite my nerves. Tonight's movie is none other than *Despicable Me*. I click play and toss the remote on the ground, willing my anxiety to calm down.

Stella plops herself down right beside me, and I jolt in surprise. She could have had an entire couch to herself, yet she chose to snuggle up next to me, a complete stranger. Her long hair brushes my arm as she makes herself comfortable, casually throwing a blanket over our legs as if we didn't just meet a few hours ago.

I marvel at Stella's easy demeanour, one that doesn't reflect some-one who is experiencing her first friend hangout in three years. Willing my body to follow her lead, I shuffle down on the couch and soon laughter fills the room as Gru and his minions' villainous exploits unfold on-screen.

My nervousness from earlier all but dissipates as the screen turns to credits and Stella snatches the remote from the ground, pressing play on the sequel before I can think of going to bed. A foreign feeling fills my chest, and it takes me a moment to identify what it is: excitement. Excitement that I may have found a new friend, and maybe, just maybe, a dash of excitement for the year ahead.

Because as far as first days go, this one didn't turn out so bad.

CHAPTER 4

Wes

Sweat drips down my neck as I sprint across the field.

I would say we are finishing practice with a friendly rally but considering all three rookies got put on the same team, it feels more like a test than anything. Seeing Cody's defence line closing in on Hunter's breakaway, I quickly swerve right, raising my stick to signal a pass. Without hesitation, Hunter tosses me the ball and I catch it easily in my stick's mesh netting. Swivelling and putting all my power into my throwing arm, I hurl the ball as hard as I can towards the net, holding my breath until I see it glide past the goalie's outstretched hand.

My team breaks into cheer and Cody runs up to slap me on the back, "Keep that up and we might win some games this year."

Turning to address the rest of the team, our team captain waves everyone in, "Excellent hustle today, boys. Both teams did great but I'm afraid a deal's a deal." Groans go up from the guys wearing blue jerseys.

"Red team can hit the showers, blue team you're on clean up duty. Pack up the equipment and don't forget the 100 push ups." Taking a second to hand out a round of high fives, I split off from the red batch and circle back to help the losing team pack up.

"Wes, I didn't know you were coloured blind. The jersey on your back means you're clear to go." Cody points to the group of guys heading towards the showers.

I shrug, continuing to bag lacrosse sticks. "Doesn't matter what side I'm on, Cap. If my teammates lose, I do too." Cody looks at me for a moment then nods.

"In that case, don't forget the push ups." I give him a salute, and with a laugh, my team captain wanders over to help dissemble the nets.

ele

Shaking wet hair out of my eyes, I walk out of the men's locker room and spot none other than the girl who ghosted me scurrying down the hall, arms teetering with books.

"Lou! Hey, I was wondering when I'd seen you again. Makes it a little more challenging when I'm left on read." Quickening my pace to catch up, I shoot her a grin to let her know I'm joking.

Lou winces, her shockingly pretty eyes meeting mine, "Sorry about that. I was pretty tired... and didn't want to get knocked down for a second time that day."

She gives me a hesitant smile and I bark out a laugh, pleased she's just as snarky as I remember.

"Hey, anytime you want to test the limitations of gravity with a strong, independent man, you know where to find me." I shoot her a wink and get an eye roll in return.

"Did you really just describe yourself as an *independent* man?"

"Sure did. Although I accept other adjectives as well. Panty-dropping sexy. Built to perfection. Irresistibly charming. Whichever you prefer."

"Noticed you left incredibly modest off that list." Lou shifts the books in her arms, and one topples out of the pile.

"Hey, even a mere mortal like myself understands we all have weaknesses. The trick is knowing what they are and using them to your advantage." Noting the confusion on Lou's face, I snatch the book off the ground and hold it out as proof.

"Take your inability to carry normal amounts, for instance. You managed to get the attention *and* number of the best-looking freshman on campus." Carefully placing the fallen book back on her pile, my lips tug into a smirk, "I'd say that's using it to your advantage."

A fiery glint lights up Lou's eyes, and suddenly I can see different shades of grey swirling around her pupil, "Last time I checked, it was *you* who offered to help yesterday and you got *my* number while flirting with my mother."

Looking down at Lou's slight frame, an unconventional beauty are the words that come to mind. Her nose is a touch on the small side, the placement of her misty eyes slightly too wide, and her bottom lip is a little too full for the top one. Yet there's something inexplicably beautiful about the girl standing in front of me.

Maybe it's her ability to ghost me.

"Exactly my point. Your weakness resulted in me putting in all the effort. A job well done Miss Trip." My grin grows wider as Lou huffs, her irritation levels visibly climbing.

"Do *not* call me that. And your inability to use logic in an argument leaves me with nothing else to say." Spinning on her heel, she storms in the opposite direction.

Unable to help myself, I cup my hands around my mouth and make one last parting shot to her departing figure.

"Any chance you could give me your mom's number?"

Lou

The nerve of that guy. I mean really.

Best-looking freshman on campus? Come on. So maybe the dark hair, emerald eyes, and dimples would place him in the top ten. But *best?* Please. The dimples are more annoying than anything.

Barely managing to keep the stack in my arms from toppling over, I hurry across campus, heading back to my dorm. I agreed to accompany Stella to the opening session of rush week this afternoon, and it's not exactly something I'm looking forward to.

Rush week happens every fall with the goal to convince freshmen that the perfect university experience is one club membership away. Just like the movies, rush week gives socially awkward students like me the chance to try something new and potentially make lifelong friends in the process. Or so they say.

As of right now, the sheer thought of succumbing to Taber's social marketing strategies is enough to make my stomach cramp up in knots. Joining a club means another first day full of new faces. It means my outsider status coming back to haunt me once more, and I'm not sure I'm ready for that.

Dread pricks my skin as I consider the sickening possibility of Stella witnessing my inability to fit in anywhere. The friendship I've forged with my roommate in the last 48 hours has quickly become my most prized possession. It's been three long years since I've called anyone my friend, so I don't want to risk this one by following the freshman status quo.

Making up my mind that I will not, in fact, be joining any clubs this afternoon, I find I can breathe easily again. Crisis averted.

Uncomfortably shifting the books in my arms for the tenth time, I somehow manage not to drop a single one. I take a glance around, instantly slowing my hasty march to a brisk walk as the scenery around me takes a turn for the better.

Instead of walking through the winding hallways and past the school cafeteria, I decided to take a shortcut outside. It seems as though my shortcut led me to a courtyard of some sort, as the concrete beneath my feet turns into cobblestones that follow an explosion of flora down the pretty path. Taber must have a garden club because the rows of vibrant, blooming flowers display a level of precision and care I have never seen before. Fall-coloured aspen trees line the edges of the path, creating a wall of seclusion from the busy bustle of the university. Stone benches jut out every few feet, and I spot a couple of them occupied by students reading.

It's so... peaceful. I love it.

Making a silent promise to myself to return to this slice of tranquility, I take one last look at the breathtaking flowers, and quicken my pace to go meet my roommate.

ell

"I can't believe the two of you keep bumping into each other! I swear other than you, who I live with, so it doesn't count, I haven't seen any of my friends who live on campus." Having filled Stella in on my box collision with Wes yesterday, she's now up to speed.

"Ya, well, every time I see Wes my personal belongings somehow find their way to the ground." I solemnly shake my head, mentally cursing my inability to carry normal quantities like a normal person.

"You better be careful, Lou. If this guy is as sexy as you say he is, then the next personal item that falls to the ground might be your panties."

My jaw drops, "Whoa, whoa, *whoa*. Let's backtrack here. I most certainly did not call Wes sexy. I said he has dimples and knows how to use them. That's it, that's all. Definitely no sexy in that description."

I shudder in mock horror while Stella bursts out laughing.

"Honey, if a man has the confidence to not only use his dimples but use them effectively? That right there is the definition of sexy. Based on your description, Urban Dictionary probably has a picture of Wes next to the definition of sex appeal." Stella claps her hands with glee and I focus on not blushing. Now I can't stop picturing those stupid dimples and crap if they aren't the teensiest bit sexy.

Hasty to change topics, I use the age-old deflection technique: compliments.

"I really like what you did with your hair today, Stella."

Working like a charm, my roommate beams and proceeds to give me a list of all the braiding styles she can do. I wasn't lying with the compliment, her platinum mane looks extra gorgeous today. The French braid running along the top right-side ends with an invisible elastic, the rest of it flowing freely down to the tip of her white cargo pants. This girl must own every style of black tank top ever made, because the top she's sporting today is identical to the one from move-in day except for the criss-cross straps going down the back.

If I was impressed by Stella's arm definition, I am in awe of her sculpted back. You can't tell where my arms connect to my shoulders, let alone have a map of gym-made markers sectioning off each muscle group in my back. I feel exhausted just looking at it.

Taking a look at my own outfit choice, I am pleased I went with an oversized Blink-182 concert t-shirt. All back and shoulders are covered, so I don't need to worry about looking like a limp noodle next to my fitness model roommate. The mom jeans my shirt is tucked into were once blue, but now can only be described as distressed. They were originally frayed back in tenth grade, but after many years of use, the frays became... well, holes. Hence why I call these my favourite pair of "ripped" jeans.

My self-assessment comes to an abrupt halt when we reach the foyer. I thought movies were prone to exaggeration but it turns out Taber University likes to go even bigger. And by bigger, I mean brighter. As in hundreds of different colour schemes assaulting my vision. Organized in columns, rows and rows of booths line the foyer, each with their own explosion of neon banners and posters representing some sort of club theme.

At least that's what I think is going on. The noise level has hit a point where it might be affecting my visual discernment.

Somehow, I manage to hear Stella squeal over the deafening noise. What my roommate lacks in height, she more than makes up for in energy. I feel small hands grab my arm and the next thing I know, I'm being dragged to the booth in the farthest corner.

Up close, it's a bit easier to figure out the individual themes. This one appears to be a cannabis club, with cartoon leaves winking at me from bright green posters. There's only one guy working the booth and he throws us the peace sign.

"Ready to join the hotbox gang? Been dying to unleash your inner pothead? No problem my dudes. Just leave your email and I'll send you the addy for our weekly doobie break."

Biting my lip to keep from laughing, I sneak a glance at Stella who unsubtly coughs into her hand, "So, um, the gang just meets up and gets high together once a week? No meetings or real... purpose to this club?"

We wait a good five seconds for the doobie master to rabidly shake his blond locks back and forth. Not sure if that's a no, or if he's trying to find the answer buried deep in his skull.

"Homies, you've got this all wrong. Mary Jane *is* the purpose of this club. Uni gets hella stressful, and when you need a quick trip, company with fellow hash lovers only makes it *better*." Abruptly shoving his chair back, our new friend attempts to stand up on the chair but wisely wobbles back to the ground. He turns a bloodshot gaze on us, placing a hand over his heart.

"CanDoobies For Life isn't about *us*. It's about smoking for those who *can't*. Like our poor brothers down in the US of A. Doobies aren't even *legal* down there for everyone. Can you imagine? Fucking cruel, man. Fucking cruel."

Barely holding it together, Stella nods in sympathy. "That is unfortunate. Well, we best be going, but thank you for your time, uh..."

"Chaz. Sick t-shirt by the way. Blink rocks." Throwing me another peace sign, I give Chaz a feeble thumbs up in return.

A fresh wave of students descends upon the CanDoobies booth, and we make our escape just as Chaz begins his welcoming spiel once more, "Looking for a good-time high? Need a doobie brother or two? Just leave your email here..."

"Oh. My. God." Stella claps a hand over her mouth as we pull away from the booth.

"Did you see him trying to stand on that chair? I thought we'd have to call the emergency help line." I bend over, clutching my stomach in laughter.

"Forget the chair. How about the fact he calls himself Chaz? His real name is probably Chase but he decided to shorten it and add z, so it looks cooler." The attempt to straighten myself goes out the window as another wave of laughter hits me. Wiping tears from my eyes, I fan my face to cool my cheeks down.

"We've already hit the highest booth. It's a downhill trip from here." Stella shakes her head at my terrible pun and links her arm through mine.

Watching the endless mass weave through booths, you wouldn't think Taber is one of Alberta's smallest universities. Students of all ages are streaming in from every direction, immediately becoming part of the surrounding chaos. Chatter and laughter fill the air, as if the university itself has sprung to life and hums in tune with the student body.

Overwhelming? One hundred percent. Yet, strangely fascinating at the same time. Boys and girls of all shapes and sizes bounce from table to table, making conversation and connections with complete strangers. The dread from earlier feels present but faded. I think the neon overload and club-joining atmosphere has naturally released some of my tension.

It could also be that everyone seems so... comfortable in their own skin. A foreign concept to me, but one that warms the heart to see.

While I manage to avoid leaving my email at any of the booths we've looked at so far, Stella has somehow signed up for every single one. Well, with the one exception of Chaz's booth.

If I'm being honest, most of the clubs seem interesting, if not fun, and if I wasn't so paranoid Taber will turn into a re-enactment of high school, I would probably would sign up for a couple of them. Well, I can say with absolute certainty that if I wasn't so anxious, I definitely would have left my email at the Punk Rockers booth.

Giving a shoutout for anyone with a love for alternative music, the booth features monthly get-togethers where live music, trivia games, and overall audience participation are encouraged. The spokesperson working the booth even had on the same Blink t-shirt as me. If I was a believer in signs, that would have been my cue to join. Yet, even after Stella wrote down her email and followed them on social media, I couldn't bring myself to do the same.

High school taught me one thing and one thing only: I don't belong. So, there's no point in signing myself up for disappointment in hope this one might be different. Because it won't be. I've been down this road before and it always ends the same way.

Despite my commitment to avoid all club commitments, I'm still thinking about the Punk Rockers four booths down. Hard not to, when I'm doing my best not to grimace at the swing dance poster in front of me. Do people actually sign up for this?

To my utmost horror, Stella throws her name down for this one as well, oblivious to the future embarrassment she will be facing. I gawk at her, watching as she happily turns to me and tries for the tenth time to convince me to join.

"You've got to give this one a try, Lou. Think about it, we could be partners! Bet I could easily swing you from hip to hip." Stella mimics the motion, tossing an invisible person from one hip to the next. Applause breaks out from the freshmen a few tables over and Stella drops into a bow for her admirers. I'm still staring at her in horror when she takes my hand and leads me to the corner where the line for free snacks snakes around the corner.

"Alright roomie, what's your deal? We've been here over an hour, and you haven't written your email down once..."

"Stella? Hey, I thought that was you."

I'm saved from interrogation when a stocky blonde guy wanders over from the snack line. When student budgets are present, there will always be a line when it comes to free food.

"Oh hey, Cody. I didn't see you at the gym this morning. Second day and already slacking, huh?" Her tone is teasing but the glint in her eyes doesn't look so friendly. Feeling like I've walked into the middle of something, I shift awkwardly from side-to-side as the gym offender shrugs and smiles in response.

"Practice started earlier today and I wanted to check out the new rookies. I would have skipped if I knew my absence would bother you so much."

Stella laughs, the spell seemly broken as she playfully slaps his arm. I try not to stare at Cody's insanely broad shoulders, which give the term a mountain of a man a whole new meaning. His arms aren't any smaller, and the veins running down his forearms attest to that fact. If Hugh Jackman was four inches shorter, two inches wider, sported a blonde fauxhawk, and lost the accent, Cody would be a shoo-in for his next movie.

"Cody, meet my room-

"TRIP!" I groan as familiar tussled dark hair and sparkling green eyes come into view, "I almost didn't recognize you without bags, books, or boxes weighing you down." Throwing me a wink, Wes saunters over to give Cody a side bro hug.

"Cody, this is my good friend Trip. I make her a little nervous, so she has a tendency to drop things around me."

I grumble under my breath, purposefully ignoring the dimpled grin sent my way. Turning his attention to the one person he hasn't met yet, Wes turns towards Stella and sweeps into an extravagant bow, "And who might be this flawless friend of Trip's? Milady, it is my greatest pleasure."

I wouldn't have pegged Wes as a Duke from the eighteenth century, yet here we are.

My roommate giggles and ducks into a curtsy, "I'm Stella. You must be Wes. *Trip* has told me so much about you." Seeing my glare, she blows me a kiss.

Cody, who'd been silently watching the exchange up to this point, sticks out his hand, "Nice to meet you, Trip."

Gritting my teeth, I shake his hand. In my peripheral, I can see Stella biting her lip trying not to laugh. I turn my volatile stare onto Wes, but before any permanent damage can occur, Cody takes control of the conversation.

"So, have you ladies found any clubs to join?" I instinctively stiffen, knowing what's about to come.

"We sure have! Well, I've signed up for a few. My roommate is a little pickier with who she hands her email out to." Cody chuckles and his response sends buried emotions rushing to the surface.

Blinking rapidly, I duck my head and stare at my converse, willing the burning sensation to fade. Oblivious to my melodramatics, Stella and Cody continue to chat away. I take a few deep breaths, trying to compose myself.

When I finally look up, a pair of sparkling emeralds stare back at me.

Without a word, Wes takes my hand and leads me away from the gym duo. I swallow thickly, embarrassed he witnessed my emotional moment. Opening my mouth to apologize, I don't get the chance to say anything before Wes performs his most shocking charade yet.

He pulls me into a hug.

Wes

I didn't plan on hugging Lou, but damn if it doesn't feel right.

Seeing her eyes fill up with tears seconds earlier just about broke my heart. Unlike most guys I know, crying girls don't freak me out, and I don't do the whole pretend-I-didn't-see-anything act. Dealing with my sister's hormones over the years gave me a sixth sense for when people of the opposite sex need comforting. Sounds creepy, but I promise it's strictly platonic.

For two painful seconds, Lou remains stiff in my arms before folding herself into my embrace. Was I worried she would pull away and march off? Not in the slightest. I am the world's greatest hugger and that's before you take my incredible physique into consideration. Human form of catnip, at your service.

Resting my chin atop Lou's head, I'm suddenly distracted by the amazing smell coming from her hair. It's not fruity exactly... I got it. It's coconut with a touch of vanilla.

Shit. I've just found my new favourite scent.

Inhaling Lou's hair like it's a line of cocaine, I'm suddenly aware of two perky breasts pressing against my chest. She hasn't made a move to pull away, but suddenly the lack of space between us is getting a little too comfortable. I loosen my hold and take a couple of steps back, not wanting to ruin the moment with a surprise semi.

See? Strictly platonic.

Lou blinks at me as a pink hue tinges her cheeks, "I'm so sorry, I just... thank you. I really needed that."

The surprise in her eyes when I don't make a smart-ass comment is enough to make me feel bad.

"Anytime. I mean it. University is a tough time for everyone, don't let the partying and club memberships fool you." My words hit their mark and Lou visibly relaxes, dropping her shoulders and nodding slowly.

"You seem to be doing okay. With adjusting, I mean. I've never seen you as anything other than ridiculously confident."

I smile, beckoning her closer, "I'm going to let you in on a little secret, Trip. Wait, is it okay if we keep the nickname?"

When in doubt, always go for the consent route. In my experience, 98% of the time it actually increases your chances of success.

Hey, consent is sexy. You heard it here first.

With an eyeroll, Trip nods her approval and adds another tally to my consensual scoreboard.

"Alright, I'm going to let you in on a little secret, Trip. You can be whoever you want to be." I say the last part slowly, allowing time for digestion.

"I know that. That's why we're all here. To study, graduate with a degree, then go on and pursue whatever we want to do." I shake my head, remaining patient with my padawan.

"Listen carefully. Here, at Taber University, you can be whoever you want to be. You can be Lou, you can be Trip, you can be any version of yourself you can imagine. Think of it as a clean slate. No one knows you and no one knows who you used to be. All of us are at Taber to figure out who we *want* to be, and that's why most people go buck wild their first year. Because they want to try new things, test the limit to see what works and what doesn't. Basically, the next four years are a test drive to figure out what person you want to be moving forward."

Fuck. Someone call me Hamlet because if that wasn't a glorious monologue, I don't know what is.

Lou chews on her bottom lip, undoubtedly overwhelmed by my display of philosophical wisdom. I would make a fantastic Jedi.

"I've never thought of it that way, but you're right."

I tilt my head, giving her a look of complete innocence, "Sorry, I missed that last part. Would you mind repeating that?"

Lou smirks, "Nice try, Wes."

Note to self: the innocent face needs some work.

CHAPTER 5

Lou

You can be whoever you want to be.

Wes' words echo in my mind as Stella and I make our way round the remaining booths. As dumb as it sounds, his simple concept has never once crossed my mind. After high school's isolation, I simply resigned myself to the fact that I will always be the one who doesn't fit in. But what if that person was simply the high school version of myself? What if there is a version of myself who finally finds her group? A version of myself who finally finds her people?

The thought sparks a light in my chest and suddenly I'm looking at the students bustling around me in a whole different light. Instead of tacky posters and students dividing into cliques and clubs, a sea of multi-faceted individuals take their place. Individuals, who like Stella, aren't subjecting themselves to one sole membership.

I can't believe I never noticed this before.

Looking across the booths, I see a girl with brown braids and glasses chatting amiably with a sorority spokesperson. The Delta member is a gorgeous, plus-sized black girl, whose cackle can be heard from across the room. From my vantage point, the two girls look like polar opposites in looks and personalities, yet the one with braids happily throws her email down and snags a brochure on the way out. Had this been high school, there is no way either party would have spoken to the other, let alone been Greek sisters.

As Stella and I finish our last booth, a thread of fear weaves inside me. Grabbing my roommate's hand to stop her from heading to the exit, I fretfully ask my new friend a favour, "I know we've been here a couple hours... but maybe we could do a quick re-tour? A super quick one, I promise. It's just... I've decided there's a few clubs I want to join."

I hold my breath, desperately hoping she won't be angry. Worst case, I can always venture out on my own. Probably. Maybe.

Thankfully, I don't have to worry for long because the smile that cracks across Stella's face is as bright as a beam of sunshine, "I thought you'd never ask! Not going to lie, we were going to keep doing laps until you signed up for at least one."

A wave of relief washes through me and I laugh, feeling lighter than I have in a long time.

—ele—

I would love to say my change of heart had me signing up for clubs left, right, and centre like my vivacious roommate, but that wasn't the case. My social anxiety didn't just disappear with one pep talk, but it did calm down to varying degrees. By the end of our second go-round, I gave my email to no fewer than four booths. One of them being my beloved Punk Rockers. It's not quite the running leap I had in mind, but it's a step. A small one, but one in the right direction.

Stella and I are finishing the day off with dinner at Taber's cafeteria when my roommate tries to kill me, "Did you and Wes find a corner to make out in when you disappeared today?"

The bite of poutine I was in the middle of swallowing changes direction and goes straight into my windpipe. I start hacking, and with a few back slaps from Stella, the fry frees itself from my airway. I gasp with relief, sucking precious oxygen back into my lungs.

"We did NOT make out. When we got separated, I was having a moment and Wes was nice enough to comfort me."

"Would have been nicer if his tongue was down your throat."

I throw a fry at Stella's smirking face, "Get your mind out of the gutter. We're friends, that's all."

A perfectly shaped eyebrow cocks at me, "Oh, so you're friends now? I thought he was irritating."

"He was! I mean he is. Irritating." I wince, hearing how weak that sounded. I try again, "Wes annoys me with his sparkling green eyes and flirty tendencies, but otherwise he's a good friend. He didn't need to give me a hug today in the middle of the foyer, but he did. I think that qualifies as solid friend points."

Stella's mouth drops open, "Hold up. First off, you literally listed his attractiveness as his only flaw. Second, why did you not tell me before now you two hugged?! This is the stuff I live for. And third, what triggered the hug? I feel like I'm missing the whole puzzle at this point."

I sigh, willing myself to open up. *Pick the version you want, Trip.*

"I'm sure you noticed I get a little... hesitant to join things." The kindness in Stella's eyes encourages me to continue, "High school was tough for me. Really tough. By second semester of tenth grade, I was counting down the days until graduation. The cliques at my school were brutally exclusive and I didn't belong to any of them. Any time

I tried out for a team or joined a club, I was ignored. Doesn't sound so bad, but when you're a teen struggling with acne and hormones, the inability to fit in feels like the end of the world. And now... well, I guess a part of me is scared Taber will turn into a second round of high school."

Nothing like dumping three years of teenage angst onto my new roommate while she eats her grilled chicken and spinach salad. Can we get the cheque please?

"Oh, Lou. I am so sorry that happened to you. The kids at your school sound like dicks, no offence."

I laugh, "None taken."

Reaching across the table to grab a hold of my hand, Stella stares intently at me, "I promise university is going to be different. I'm new here as well, and together we'll make the most of it. There are no cliques at university, maybe a few bromances on the varsity teams, but even those guys aren't so bad. Look at your Wes. Or Cody."

"He's not my Wes. Wait, Cody's on the lacrosse team as well?"

Stella nods, "He's team captain this year. Played with my older brother last year and now they're the best of friends." Rolling her eyes, she diverts the conversation back to reassurance, "My point is you don't have to hold back at Taber. You can try as much or as little as you want."

Giving my hands a squeeze, she sits back in her chair.

"You can be anyone you want here, Lou. No one is going to judge you."

The similarities between Stella's pep talk and the one Wes gave me earlier is enough to give me goosebumps. There must be something in the air here because I've never known so many young adults so full of wisdom. Not that I know that many young adults, but still. Creepy.

"Thank you, Stella. Now, one last question before we hit the dessert table." Eyeing up my admittedly unbalanced dinner, Stella waves a hand for me to continue.

"Do you have to look like an Abercrombie model to be a varsity athlete or is it just the lacrosse team?"

"Now that my dear Lou, is a question I'm dying to know the answer to."

Wes

You know when you have a question about a person you don't want to talk about so you end up asking about a *different* person hoping it will eventually come back around to the one you *actually* want to talk about? A complicated process, I know, but luckily stealth and subtly are my specialty.

Like any veteran, I make sure all factors are taken into consideration.

Location? Check. Weight room with the team. Nothing like a testosterone pump to get a conversation going.

Target? Check. Cody is making his way over to the dumbbell rack, which is next to the bench press, where Nico and I are currently stationed.

Damn I'm good.

"Hey Cap, what's the deal between you and Stella?"

Stopping mid-bend on his way to the heavier weights, Cody straightens and looks me dead in the eye, "What's the deal between you and *Trip*, Wes?"

Shot down before I step on the battlefield.

I take a second to help Nico lift the barbell off the rack, "Oh you know... anyways, I was just wondering whether you think Trip likes me." Laughter splutters from the bench beneath me and Cody's lips start to twitch.

Shit. I'm not living this one down any time soon.

"When you say like do you mean… like or like *like* you?" Nico sounds like he's having a full-on asthma attack by this point, so I make no effort to help him re-stack the barbell. The laughing traitor can do it himself.

I know Cody's taking the piss out of me, but the fact he's managed to keep a semi-straight face throughout this exchange is something I can't help but admire. The guy's either got impressive self-control or some seriously strong face muscles. My bet's on both.

"Ha-ha. What I mean is… do you think Trip sees me as a friend? I joke around with her a lot, and I just want to make sure I don't come off as a total douchebag."

It was the look of surprise that got me. The fact Trip genuinely seemed shocked I am capable of being a nice guy hurt more than I care to admit.

Cody falls silent while I finally relieve Nico of the bar. I look up to find him staring thoughtfully at me. He nods to the dumbbell rack, and I head over, getting a slap on the ass from Nico.

"Don't worry honey, I'll always love you. Total douchebag and all."

I flip him off and approach my captain, suddenly nervous of what I'm about to hear.

"I didn't think you came off as rude, Wes. I thought you were your usual cocky-as-hell, charming self. But if it's really bothering you, then you should ask her yourself. The most honest answer will always come from the source."

No wonder my sneak attack was a failure. The man is a white Gandhi.

"Thanks, Cap. I appreciate the input."

Cody slaps me on the back and bends down to pick up his dumbbells.

"Anytime, Wes. I hope you find out whether Trip *likes* you or not."

I'm cruising like a newborn sailor through my first week of classes when Friday decides to drop the anchor in the form of Professor Lee Anderson.

"Some of you are here today because this course is mandatory. Others chose Intro to Psychology as an easy way to check off their science requirement. Is that correct?"

The crisp voice echoes through the auditorium, drawing chuckles and sheepish nods from students. Between the tight suit, polished shoes, and sweet looking goatee Anderson looks more like an investment broker than a psych prof. As a business student myself, that fact should give me a sense of companionship with the man pacing the floor, yet for some reason it puts me on edge.

Call it foreshadowing.

"Well, I'm here to tell you that either way, this course will not be a GPA booster. In fact, I'd be surprised if most of you walk away from this class with a B, never mind an A. In the world of science, there is no such thing as excellence. Brilliant minds spend years analyzing the same data over and over and they still come up short. The simple truth of the matter is: life isn't fair. Therefore, I'm taking it upon myself to be the first professor to treat you students how *real* scientists are treated: with much criticism and little reward. You will be asked to review work. You will be asked to redo work. Most of you will hopefully attain the satisfactory level, a few of you may even hit the exemplary level. But one thing I can promise you is none of you will achieve the excellence level. And that is the greatest lesson I can give you."

Taking a pause to drink water, Anderson sweeps his gaze around the room. I fight the urge to flinch when his gaze lands on mine.

Full disclosure: I'm one of those students who took this class because I thought it would be the easiest choice for my science requirement. Bio, chem, and physics require way too much effort so that left the choice of geology or psychology. And come on, serial killer documentaries versus rock formations? It's a no brainer.

"If you are unable to handle my grading mindset, then you are welcome to drop the class. Those of you who choose to stay, however, will undergo such growth and development that your perspective of this fine institution may change, perhaps even your perspective of the world."

The hot brunette I was chatting up earlier shifts her laptop so I can see the screen. All geology classes for this semester are full, leaving only the main three sciences as remaining options. Each with an additional three-hour lab, and in the case of physics, a one-hour tutoring session on top.

Fuck. I should have given those minerals a chance.

"Today we will begin by taking a look at-

BANG! The auditorium door flies open and a frazzled looking girl stumbles in, arms overflowing with textbooks and a box that looks suspiciously like the cafeteria's poutine. The golden streaks highlighting the chestnut hair are a dead giveaway as I watch my favourite pack mule juggle her way to an empty seat in the front row. Catching Trip's eye, I blow her a kiss and grin at the scowl I get in return.

This class just got a little bit more interesting.

CHAPTER 6

Lou

That arrogant, son of a bi-

"And what might your name be, Miss?"

I look up to find an impeccable goatee towering over me. Sneaking a glance at my watch, I wince. Twenty minutes late. I knew I should have grabbed lunch after class. Hunger be damned.

"Lou Mackenzie, sir. I'm so sorry for being late, it won't happen again."

"I see." I slump in my seat as the professor turns to address the rest of the class, praying my face isn't as red as it feels.

"Today's lesson is on a term called operant conditioning, a learning process that occurs when two repeating stimuli are repeatedly paired. I originally prepared a PowerPoint with some videos to go over with everyone, but thanks to Miss Mackenzie, now we have the opportunity for a real-life demonstration." I freeze, feeling the entire auditorium look in my direction.

"The first stimuli of our demonstration is a student turning up late to class. Now, if this response is met unchallenged, there is no reason for such behaviour to change. Thus, using the general idea of operant conditioning, to reinforce the knowledge that tardiness will not be tolerated in my class, I condemn each and every one of you to a ten-page paper defining the advantages and disadvantages of such conditioning in a domestic setting. The paper is due on my desk by 9am Monday morning and will account for 20% of your overall grade. Remember to cite your sources. Now, please open your textbooks to page 367..."

The professor's voice drones on as I slide further into my seat. The stares have turned into glares, and the animosity flowing my way feels strong enough to start a fire. The guy on my right shifts his chair as far away from me as possible. He can probably smell the shame wafting from my poutine.

The rest of the class goes by at a snail's pace and as soon as we're dismissed, I launch out of my seat and make a break for the exit. The last thing I need is a black eye from one of my classmates.

I head straight for the courtyard, hoping it will be far enough away to hide from my classmates' hostility so I can finally eat my lunch. After all that, I still didn't cure my hunger because I was too scared it'd turn into another conditioning moment.

Well class, given that Miss Mackenzie insists on eating her carbs instead of taking notes, every one of you will have to go on a carb-free diet for the rest of the semester.

I groan at the mental picture, finally opening the box to Taber's ridiculously delicious poutine. The cheese and fries are soggy from sitting so long in the gravy and the cold temperature gives the whole thing an odd texture, but right now it's the best thing I have ever tasted.

Who knew tyrant teachers could build such an appetite?

I moan when I find a lukewarm fry and out of nowhere a male voice interrupts my courtyard feast, "Normally I have to put in a lot more effort to get those sounds from pretty girls, but I'm glad my presence does it for you."

My head snaps towards the sound, and I blink as my seated gaze meets a black t-shirt. A *tight* black t-shirt. One that stretches across broad shoulders, perfectly formed pecs, and hints at a six-pack underneath. Registering the specimen before me, my thought process all but obliterates as boyish dimples flash my way.

Trying not to focus on the fact this gorgeous guy just called me pretty, I do my best to look annoyed.

"I doubt you have to put much effort in when it comes to girls, Wes. Why are you here?"

"Hey, it's not my fault I'm naturally charming. I've been told I have a yellow aura. Never been very good with aura distinctions but apparently that's a good one." With a sigh, Wes plops down next to me on the bench.

I stiffen, trying not to let his leg brush against mine.

"I came to see if you were okay. It wasn't cool for Anderson to call you out like that, let alone make you a target for every wannabe partygoer this weekend."

"Oh." I'm ashamed to say I am once again surprised by Wes' kindness.

This is the second time he's put in the effort to comfort me, to make sure I'm okay, but it still feels like a shock to the system. Maybe it's because I'm not used to the whole having-friends thing. The last three years was me searching for quiet places to escape and isolate myself from the endless strain of loneliness. As dumb as it sounds, I found it easier being alone than being invisible in a group of people.

Having people like Stella and Wes in my life, friends who go out of their way to show they care, feels... unnatural. I've been living in my protective bubble for so long, I think I've forgotten what friendships are supposed to be like.

"I appreciate the check-in, Wes. I'm doing alright, mostly feel guilty for ruining everyone's weekend. I'm definitely public enemy number one right now."

Wes nods without hesitation, "Oh, for sure. I wouldn't be surprised if your name gets changed to She Who Must Not Be Named."

I laugh despite myself. Other than Stella, I've never found anyone so easy to interact with before. It's as though Wes' outrageous confidence gives me a safety net. I don't have to worry about my own social skills because I know the social butterfly next to me will make up for it.

Throwing his arm around the back of the bench, Wes leans back and takes in the scenery, "This place is gorgeous. How did you find it?"

"I took a shortcut after grabbing my textbooks the other day. Aren't the flowers amazing?"

"They're incredible. I've never seen marigolds so vibrant."

It takes a second for my brain to register the name drop.

"A big flower guy, eh?"

Wes drops his voice to a whisper, "Don't tell the boys, but I could name every flower present."

My jaw drops, "No way."

"Way, I'll prove it to you if you want."

Unable to stop myself, I start randomly pointing at different flowers.

"Pansies. Violas. Daisies..." Coming up with a different name for each one, turns out Wes has been a closet plant mom this whole time. Mind you, I have no idea if the names he's rattling off are real or if he's making them up. Other than colour differences, the flowers all look the same to me.

Once we go through the entire row lining our stone bench, I finally give the game a rest.

"That is amazing. Do you study garden books in your spare time?"

Grinning, Wes shakes his head, "My botanical knowledge is thanks to my younger sister. She's a garden geek, so every year I give her a different flower for her birthday. Problem is, she started the obsession back when she was five, so I used up the easy ones early on. Now I have to look for three syllable monstrosities and cross check the ongoing list I have."

I smile at the memory, "I'm sure she looks forward to that every year. How old is she?"

"Turning seventeen this year. There's only thirteen months between us." Wes pauses to wipe fake tears from his eyes, "They grow so fast. Soon Lacey will be embarking on her own university adventure."

I shake my head with a laugh. Wes and his theatrics.

Smiling, Wes bumps his shoulder into mine, "What about you? Any annoying siblings back home?"

"I'm afraid it's just me, myself, and I. Although sometimes my mother acts more like an older sister than my mother."

A playful grin tugs at Wes' lips, "Oh, I remember your mother. Still waiting on that number, you know."

"Oh my god. Don't be such a creep."

I slap his arm, forgetting my no-touching rule when it comes to Wes.

As ridiculous as it sounds, I implemented this rule to ensure nothing happens between Wes and me. Stella heard some rumours about a new all-star rookie who's been making his way through the female population of campus, and although names weren't mentioned, given

Wes' natural swagger and boyish charm, it doesn't take much to put two and two together. Not that there's anything wrong with promiscuous activities, but it doesn't exactly scream boyfriend material. And knowing my luck, Wes would be my first, I'd fall madly in love, then he would move on to the next girl he knocks over.

I've lost enough friendships over the years, I don't want to lose this one too.

My hand appears to be a little behind on the memo because instead of slapping Wes' arm and moving away, it decides to stay resting on his bicep. We both look down at my traitorous fingers and before I can snatch my hand away, he looks up and catches my eye.

I'm not sure if emeralds were ever used in hypnosis, but Wes' eyes sure as heck could have been. The sparkling green beckons me closer and without realizing it, I start to lean in. His gaze flicks to my lips then back up to my eyes.

"Trip, I-

"There you are! I've been looking all over for you. Oh, hi Wes." Stella's voice breaks the trance and I fly off the bench, jumping away from Wes and his mesmerizing eyes.

I hear Wes slowly get up behind me and I will myself not to look back. I can feel the blush rising to my cheeks and the last thing I need is to become a full-blown tomato from making eye contact with the guy I almost kissed.

Oh my god. I almost kissed Wes.

The headache forming at the base of my skull feels like a neon sign with the words THIS IS WHY WE HAVE A NO TOUCHING RULE pounding repeatedly against my brain.

"Stella, I'm so sorry. I totally forgot we were supposed to meet in the library." After the psych disaster and my impending hunger, our study session completely slipped my mind.

Worst. Roommate. Ever.

"It's no biggie, I'm glad Wes was here to... keep you company."

The raised eyebrow and pointed look tells me there will be a debriefing happening very soon.

Remaining uncharacteristically quiet in the background, Wes finally pipes up, "Stella, it's nice to see you. Trip." He throws me a brief smile, dimples noticeably absent, "I'll see you around. Enjoy the rest of your day ladies."

And with that, Wes turns and walks in the opposite direction. Tamping down the disappointment building in my chest, I turn to see my tiny roommate plant her hands on her hips.

"You've got some explaining to do, Missy. And you better not skimp out on the details."

CHAPTER 7

Lou

I'm going to be arrested.

The scraps of fabric lying on my bed looked innocent enough until Stella informed me they were my outfit for tonight. One she personally picked out.

I must have been a worse roommate than I thought because the clothes - if they can be called that - Stella picked can only be described as publicly indecent. And I'm pretty sure that's a felony.

"Stella, you can't be serious." I hold up the black square of fabric, frowning at the five inches of material in my hands, "I think you mistook this neck warmer for a shirt. Seriously, it doesn't even have arm holes."

I peer through the opening as if sleeves will magically appear on either side. The fabric is soft and stretchy, but that doesn't escape the fact it barely covers my hands, let alone my torso.

Stella snatches the top from my grasp. "It's a bandeau, Lou. Like a tube top except smaller."

"But why would anyone want *smaller*?" Bewildered doesn't begin to cover my current state. Stella sighs, sits on my bed, and pats the space next to her.

"My dear Lou. You have so many things to learn."

My mattress topper dips as I join her, and I brace myself for the parent/roommate lecture about to come.

"Remember when you agreed to go dancing with me this weekend?" I nod, already regretting that decision, "Well, tonight we are going clubbing. Clubbing is where people our age go to drink, dance, and let loose. Lucky for us, there's only one club near Taber's campus so it's bound to be full. Full is good, because the more people there are, the less awkward it feels to dance."

I nod again to show I'm listening. Not following per say but listening.

"You know the movie Dirty Dancing? Picture that but university students. Lots of grinding, the occasional make out session, and roommate bonding. Basically, it's a lot of fun."

Fun sounds like infectious diseases and a dash of humiliation but I wave a hand for her to continue.

"This right here." She shakes the neck warmer in my direction, "Is what we mortals call the secret weapon. We dress up, look sexy, shake our booty, *and* score free drinks all night long. It's the ultimate win-win."

Like an obedient student, I raise my hand in question.

"No, Lou. You are not allowed to wear an oversized concert tee to the club. First off, you would die from hyperthermia and second, you agreed to let me choose the outfits for tonight."

I lower my hand then slowly raise it again.

Sighing, Stella nods her permission.

"Why do we need free drinks if you're not drinking?"

Seemingly pleased with my question, she smiles and pats my hand, "Oh, honey. We're getting the drinks for *you*. Trust me, you'll thank me later."

Well, that's reassuring.

Joking aside, the consumption of alcohol has never been something that scares me. I know my limits - a feeble four, but hey, it's better than some - and have never veered into the memory-loss territory. As far as drinking goes, I am somewhat sensible.

Stella, on the other hand doesn't drink at all. She told me her vigorous workout routine leaves little room for hangovers, so she's happy to be the designated driver. Her excuse sounds flimsy at best, but I'm not one to probe.

Accepting my defeat, I groan and flop on the bed. Seeing my surrender, Stella lets out a shriek of excitement and I can't help but smile. If nothing else, tonight will be good roommate bonding. And really, it's just dancing.

How bad can it be?

ele

My expectations start to lower as soon as I see the neon red BA$$ sign. It's safe to assume anyone who puts dollar signs in their company name probably doesn't have the most professional work setting. And if the scantily clad girls lined up in front of me are anything to go by, BA$$ checks off all the boxes for questionable business management.

Standing in line outside the building, I can feel the pulse of the music vibrating through the concrete beneath my sneakers. The good news is my bandeau and skinny jeans look conservative compared to the lingerie and fishnet stockings around me. The bad news is I didn't bring earplugs.

Stella's silky hair brushes my arm as she laughs with the new friend she made two minutes ago. For the first time ever, Stella's hair doesn't have a single braid in it. Instead, it's pulled up in a high pony with strands strategically wrapped around the elastic band. Even put up, the impressive length hangs to her low back, swishing back and forth like a hair extension commercial. The top she's got on glitters under the streetlights, the black sequins glistening against her light skin and outlining the muscles rippling down her arms and upper back. She looks intimidatingly beautiful.

Although I prefer my baggy shirts and mom jeans, I am glad Stella didn't budge on the outfits. I would have stood out like a sore thumb before we hit the dance floor.

If you thought my social skills are bad, wait until you see my dance moves.

"Lou, meet Porsche. Poor girl has the worst luck with roommates. For a second year in a row, she got a sleepwalker!"

"That must be... tiresome." Falling back on a terrible pun, I look at the girl in question and try not to let the shock show on my face.

When someone is named after a luxury vehicle, you can't help but picture them... well, drop-dead gorgeous. Because really, who names their kids after sports cars? Celebrities and other outrageously beautiful people. Looking at the small Japanese girl in front of me, her round glasses and plain face is slightly... underwhelming. She's undoubtedly cute but far from eye-catching.

Porsche laughs at my weak joke and I immediately feel bad for having such thoughts. Anyone who laughs at my feeble attempts at humour deserves to be admired, not judged by a parent's poor name choice.

As we inch up the line, Porsche shakes her head morosely, "I thought first year was bad with the drawer banging. That was nothing compared to this year. Every night my roommate sleepwalks out of her room but can never find her way back. Half the time she ends up on our living room sofa, the other half she tries to break into my room thinking it's her own. The first night I forgot to lock my door and she crawled into bed with me. Fast asleep, eyes wide open. Scariest moment of my life."

I gasp, "Oh my god. My heart would have stopped."

Nodding in agreement, Stella draws a cross on her chest. "Death by fright. In the dorm. By the roommate."

"Death by the *unconscious* roommate." Porsche corrects, causing us all to break into laughter.

When we finally reach the front, a burly bouncer scans our IDs, and we walk through the entrance. The pulsing beat I could feel outside gets turned up to an ear-splitting level, the low vibrations turning into lyrics thundering against my shoes and inside my skull.

It's like dunking your head under water, except instead of submersing yourself into a world of peace and tranquility, BA$$ submerses you into a world of chaos and noise.

Permanent hearing damage here I come.

A long bar stretches across the back of the room, with a small seating area with tables and chairs filling up the section nearby. The dance floor itself is elevated two feet off the ground and fills the remaining space, with two shabby-looking bathrooms poking out of the right-hand corner. What BA$$ lacks in sophistication, it more than makes up for in popularity. The place is packed.

Squealing with excitement, Stella grabs me and Porsche, and drags us all towards the gyrating mass on the dance floor. Endless bodies and humid air fill my senses as we squeeze past clumps of people, finding a few feet of minimal space near the centre. The few lights located above the bar don't make it to the elevated platform, so the only light on us are the glowing shades of blacklight. Stella's platinum ponytail lights up like a Christmas tree, thankfully making her easy to spot. The last thing I need is to get lost in the drunk mass around us.

A new Ed Sheeran song pumps through the speakers and both members of my girl squad start moving as though they've been dancing their whole lives.

Confession time: I've never danced before.

I mean, technically at school I learned the four square and a couple steps of the jig, but I've never danced, like, for fun before. Music was never important in my household growing up, and by the time I became a teen, my love for alternative rock was ingrained. Don't get me wrong, I can play the air guitar like the best of them, but when it comes to swinging my hips? I am a newbie. Fresh on the dance floor.

Now that we're here, I realize I should have taken the time to google tips and tricks for beginners. Or at least watched a Shakira music video. Because it turns out, faking it is a lot harder to do when you don't know *how* to fake it.

Deciding to learn from my squad, I study Porsche's movements for a few seconds. The rapid succession of arm bends starts to give me a headache, but I force the throb aside and do my best to follow.

"Ow! Watch the flailing, Uma Thurman." I wince apologetically at the cute guy standing nearby. Cross arm movements off the list.

Turning my attention to Stella, my eyes widen as I take in her effortless hip sways. Back and forth, side to side, clockwise, counter clockwise, my roommate's lower body never stops moving. Throwing me a wink and twirling around, Stella looks like she's having the time of her life. All I can do is stare, mesmerized by her fluidity.

At the moment, there are only two things I know for certain: Stella's hips do not lie. And I may have a new girl crush.

Focusing on Stella's movements, I try to swing my hips from side to side. Too much momentum carries me far right, and I take down the brunette beside me.

"ARE YOU OKAY?" Screaming in my ear, Stella hauls me off the sticky ground. My pants feel strangely damp, and I pray to God it's just spilt beer. I don't want to know what other substances are on these floors.

I nod yes to Stella's question, and over her shoulder I catch sight of a couple dancing as if their lives depended on it. The guy's hands are around the girl's waist, pulling them flush together while they move perfectly in synch. I say move, but I guess the technical clubbing term would be grinding.

I'm not the only one watching the couple grind against each other. The crowd as a whole seems to be captivated by the striking couple. The confidence oozing from them seeps into the energy of the club itself.

The girl's dark cornrows contrast beautifully against the guy's bright white shirt - cue the blacklight glow - and his fair skin is barely visible as her hands clutch his midnight-coloured hair. Doing a double take, I register the dark locks the girl is holding on to and flick my eyes to the biceps circling the girl's torso.

It's Wes.

Wes

This chick can move.

I'm always down for grind time, but every once in a while, you find a partner who fits perfectly against your body, and the whole night gets taken to the next level.

Here's some Wes wisdom for ya: clubs are a fantastic source of foreplay. I can sense your disbelief but think about it: the alcohol, the hormones, the over-stimulated senses, the flirting, the dancing; my list could go on forever. Clubs are the perfect way to scout out a good lay. You can test what fits without so much as taking off a shoe. No muss, no fuss.

The best part is most girls are here looking for the same thing: no strings, no promises. Hell, half the time I don't even get a phone number by the end of the night. It's purely symbiotic, where two horny parties come together as a means to an end.

Pun intended.

Honestly, Simone's ass rubbing against me is just what I need to get the whole courtyard situation out of my head. How my innocent intentions to check on a friend almost turned into a make-out session is something I still do not understand. One second I'm using my big brother status to name all the flowers, the next I'm being pulled like a magnet to Trip's slightly too full bottom lip.

Shit. Now, I'm thinking about that bottom lip again.

Grind time. Focus on grind time.

I roll my hips in time to the music and Simone is right with me. Damn. If this keeps up, this might be the best night I've had in a while. I lift my head to nuzzle her neck and see a flash of neon hair.

Keeping my hips moving in time to the beat, I do a sweep of the room, my eyes landing on platinum hair whipping back and forth in the highest ponytail I've ever seen. I smile, immediately recognizing Stella's tiny stature. My gaze drifts over to the two girls she's dancing with and I'm instantly amazed by the Asian's TikTok moves. Her arms hit every musical beat, and there's no awkward transition from one move to another. Consider me impressed.

I shift my gaze to the third girl in their group and I try not to cringe. The poor girl shuffles painfully from side to side, completely out of time with the rhythm. I bet she doesn't normally listen to pop music.

Studying the girl from across the room, something strikes me as familiar. Loose golden-brown curls fall around her pretty face, the sexy bandeau emphasizing a decent sized rack, the black skinny jeans showing off her long legs. I'm intrigued, even while half my attention is on Simone, and that's before me and the terrible dancer make eye contact.

The girl I can't get out of my head is here.

The realization drop kicks me in the face and I stumble over the next two beats of music. It's not hard to fall back in rhythm with Simone, but suddenly, I don't want to fall back in rhythm with her. There's someone else I want to see.

Abruptly stepping out from Simone's embrace, I give her a quick kiss on the cheek, and she nods in understanding, "If you change your mind, I'll be at the sorority house tonight. Maybe with company, maybe not."

Giving me a smile full of bad intentions, Simone winks and wanders off in search of her next partner.

Taking note of that tidbit of information, I turn and make a beeline for Trip. Like a drunken sailor, I stumble my way through the crowd until I reach my grey-eyed siren.

"Someone's quite the irresponsible student. Don't you have a ten-page paper to write?" Bending to yell in her ear, my senses are immediately overwhelmed by her coconut vanilla shampoo. Jesus, where does she buy that stuff?

"I could ask you the same thing." The wry look on her face brings a grin to mine. I can't remember the last time I enjoyed riling someone so much.

The wrinkle that forms between Trip's eyebrows? Gets me. Every time.

"I finished my paper two hours ago." Her eyebrows shoot up and I shrug with nonchalance, "Procrastination isn't my style."

"You mean you're a nerd."

"That depends. Are you into nerds?" Trip recoils as if my sexy studying habits are contagious.

"Not where you're concerned."

I clutch my chest and stumble back, bumping into dancers around us. Trip snickers at my antics.

"WES! IT'S SO GOOD TO SEE YOU!" Stella screams in my direction and I throw two thumbs up in her direction. With a quick wave to the TikTok star, I turn my attention back to Trip.

"Why aren't you dancing?" I lean back down to her ear, partly so I can smell her shampoo again but mostly so she can hear me over the thumping bass. Which seems to be getting louder. Or maybe I'm getting sober.

"I am dancing."

I narrow my eyes in concentration. Unless she counts the barely visible side shuffle she's got going on as dancing, I see nothing.

"Sorry, but last time I checked a nervous tick doesn't count as dancing. You look like you need to pee."

She immediately stops shuffling and puts her hands on her hips.

"I don't remember asking for your opinion."

"Touché, but wouldn't you have more fun if you let loose a little?" She mumbles something, ducking her head.

"Sorry gorgeous, I missed that."

The glare returns full force, "I said, I don't know how to dance. There. Happy now?"

It takes a second for her words to sink in.

"You mean you've never gone clubbing before?"

"No, I mean I've never danced before. Besides high school gym classes, the whole move-your-body-time-to-the-beat thing is something I've never done. Or been taught. I *literally* do not know how to dance. Especially in an unsupervised setting."

I pause to do something I've never done before: I think before I speak.

Choosing my next words carefully, I throw out a suggestion, "Okay. Between the two of us, we can get through this. Let's break it down step-by-step."

Grey eyes watch me skeptically.

I point to her converse, "First thing is the feet. I want you to step-touch your right foot to your left." She follows my movements and I feel a strange surge of pride.

"That's it! Perfect. Now, let's add a little motion to the upper body. Shoulders, arms, anything you want." I throw up jazz hands to make her laugh.

The burst of laughter works just as I'd intended, sending a boost of confidence straight to her dance moves. Stiff arms and legs start to move vigorously, and I'm pretty sure I see an attempt at a hip swing. Hard to tell for sure, because her jerky movements are similar to those of a seizure victim, but hey, you can't expect someone to move like JLo after five minutes.

"Wes, I think I'm getting it! I'm dancing!"

The joy radiating from Trip as she tears up the dance floor with her God-awful moves has me grinning so hard my cheeks ache. There's nothing better than seeing insecurities fly away and confidence take its place. From rookies on the lacrosse field to girls who've never danced before, the real magic happens once we forget to be self-conscious.

"Hey man! Didn't think I'd be seeing you here tonight." A hand claps my shoulder and I turn to see Hunter shaking shaggy hair out of his eyes.

He told me the young Justin Bieber look is back in style, but looking at the trendsetter, I'm not so sure. Guy looks more like a golden retriever in need of a haircut than a prepubescent popstar. His pale blue eyes sweep the room, looking glazed and a little confused.

Not going to lie, if it weren't for his varsity status, Hunter would be a full-on stoner. As it is, he can only smoke for a couple more weekends before our tournament season begins. It's safe to say Hunter has been making the most of these last few weekends.

"Gotta let out the rookie stress somehow." My response draws a laugh from Hunter and he turns his attention to the girls. Something tightens in my chest as his gaze passes over Trip, only easing once Hunter's stare moves to linger on Stella.

The relief in my chest is unfamiliar, the source completely unknown. Either my five minutes of teaching has transformed me into a possessive dance mom, or I was experiencing my first bout of jealousy.

Nah, it was definitely the dance mom theory. When in doubt, always go for the MILF.

Getting momentarily distracted by Stella's hip control, I don't notice the other person join our dance squad until Trip speaks up. Well, screams at the top of her lungs is more accurate, but you get my point.

"HEY CODY! IS THIS A TEAM OUTING OR WHAT?" I whip my head around to find my team captain glowering in our direction.

Shit. Are rookies not supposed to club during off-season?

Perspiration forms on my forehead as I see my chances of winning rookie-of-the-year slip through my fingers. I should have followed Nico's example and stayed home tonight. I've never seen Cody look so harsh. And the guy's got a *jawline* for crying out loud.

"Hey, Trip. I was checking on my pups to see if their leashes needed to be reined in." I try not to flinch as I meet Cody's unforgiving gaze. Thanking my lucky stars, I swiftly register that Cody isn't looking at me, but rather over my shoulder. I turn, following the flickering embers of death his stare leaves in its wake.

Dancers, more dancers, Hunter lip locked again, dancers... Wait. My gaze shoots back to Hunter and the girl he's playing tonsil lacrosse with. Well, would you look at that. Hunter's tongue has found its way down Stella's throat.

For the record, there is nothing wrong with a good game of taste mingling. I'm all for sharing the love whenever and wherever the need arises. But looking at Cody's expression, he does not feel the same. Although it is strange that Hunter's sexual prowess at the house party the other night didn't bother him. Unless... oh. *Oh.*

Someone call me Sherlock because I just cracked this shit wide open.

The captain's got a thing for Trip's feisty roommate.

Feeling smug about my mental boy plus girl calculations, I'm about to crack a joke when Cody heads straight for his lip-locked Juliet.

Crisis mode: Do I run to the convenience store for popcorn or call the ambulance for Hunter's soon-to-be dead body?

Turns out, I don't have time to grab my phone for a video because in the blink of an eye, Cody grabs Stella mid make-out – the saliva trail was there, believe me – and throws her over his shoulder, carrying her to the exit. Her kicking legs whack a few people on the way out and after recovering from my shock, I snag Trip's hand and we follow the fuming couple outside.

The exit door bangs open with a wave of cold air and fresh oxygen. You don't realize how muggy it gets on the dance floor until you're back outside.

Finally putting Stella back on the ground, the furious roommate whirls around and lays it out on my captain.

Upper chest punch, "How dare you *think,*" torso punch, "you have the *right,*" abdomen punch, "to carry me like some sort of *pet.*" Big yikes. That one was borderline pelvic bone. Protect the balls my man, protect the balls.

Finishing off her impressive boxing career with one last shot to Cody's stomach, I make a mental note to never get on Stella's bad side. Even my abs aren't hard enough to take that beating.

Cody remains silent and still, patiently waiting for Stella to finish her pummelling. Only once the raging pixie finishes does he hold up his hands in surrender, "Look Stel, I'm sorry for making you feel like a pet. But I'm not sorry for getting you away from that creep."

The chest punches must have given him a concussion because the creep in question is one of the rookies Cody personally picked for the roster this year. Talk about awkward.

"I made a promise to your brother when he made me captain. I promised him I would look out for you, keep you out of trouble. What do you think Mo would have said if he saw you tonight?"

Hold up. Did Cody just say *Mo*? As in Taber lacrosse royalty, *The* Mighty Mo? He's Stella's older brother? Shit, I didn't even know there was more than one O'Brien prodigy.

"That's not up to you, Cody. And if Mo were here, he couldn't say a damn thing about my situation because his wild streak lasted *four years.*"

She's not wrong. Mo wasn't known for being mighty only on the lacrosse field. Rumour has it the guy was the hardest partier Taber has ever seen. Apparently, he ran the naked mile along University Drive after hitting four funnels and beating a bunch of frat guys at beer pong his freshman year. And that's just the tame stuff. When it came to girls?

Left, right, and centre. There was no 'some Mo didn't try out. The man is a *legend*.

Sighing, Cody runs a hand through his fauxhawk, "You're right, I may have overreacted. I apologize if I ruined your night." And there's the even-headed team captain I'm used to.

No matter how pissed or how tired Cody may be, there's never been a time when I haven't seen him smooth things over with his natural peacemaker tendencies. Except for the fireman carry – which, for the record, looked hella sick – Cody is the politest person I know. Even when he's being painfully honest, he always manages to deliver it in a way that leaves a positive impact.

Basically, he's the master of the compliment sandwich: Outer slices lathered with compliments while criticism is cleverly stashed in the middle.

I've said it before, but I'll say it again: the man is a white Gandhi.

Silence descends the group as Cody's apology hangs in the air. With a sigh, Stella pats him on the arm, "I know you mean well. I'm sorry for punching you. But the next time you lift me off the ground like a damsel in distress, my fists of fury will aim lower. *Much* lower."

The threat has me instinctively shifting to cover my package but Cody just tilts his head with a smile. Jesus. The guy must have balls made of vibranium.

"We're good?"

Stella replies with a sigh, "Ya, we're good."

I make eye contact with Trip and raise my eyebrows in question. Shrugging, she mouths *Gym Bros* as if that explains the assault charges we just witnessed.

CHAPTER 8

Lou

Saturday mornings are not my thing.

Actually, that's completely inaccurate. Saturday mornings are totally my thing. Who doesn't love sleeping in after a long week of morning classes? However, when my Saturday morning starts with a grumpy roommate and a looming ten-page paper, it quickly becomes not my thing.

Even though Stella told Cody they were good, in her mind, they most certainly are not. I know because she told me in those exact word, many, many times on the drive home and now again over breakfast.

"The nerve of that guy. Doesn't he realize we live in the 21st century and you can't throw people over your shoulder like some sort of caveman? I may have told him we're good, but in my mind, we most certainly are not."

I mentally add another tally to the Hating Cody scoreboard. If Stella keeps this up, we'll hit rant fifteen by lunchtime without breaking a sweat.

I poke at my breakfast mac n' cheese and try to think of a response I haven't said yet.

"Totally ridiculous." Hmm, that one sounds familiar. I may have used that line when we were brushing our teeth this morning.

"Right?! God, he makes me so mad..."

My phone buzzes on the table and I swiftly grab it. I've been waiting for this call all week.

"Sorry, I've got to take this, it's my dad. Meet you back at the dorm?"

Stella waves me away with a flick of her protein shake, "No rush. Say hi to your father for me."

I shoot her a smile, snatching up my bag and pressing accept on the FaceTime call as I head to the courtyard.

"Hi sweetie." My dad's smiling face fills the screen. "How's my favourite university student?"

I shake my head with a smile, "Dad. We both know I'm the only university student you know."

"Ah but that doesn't mean you're my favourite, now does it." I can't help but groan. Some things never change.

"Enough joking around, I want to hear about everything. Tell me about your roommate. About the disastrous state of your bathroom." Laughing, I answer each of his questions.

Due to the nature of his new job, I don't get to see my dad as much as I used to. He's an ecologist, so he gets paid to study the relationships between organisms and their environment. Last spring, he got a promotion to be one of the scientists who travel around Canada, conducting research on various ecosystems. The opportunity, not to mention the extra salary, made the decision to accept an easy one. Sadly, it also means the time my mother and I get to spend with him is cut in half.

"Anyways, how are you doing? What's Yukon like?"

Another bonus of this promotion is I get to hear about every corner of Canada. Most of the time our calls end with me adding locations to my vacation bucket list, other times I am putting them on my don't-step-off-the-plane list. The trick is to have balance.

"Yukon is amazing; you would love it here. I get to see the northern lights every night, and nature stretches as far as the eye can see." I sigh at the image, and suddenly my father's voice drops into a serious tone.

"But let's not talk about work, are you really doing alright, Lou Bear?"

High school may have taken years off my social development, but I swear it took even more years off my parents' stress-producing organs. The sad part was there was nothing my parents could do to help me make friends, just like there was nothing I could do to reduce the worry my parents carried day-in and day-out.

No one enjoys being the social outcast, but when your own parents are aware of the struggle it makes it so much worse. The stress sinks on both parties until I feel guilty for not being normal while my parents feel guilty for not being able to help. It's the ultimate lose-lose situation.

"I'm doing well, dad. I really am. Besides Stella, I've managed to make a couple of other friends too. University is different from high school, no one cares about cliques or popularity anymore. It's as though the social hierarchy has finally flattened out."

Relief relaxes the lines around his eyes, "I am so happy to hear that. And I want you to know, I am proud of you. You've really put yourself out there and already you are doing so much better than last year. Now, I hate to say goodbye Lou Bear, but I've got an incoming call from one of our shareholders. Let's try and talk again soon, okay? Miss you!"

"Miss you too." The words barely leave my lips before the call ends. And just like that, my dad disappears for another few weeks.

I love catching up with my old man, but the yearning to see him is always so much worse after we talk. I know from experience that the homesickness eventually fades, but right now my heart feels too heavy for my chest.

Closing my eyes, I take a moment to breath in the tranquility of the courtyard. About three breaths in my Zen gets broken when my phone chirps with an incoming message. I grin, thinking it's my dad forgetting to tell me about some new insect he discovered, but when I glance down at my screen it's not his name flashing up at me.

WES: How's that paper coming along?

Laughter bubbles up in my chest. I don't know how he does it, but Wes has impeccable timing when it comes to lifting my spirits.

ME: Finishing up the conclusion as we speak.

WES: I can smell the lie from here.

Laughter spills out of my mouth because he's caught me. I haven't thought up a topic for my paper, let alone started the writing process. When it comes to procrastination, I am the master of all masters. Not that he needs to know that.

ME: I'm serious. Operant conditioning has never been more interesting.

Typing bubbles fill my screen instantly.

Wes: Not even I can make operant conditioning interesting. Send evidence.

ME: Sorry, I'm not a pic sending type of girl.

I smile victoriously. He set himself up for that one.

My phone dings again, dragging my attention downward. I open the message, gasp, and hurl my phone across the cobblestone path.

Instantly realizing my mistake, I scramble towards the flower bed to find my phone.

Cursing my stupidness, I breathe out a sigh of relief when I see my device safely waiting for me in a pile of dirt. Carefully brushing off the screen, I re-open the last message Wes sent me. It's a picture, one I barely looked at other than to register his skin was showing and throwing it away in panic.

Why my immediate thought was *AHH NUDES!* I do not know. Especially considering the message is from a *friend*. An annoyingly attractive friend who uses dimples to his advantage but still. A friend.

Blowing the photo up, turns out Wes didn't send me nudes at all. Shocker.

Instead, the photo is a solid PG shot of his ten-page report lying mockingly on his bare chest. The only reason I know his chest is bare is because the tiniest bit of shoulder pops out the righthand corner. I almost lost my phone because of Wes' ten-page psychology paper. Ridiculous.

I type back a response and put my phone away. With a heavy sigh, I take one last glance around my personal Eden and start walking back to the dorms.

Those ten pages aren't going to write themselves.

Wes

Nerd.

"Uh oh. Someone's got a crush." Nico's voice pulls my attention away from my phone screen.

I look at him with a smirk, "Mrs. Montez and I blew by the crush stage years ago."

My best friend rolls his eyes, "Not even my mother puts a grin that big on your face."

Busted.

The curse of a childhood friend is they always know when something's up. In the twelve years we've known each other, I have never once gotten anything by Nico. He sees right through my charades, from the time I lied about stealing his last cookie in fourth grade to the reasoning behind my prom date last year. No matter what I show the outside world, Nico always sees beneath the surface.

"Let me guess." He taps his chin thoughtfully, "This girl's name may or may not rhyme with Slip."

See what I mean?

I sigh with defeat, "You may be on to something."

Pumping his fist in victory, Nico draws looks from the other benchwarmers lining the sidelines. I lean forward, making eye contact with one of the sophomores, and give him a big thumbs up so he knows the crazy comes in a duo.

Never abandon a brother. It's part of our bro code.

Nico shifts his attention back to the skill demonstration the seniors are putting on and bumps my shoulder.

"So, what's the deal? I've never seen you gush over text messages before."

I scoff, "Smiling at a comment does not qualify as gushing, thank you very much." I pause for a moment, taking the time to admire a backwards pass Cody just pulled off. The guy's got moves.

"I don't know, man. Trip and I are... friends, but it's like half the time I don't think she even likes me while the other half just clicks. Like on a different level." I hesitate before adding, "And we almost kissed in the courtyard the other day."

There's no point in me holding back information because Nico is bound to find out eventually. He's got perceptive powers that could rival Wonder Woman's lasso of truth: the more you resist, the more it hurts.

Think friendly intervention with a side of emotional torment.

"So, what I'm hearing is you're insecure about where you stand in this friendship and are unsure whether you want this connection to stay friendly or become something more."

And just like that, Nico takes the jumble in my brain and lays it all out on the table in a clear, orderly fashion.

Lasso of truth, I'm telling you.

"Pretty much. Where does that leave me?" Nico takes a moment to cheer for the goalie's save. I'm not sure which side we are supposed to be cheering for, so we're keeping the enthusiasm equal.

"That depends on you, Wes. Where do *you* want this to go?"

Talking in riddles is all fun and games until you're the one in the hot seat. Then suddenly those answer-questions don't seem so fun anymore.

Luke, my man, I am so sorry. Dealing with Yoda must have been a bitch.

Taking my silence as confusion, Nico does his best to clarify, "What I'm trying to ask here is are you happy being friends with Trip or do you want more?"

"That's the whole issue. We were solid buddies until the courtyard situation and now I'm feeling all these things I shouldn't be feeling and noticing all these things I shouldn't be noticing."

"An example being..."

"The shampoo she uses."

Nico takes his eyes off the field to stare at me.

"The *shampoo* she uses?"

I shake my head impatiently, "That's what I just said. Every time I'm close to Trip all I can smell is this amazing coconut vanilla combo. It messes with my head."

Nico's lips start to twitch and I can tell he's struggling to keep a straight face, "Right, of course. So, Trip buys nice shampoo. Anything else?"

"Well, when we were at the club the other night, I kind of... well, I wouldn't say kind of, it was more of a fleeting feeling..." I trail off, suddenly nervous about voicing it out loud. Is it normal to be scared of an emotion?

"Come on, Wes. It can't be worse than fangirling over hair product."

He's right yet so wrong. This one feels so much worse.

"IkindofgotjealouswhenHunterlookedatTrip." In one breath, I push the terrifying truth past my lips as fast as humanly possible.

"I can't tell if that was one long word or an entire paragraph thrown together. Let's try that again, but this time slowly."

Fuck, this is painful. Pretty sure I can feel emotional bruises forming.

"When Hunter checked out Trip at the club, before making a move on Stella, I felt... uncomfortable."

Nico blinks, "By uncomfortable, do you mean jealous?"

The agony. Make it stop.

"Fine. Yes, I was jealous. But it didn't last longer than this." I snap my fingers in front of his face.

"But it was there?" Any sign of mirth disappears from his dark eyes as they intently scan mine. It feels like he's cataloguing every micro expression crossing my face.

"It was there." I hang my head in defeat and Nico slaps my back in glee.

"Your first adult crush. Congratulations my boy."

"Very funny. Thank you for the therapy session."

The beaming smile across Nico's face doesn't waver as he gives my arm a supportive squeeze.

"Hey, you know I'm joking. Honestly, try not to overthink this thing with Trip. Put in the effort to hangout more, just the two of you, and see how things go. What's the worst that can happen?"

The man's got a point. I've already turned into a babbling fool from one almost-kiss, so my pride and dignity are no longer a consideration.

"Yeah, thanks man."

Cody signals for Nico to switch out with the senior goalie, so he gives me one last pat on the back before running onto the field.

I shuffle down the bench, thinking over Nico's advice.

As far as suggestions go, his hangout idea is a pretty good one. In theory, the more time I spend with Trip, the less power her coconut vanilla spell will have over me. Like alcohol or caffeine, I'm going to build my Trip tolerance, so soon those misty grey eyes and full bottom lip will be a decaffeinated, distant memory. Brilliant, right?

Shit. I need to get laid.

CHAPTER 9

Lou

University may be a social improvement from high school, but the workload per class certainly isn't.

The issue lies with the cruel nature of week one: the ultimate tease. Exception being Professor Anderson's class, the first couple weeks of university were a breeze. A delight, even. I would go as far as to say some assignments were even enjoyable.

Introduce week three: the ultimate scramble. As we head into the end of September, professors have realized how far behind we've fallen on the course outline (why it took them three weeks to figure this out remains undetermined) and have kicked into high gear. All at the same time.

The laidback course vibes are a long-forgotten memory. I can't remember what it feels like *not* to have eight assignments, four exams, oh and five assigned readings due every week. My courses and I went from having a healthy relationship to a downright toxic one.

It will come as a surprise to absolutely no one that my powers of procrastination are quite the detriment in this never-ending game of time management. The lecture my mother gave me all those years ago is finally starting to sink in.

My cause isn't helped by the amount of extracurricular activities Stella drags me to each week. True to her word, my roommate has put in her best efforts to make my Taber experience as enjoyable as possible. For her, that means dragging me to every art show and local theatre production Taber has to offer. She even managed to drag me to one swing dance practice, but after a spectacular near-concussion experience, we decided that was my first and last time swing dancing.

The upside is Stella's plan seems to be working social-wise, familiar faces now smile at me in the halls, but the downside is my time spent studying has seriously diminished. And by seriously diminished, I mean it's non-existent.

To be fair, we do have study sessions. However, the serious intent of said study sessions only last for about five minutes before Stella starts playing music, dancing in her seat, and eventually convinces me that our time could be more productive doing an activity that does not involve textbooks.

Case in point: what does doing handstands in an empty football stadium have to do with chemistry? We spent two hours doing the former and I still cannot tell you.

After I bombed an online quiz last weekend (re: forgot to take it), I had to sit my spirited roommate down to negotiate a contract: She can plan two outings each week, one during the weekdays and one during the weekend, and in return, an hour and a half of quiet time is allocated to five afternoons a week.

For me, this means studying and getting assignments done, for Stella this means dance partying with earplugs in behind her closed door. When I first noticed Stella's studying habits, or lack thereof, I was concerned. There's a mandatory number of classes a student must take to stay eligible for residence, so I started to worry that my bubbly roommate might be on the verge of failing her classes.

I'm not one to broach uncomfortable topics, but after a few days of internal debate, I finally worked up the courage to bring up the topic during tonight's movie night.

"Stella, I've got a bit of a personal question for you."

Grabbing the remote to click pause, my roommate turns her full attention on to me.

Deep breaths, Lou. Be brave.

"I don't know how to say this...are you doing okay in your classes? Grade wise, I mean. I don't mean to pry, it's just I've never seen you study." My throat thickens traitorously and suddenly I'm blinking hard to hold in my tears, "And if you drop too many classes you might have to move out of residence and I... I don't want to be here if you're not going to be here." A single tear leaks out and I quickly wipe it away with my sleeve.

To my utmost horror, Stella bursts out laughing.

"Oh Lou, I'm not going anywhere! First off, I would never leave you to fend for yourself in these dorms. What if your new roommate sleepwalked? Or left their toenail clippings in the sink?" Pausing to shudder, Stella continues, "Second, I currently have a 4.0 GPA in all my classes, so there's slim chance I'll have to drop out."

My mouth drops open, "But how? I don't think you've opened a textbook in my presence."

Stella pats my hand reassuringly, "I'm sorry, I should have explained sooner. Every morning I'm up at 4:30 and hit the gym for a couple of hours. We always head to breakfast around 8:45, so I come back to the dorm, hop in the shower, and get all my homework for the next day done."

Shrugging, she flicks a platinum strand over her shoulder. "I've always been a morning person and I find it easier to focus after working out. I'm borderline ADHD and find it hard to sit still. I'm so sorry for distracting you during our library sessions, though."

My brows pull together, brain struggling to process the new information.

"So, you hit the gym and get all your homework done... before I wake up?"

At her nod, I feel my level of laziness reach new heights. Of course, I'd noticed Stella always looks picture perfect when we head down to breakfast, but I just assumed she was one of those people who wake up looking gorgeous.

Studying the girl across from me, I notice for the first time the dark circles hiding beneath her concealer. Doing some quick math in my head, I calculate Stella can't be getting more than four to six hours of sleep each night. Even for a fitness guru/time management genius, that seems a little extreme. The only reason someone remains conscious for twenty hours a day is if there's something in their unconscious keeping them awake.

An uncomfortable question suddenly hits me: How well do I really know my roommate?

Shaking away the unsettling thought, I lean over to give Stella a hug. Before I can let go, she pulls me close and whispers in my ear.

"You're my sister, Lou. And family doesn't abandon family."

Wes

Operation Build Trip Tolerance got put on hold when first semester decided to ambush me behind an alley and beat me to a pulp. I would say I'm speaking in metaphors, but my brain tissue is still in recovery.

Whenever someone congratulated me on the varsity status, I assumed they were impressed with my ability to make it on the team. Turns out, they were congratulating me on willingly signing up for a juggling act that only gets worse with each passing week.

Scheduling master, I am not.

My problem is I love to be prepared. Like the psychology paper I crushed out in four hours, anytime there's a big assignment I just sit down and get it done. No point in wasting time and energy stressing over something that's easily checked off.

Are hefty assignments a pain in the ass to get done? Of course. Hence the adjective choice. But sitting down and grinding for a few hours makes the rest of your week and weekend so much easier. Sure, I fall into the eager student category but let me put it to you this way: would you rather be nursing a hangover Sunday morning by writing a ten-page essay, or would you rather be watching Netflix and catching up on some ZZ's?

My point exactly.

The obstacle I'm currently stuck on is the balance between training and school. My homework strategy works perfectly until I've got a 4PM lacrosse practice that cuts my homework time in half. Then by the time I shower, pack up my equipment, walk back to my dorm, and make some dinner, about three hours has gone by and the thought of sitting down and finishing the assignment is the last thing on my mind.

My jock and nerd tendencies are clashing against each other, and it feels as though there's not a thing I can do about it.

Musing this dilemma in my usual seat for psychology, I see Trip enter the auditorium. Her standard ponytail swings softly behind her as the four books shift precariously in her arms.

Without thinking, I push my chair back and holler, "TRIP! OVER HERE!"

Not my most subtle approach, but hey, it gets her attention.

Startled, she looks in my direction and I make an impatient *get over here* hand gesture. I see her eye roll from across the auditorium and I have to bite back a grin when she starts making her way towards my row.

I sit back down in my seat and it's only then that I realize both chairs on either side of me are full. Looking up and down my row, not a single chair stands empty. The only spots open are the ones I just waved Trip away from. Shit.

I quickly turn to my neighbour, the pretty brunette I befriended during the first psych class, and flash her my most charming smile.

"Serena, my beautiful queen, my unstoppable empress." I pause, making sure each word has a chance to sink in, "Would you so kindly do me a favour?"

Serena studies my dimples, tilting her head. Target has been hooked.

"I'll move. For twenty bucks."

I blink, my brain short-circuiting on how my target became the hustler within seconds.

"What happened to good will? Or helping out a friend in need?"

Serena shrugs without a trace of remorse, "I'm fulfilling my duties as an empress. Now, hand me a twenty so I can leave before your girl gets here."

And to think we live in a democracy.

"Tyrant." I mutter, pulling out my wallet.

Snatching the bill from my hand, Serena throws me a triumphant smile and sashays her way down to the front. I hope today's lecture is on ethics.

I put my wallet away and stand as Trip finally makes it to the newly emptied seat. Her head barely reaches my shoulders, and she looks up at me with a hesitant smile.

One of the things I like most about Trip is that there's nothing typical about her. From her misty eyes to her emo style, every aspect of Trip is perfectly unique. We all fall into some stereotype one way or another, but with Trip, she's an original.

She's also one of the few people who continues to surprise me. And for someone like me, surprise is... well, surprisingly refreshing.

"Am I allowed to sit down or are we going to stand through today's class?"

Taking a quick glance at today's t-shirt choice, I note Nirvana was the lucky winner. Classic.

"Mais oui, mademoiselle." Using the worst French accent humanly possible, I pull Trip's chair out with a flourish.

"Why thank you kind French man." She drops all her books onto the table with a bang and I drop back into my chair. Dropping my voice into a whisper, I make a shushing noise.

"Don't say that too loudly. The real Francophones will have my head if they hear you praising that accent."

"They couldn't handle your head if it was half the size." She playfully whispers back, and I have to physically restrain myself from taking a sniff of her hair. It's just shampoo for God's sake.

"You know, I have been told my size is abnormally large." My murmur causes a blush to stain her cheeks, but before Trip can formulate a response, Professor Anderson enters the room.

Conversation combat report: mission accomplished.

Silence falls between us as Anderson begins the day's lecture. The monologue is easy to tune out as I turn to look at the girl beside me.

One Mississippi, two Mississippi, three Mississippi...

"Quit staring." Trip whispers through the side of her mouth, refusing to shift her gaze one millimeter from Anderson's presentation.

"Not until you stop staring at the professor's goatee."

I watch her teeth grit from my side view.

"I'm not staring at his goatee, I'm paying attention."

"How can you pay attention and talk to me at the same time? Last class we learned there was no such thing as multi-tasking."

She breaks her stare down with Anderson's facial hair and turns to give me the full force of her glare.

"Did you invite me to sit here just to annoy me?"

A grin splits across my face, "Maybe."

Rolling her eyes, Trip shifts her chair to the left and starts taking notes. I follow her lead, opening my notebook and turning my attention to the lecture. Ten minutes go by, then twenty. At the half hour mark, I feel her looking over at me, no doubt curious about my lack of annoyance.

I let another fifteen minutes pass before tossing a piece of paper her way. She jumps when it hits her, and I stifle a laugh. Keeping my eyes trained on Anderson, I pretend not to notice the dirty look she shoots my way.

I continue taking notes, completely oblivious to the sound of paper crinkling as Trip unfolds the note. A couple seconds go by until the same piece of paper finds its way onto my lap.

"Excuse me miss, does this belong to you?" I hold the piece of paper towards Trip, pasting a puzzled expression onto my face. She rolls her eyes, choosing to ignore me.

Chuckling to myself, I unfold the note.

On a scale of one to goatee, how likely is it that Anderson assigns another essay due Monday?

My familiar handwritten scrawls along the top as I read Trip's response.

Goatee hands down. Good news is I showed up on time today, so it'll probably only be 8 pages instead of 10.

She's not wrong. Anderson has assigned us essays every single week, and so far, the longest one was the conditioning punishment. Coincidentally, every class since then, not a single student has showed up late. The deal is you're either seated, ready to go five minutes before class starts or you don't show up. After Trip's misfortune, we all learned the unwritten rules pretty quickly.

Have you learned to finish papers before Sunday night yet?

I toss the note over, aiming for her head. It misses and bounces off her nose onto the desk.

I do my best work last minute. You should try it sometime.

I scoff at her response.

Strategy over procrastination, honey. I dare you to try it.

I crumple the paper into a ball, line up my shot, and flick it over. Touchdown.

In that case, it's only fair you try my way. I'll finish this week's essay tonight and you have to wait until Sunday evening to get started.

I try not to flinch as I read her response. Talk about backfire. There's no way I can wait until Sunday evening to start my essay, my stress organs will collapse from the pressure. Although, I suppose there is still a way to turn this around....

You've got yourself a deal. But to make sure you complete the assignment by tonight, I'm going to have to supervise.

Surprise spreads across her face as she reads my note and I find myself holding my breath for her response.

After what feels like an eternity, a crumpled heap hits the side of my face. Resisting the urge to unfold it, I reach up and touch the spot it hit.

Ow, I mouth to her, cradling my cheek in my hands.

My charades pay off because the lip twitch Trip tries to contain turns into a full-on snort that resonates across the room. It's easily the best sound I've heard in years.

Our moment comes to a grinding halt when Anderson pauses mid-speech and looks directly at us.

"Is there something you'd like to share with the class, Miss Mackenzie?" We freeze like a couple of deer in headlights.

Serena, my money-smuggling empress now sitting in the front row, calmly raises her hand, "Sir, I was wondering about your office hours. Is there any chance you hold some online?"

The question does the trick, as Anderson's attention turns away from us and onto a long spiel of how online productivity compares to that of in person. Sending a silent prayer of thanks to the hustler in the front row, I slowly unravel Trip's message.

You're on.

Best twenty bucks I've ever spent.

CHAPTER 10

Lou

Becoming a proactive student is a lot harder than it looks.

I head to the library straight after class thinking I'll get a head start on the bet I made with Wes. Turns out sitting for two hours in front of a computer doesn't encourage productivity unless you actually start writing. Or, you know. Choose a topic to research.

I'm not even sure how I managed to kill two hours with absolutely nothing to show for. I remember reading the assignment sheet, opening my web browser, and then... nothing. Well, not *nothing*, it just so happens the moment I opened my web browser I received a notification that my favourite anime series released a new episode. And for me *not* to watch it would only be morally depleting, thus affecting my essay-writing abilities. Plus, the episode was only about forty-five minutes long... although the next hour spent brushing up on fandom feeds was probably not my best idea.

So, mistakes were made but you can't expect me to abandon all my procrastination tendencies on the first try.

I trudge back to my dorm, feeling oddly defeated. I was hoping to roll up to Wes' dorm, finished essay in toe, and slap it down proudly on his desk with a snarky remark. After this afternoon's efforts, however, the only thing I can slap down is a summary of that anime episode. Not quite the victorious image I had in mind.

I walk into the dorm and freeze. Sometime between my last class and my non-productive library session, Stella converted our living room into a dance floor. The two patchy sofas are pushed back against the walls, the TV is tucked further into the corner near our bathroom, and in the centre of it all, Stella is moving her hips in time to the music blasting from her phone lying on the floor.

"Oh-oh, that's what makes you beau- LOU!" I flinch as her singing switches to a shriek.

"Come join me. I'm practicing for this weekend." Stella adjusts the grip on her hairbrush, which I'm assuming is her substitute for a microphone. I frown, trying to remember what I'd agreed to this weekend.

"Are we clubbing again tomorrow?"

"No, silly. We're attending the first Punk Rockers convention, remember?"

I nod slowly, unwelcome butterflies filling my stomach. Out of all the clubs Stella and I signed up for, this is the one I'm most excited about. It's also the one that will hurt the most if I find myself on the social outskirts again.

"You know One Direction doesn't count as alternative rock, right?"

Stella waves my comment away, "Minor details. The important thing is there's going to be a karaoke stage, so we've got to be ready." She resumes her hip sways and I gawk in horror.

"Stella. I am not doing karaoke during our first club meeting. I can barely dance, let alone sing." And Wes won't be there to walk me through the awkwardness.

At the thought of Wes, I jolt, whipping out my phone to check the time, "Crap. I've got to run. I'm meeting Wes for an essay-writing workshop."

I shift from foot-to-foot, debating my chances of making a break for it when my tiny roommate whirls around to face me.

"Where is this essay-writing workshop taking place?"

Darn it. Missed my chance.

"I'm supposed to be at his dorm ten minutes from now." And considering his residence building is across campus, I'm going to have to run to make it on time. Nothing like showing up sweaty and out-of-breath for a study date. Er, I mean study session. Definitely study session.

"Sounds cozy. Is this a date then?"

"Absolutely not." I shake my head vehemently, choosing to ignore the fact I had the same train of thought moments before.

"Interesting. Are you wearing that to your hangout?" I look down at my Nirvana shirt clumsily tucked into my mom jeans. I check my phone again. Down to seven minutes.

"Yup. Now, I've really got to run. I'll text you when I'm on my way home." I catch the mischievous gleam in Stella's eyes as she shuffles over to give me a quick hug.

"Alright baby girl, have fun and make sure to give mama all the details when you get home. I expect a full debrief over breakfast." She playfully taps the side of my nose.

"I'll be home much sooner than breakfast, Stella."

"We'll see about that. Now, get your cute butt moving or you'll be late!"

I'm halfway out the door when she yells one last encouragement.

"Oh, and don't forget to give your boy a big smooch for me!" The door slams shut, and I pray the heat in my cheeks will be gone by the time I make it to Wes' dorm.

I arrive two minutes late, which all things considered, is pretty impressive.

At Taber University, all the varsity teams get put together in the residence buildings lining the East side of campus while the rest of the students live on the North side. The reasoning behind the separation is to help shorten the athletes' commute to the fitness centre and to help promote team bonding. The East side's proximity to the weight room and playing fields gives varsity players an extra few minutes of sleep before morning practice, and it helps to keep the noise complaints to a minimum.

Most of the teams run on a similar schedule (re: an ungodly amount of before-dawn exercise), so when 5am practices are looming, none of the players want to be disrupted by parties thrown by students who have nothing better to do with their time. Likewise, when tournament season ends and exam season begins, the athletes are ready to make up for lost time whereas the year-long partiers are ready to crack down to study. By splitting up residential buildings, Taber increases convenience while keeping the campus interconnected.

I text Wes, letting him know I arrived, and wait by the door. Each residence building has an automatic locking system with individual access cards per unit. So, my access card doesn't get me into Wes' building and his card wouldn't get him into mine. A simple system but one that ensures student safety.

I play on my phone to pass time until I hear the lock click open. The door inches open and one green eye peeks out.

"Unless you are selling alarm systems, I'm not interested."

My eyebrows creep towards my hairline, "Didn't realize you were sponsoring Taber's security systems now."

The door opens just enough so I can see exactly half of Wes' face.

"After a few incidents with a pack mule over carrying its load, I figured better not take any chances."

Fighting the urge to smile, I do my best to sound annoyed, "Very funny. Are you going to let me in or not?"

The annoyingly handsome side profile disappears and the door swings open.

"Welcome to the lacrosse quarters, Trip." Wes sweeps his hand majestically down the hall, one that is an exact replica to mine except for the colour. The lacrosse team scored an ugly burgundy wall colour, whereas Stella and I got mustard yellow. Between the two assaulting colours, I prefer the burgundy.

We hike up the stairs to the second level, reaching about halfway down the row of doors before stopping. Wes swipes his access card across the keypad and at the green light, we step inside.

I'm not sure what I expected Wes' dorm to look like, but an exact replica of my own was not it. The same ratty sofas line the two walls, facing an ancient television set that looks too old to function (Stella and I proved otherwise), and even the location of his bathroom is parallel to my own. For some reason, I pictured the varsity residences more glamorous. Or at least in a glorious state of disaster.

Looking around the room, I don't see a single pizza box, dirty dish, or any sort of overflowing garbage. The only thing out of place is a lacrosse bag strewn across one of the sofas. The overall cleanliness of the room feels underwhelming, if not boring.

"This one's mine." Wes points to the corner room, the one Stella has in our dorm. It's slightly bigger than my own, but not by much. Peeking my head into the room, I breathe a sigh of relief when I spot dirty socks peeking out from under his bed. Wes is human after all.

I take a step into his room and run smack into a huge, flat screen TV. I'd been so focused on finding evidence of dirtiness that I hadn't registered the 72" plasma screen precariously balancing on cardboard boxes just inside the doorway.

"That looks secure."

Wes laughs, "You should have seen me taping it down on move-in day. Nico just about became the first Latino Flat Stanley."

I lean forward to take a closer look and yup, I can see clear masking tape holding the boxes together.

"I can only imagine." And I totally could. When it comes to pulling off ludicrous charades, Wes is in a league of his own.

I move my eyes past the gigantic monitor and note the rumpled blue bedsheets and faded pictures taped to the wall. Between the discarded socks and the unmade bed, Wes has nearly sunken to my level of sloppiness. There's hope for him yet.

"May I?" I gesture towards the pictures and Wes gives me a nod, closing the distance between us so he can point out each one.

"That's Nico and me graduating elementary. We were in the fifth grade and our moms thought it would be cute to dress us up as if it were a proper graduation, so we ended up being the only kids wearing mortarboard hats and matching gowns. Thankfully, we both had the dashing good looks to pull them off."

I laugh, looking at the little boys in the picture playing with their matching tassels. Nico's heritage makes it easy to distinguish between the two, although even without the differing skin tones, the cheeky dimples popping out on the one's smile couldn't be mistaken for anyone but Wes.

"This one is the first time I scored a goal playing lacrosse in high school. Took days for the smell of Gatorade to wash out of my hair."

Turning to the next grainy print, I'm hit by an overwhelming sense of déjà vu. The shot was taken after the team drenched Wes, laughter breaking across his features as he sits in the middle of the puddle. The picture is almost an exact replica to the first memory I have of Wes: him laughing on the ground, sitting in a pile of my underwear.

"And this last one is from prom last year." Doing my best to shake off goosebumps from memory lane, I look at the last photo and suck in a breath. It's a graduation shot of Wes looking unbelievably handsome in a suit, standing next to the most beautiful girl I have ever seen. The two of them are laughing into the camera, Wes doing some sort of butler pose while the dark-haired beauty curtsies for the camera.

"Your date was stunning."

An uncomfortable feeling resembling disappointment settles in my chest. Wes isn't the type of guy interested in social outcasts. He's a social butterfly who attracts other, outrageously gorgeous social butterflies who ooze the same level of confidence as himself. The type of girls who are carefree enough to be captured laughing on camera.

The type of girls who had friends in high school.

Shaking his head, Wes chuckles good naturally, "You should have seen the number of guys who kept asking her to dance. Thank God my parents didn't allow Lace to attend the after-party."

I frown, trying to register the odd response, "Your parents didn't let your girlfriend attend the after-party with you?"

Wes looks at me in horror, "Lace is short for Lacey. As in my younger sister. As in blood relation."

"Oh. *Oh.*"

Wes bursts out laughing, and my cheeks redden immediately. Quickly taking another peek at the picture, I start to see the similarities I had missed before. Lacey's dark locks and porcelain skin match her brother's perfectly. Her smile is missing the dimples but the twinkle in her hazel eyes is one I've seen many times.

Feeling ridiculous for my misassumption, I decide to ask the more obvious question, "Why was your sister your prom date?"

It couldn't be because he had no other options. Our friendship might be questionably platonic, but my vision is perfectly intact.

An emotion I can't identify flickers across Wes' face before his charming smile slides back into place.

"I could tell you but then I'd have to kill you. Now, quit wasting time and show me how far you've gotten on that paper."

Wes

Nothing. She's done absolutely nothing.

I thought she was joking when she pulled out the assignment sheet in response to my comment. Turns out Trip deserves an Olympic gold medal for procrastination, because if I'm hearing right, the reason behind her lack of progress is because she spent two hours in the library... watching Netflix.

"Technically, I only spent half the time watching and the other half reading."

I cross my arms in disbelief, "You read the psych textbook for an hour?"

The blush from earlier returns to her cheeks.

"Well, no. I was brushing up on my... pop culture."

I bite my lip to keep from smiling, "I don't recall a lot of pop culture on the assignment sheet."

"Well, you obviously didn't read it thoroughly."

"Obviously." Her glare turns into an unspoken staring contest and soon we're both widening our eyes to unnatural degrees to keep from blinking. The burning sensation kicks in and I will myself not to break.

Those gorgeous grey eyes are going down.

Thankfully, Trip cracks before I have to cheat – hey, failure is not an option – and after wiping victorious tears from my eyes, we get down and dirty with psychology.

"Okay, so what topic did you decide on?" Her silence does nothing for my confidence. Sighing, I ask the more appropriate question, "Have you chosen a topic yet?"

At the shake of her head, I pull out my own outline to give her some encouragement.

Trip gasps in outrage and points at my detailed essay plan, "You weren't allowed to start until Sunday!"

"I'm not allowed to start *writing* until Sunday. You never said anything about planning. And FYI, planning is what most students do *after* they choose a topic." I throw her a wink and get a wrinkled brow in return.

Man, I love it when she scowls at me.

ele

"I think the conclusion can wait until tomorrow." I offer the suggestion helpfully, but the look that gets thrown my way makes me think it didn't come across so well.

"Right. I can finish this conclusion tomorrow, so you can win by default *and* get to finish your paper early? Nope. Don't think so." I bark out a laugh at Trip's unexpected competitiveness.

I knew she was stubborn, pack mules often are, but the competitive streak comes as a surprise. Her attitude towards our bet is one you would expect from a varsity player, the ride or die mentality high-level athletes are ingrained with, yet Trip doesn't give off the jock vibe. Hell, I shouldn't be surprised, every vibe Trip gives off is her own.

She's like my very own Rubik's cube, no matter how many times I twist the squares around they never seem to line up. And yet, every time I find a new colour all I want to do is keep twisting until I find more.

"Alright, Einstein. No need to get your panties in a twist. You've got one page to go. Keep that pretty little head of yours in the game."

Without breaking momentum with her furious typing, Trip throws a retort my way.

"I'm pretty sure Einstein didn't have a little head. And I've never understood that saying."

It takes a second for me to clue in.

"Keep your head in the game? Honey, that is the most iconic line of Zac Efron's career."

She pauses her typing to glance over, "I don't remember him saying that in Baywatch."

My gasp fills the room, "You did not just say that." Her gaze turns sheepish as it meets mine. "I'm... sorry?"

I get up from the couch and start pacing the four feet of my living room.

"Are you telling me that you have never seen the Disney TV pilot turned accidental hit movie turned unforgettable trilogy that set the basis for our *entire* generation? Does the name Troy Bolton not mean anything to you?"

Trip squeezes her eyes shut in concentration.

"It sounds sort of familiar... I'm sorry. I got nothing."

And here I thought her procrastination was bad. This is an *abomination.*

Nope, she probably wouldn't get that reference either.

"This has to be reconciled. Immediately. When you come over Sunday to supervise my last-minute scrambling skills, we are going to watch High School Musical. All three of them."

She tilts her head at me, visibly confused, "Why would anyone make a musical out of high school?"

I hold my hand out in front of me, valiantly trying to protect my heart from more abuse.

"Trip. You're killing me. Finish up that conclusion so I can revive myself." I dramatically collapse on the ground just as the door to my dorm swings open.

"Aw, man not again. Wes, what did we say about dying on the living room floor?" Nico smirks down at me from the doorway.

"Couldn't help it. Trip over there doesn't know who Troy Bolton is." Eyes widening in horror, Nico sways unsteadily into the room and proceeds to collapse in a heap on top of me. If there's one thing I can count on my best friend for, its joining in on my theatrics.

Giggling, Trip pretends to dial her phone, "9-1-1 operator? Yes, it's Lou Mackenzie. I was wondering if I could get some help down at the lacrosse quarters... cause? It appears to be a shock overdose."

"Don't forget trauma." My muffled yell is barely audible through Nico's sweater. Jesus, did he have to go all deadweight on me? Now I understand where Trip was coming from that first day.

"Ask them to send firemen. We need CPR and if I'm getting mouth-to-mouth, it better be by someone who can look sexy next to a dalmatian." Nico's comment draws a laugh from Trip as she dutifully repeats his request.

"Dude, Cruella de Vil has always been sexy." My response is more of a wheeze thanks to the muscular Latino lounging on top of me.

"Bro. Those dalmatians were dead. *Anyone* can make a fur coat look sexy. Keeping your masculinity while riding alongside a spotted hound on the daily? Now that takes skill."

Trip nods in agreement, "He's got a point."

I huff, "Tag teamed in my own dorm. I always pictured it better than this."

I get an eye roll from Trip while Nico laughs, finally climbing off me. He grabs my outstretched hand and hauls me back to my feet. Twelve years later and we're still pulling each other off the ground.

"Did you get your conclusion done?" I turn to Trip, part of me hoping she'll say no so she can stay longer, the other half already exhausted thinking about the morning practice we have tomorrow.

"I did, no thanks to you boys." Turning to my roommate, she reaches out her hand, "Nice to finally meet you, Nico. Wes has told me a lot about you."

Nico takes her hand and pulls her in for a hug, "You saved my life. We're way past the handshake stage."

As Trip laughs in his embrace, Nico shoots me an evil grin over her shoulder.

"As for Wes, well, let's just say he has told me a lot about you too."

Bastard.

CHAPTER 11

Lou

"Nico fell on top of him?! I cannot believe I missed this." Stella throws a piece of popcorn into her mouth, chewing thoughtfully. "A fair reaction to your lack of HSM awareness, though. Those movies were like the foundation of our generation."

I steal some of her popcorn and she scoots the bowl closer to me.

"You sound just like Wes. What's so important about these movies anyways?"

"It's not so much the movies themselves, it's the message within them. Our parents grew up in a time where everyone fell into a stereotypical category: if you liked sports, you were a jock. If you liked theatre, you were a drama geek. It was a more judgemental time but also much simpler. The group that matched your vibe became your friends and vice versa."

Taking a quick popcorn break, Stella continues, "Technology was a factor, but our generation wanted to branch out. We didn't want to be stuck on one setting anymore. The issue is, when you get used to being one thing, it makes it harder to try something new because it means leaving the protective bubble we build around ourselves." Stella's words hit home as she takes another popcorn break.

"So, long story not-so short, High School Musical is about putting yourself out there to pursue interests that go beyond your comfort zone." I shift uneasily on the couch, feeling oddly exposed.

"Throw in some teenage angst, spontaneous singing, a young Zac Efron, and you've got yourself a hit series that is the very *essence* of Generation Z." Stella finishes her monologue with a loud kernel crunch.

"Wow." I take a moment to let it sink in, "And here I thought Nico collapsing on top of Wes was dramatic."

With an indignant shriek, Stella starts throwing popcorn at me.

I laugh, trying to bat away her offensive measures, "Ease off the rapid fire, soldier! Target has been eliminated. I repeat, the target has been eliminated."

Finally putting her kernel ammunition back onto the ground, Stella gives me a salute and we fall over laughing.

⁕

The perks of having my psychology paper done early is my weekend feels a lot longer. It's an illusion of course, my weekend is still only two days long and there are five course readings I haven't even thought about (Monday morning's problem), but I can see why Wes promotes the whole proactive student thing. My stress levels have easily reduced 75% and my day already feels so much more enjoyable.

Instead of using my free time to work on readings, I decide to head to the courtyard to escape for a bit. Back in high school, whenever life felt tougher than usual, my go-to haven was always Brooks' plant oasis.

Priding itself on promoting eco-friendly applications, Brooks Academy was one of the first Canadian high schools to host a fully functioning greenhouse on school grounds. With solar panels on the roof and a geothermal system underground, Brooks' renowned garden centre was the school's leading source of energy. Solar power fuelled the school's electricity, while geothermal supplied heat for long winters. Their environmentally conscious efforts went as far as limiting the cafeteria menu to only offering food grown by the garden club. It was every vegan's dream, and as an ecologist's daughter, it held a soft spot for me as well.

It wasn't until a particularly bad lunch hour that I discovered non-garden club students were allowed in the greenhouse. I stumbled into it by accident, tears blurring my vision as I ran from the girl's locker room to the first unlocked door I could find. Damp streaks ran down my cheeks as I suddenly found myself surrounded by every fruit and vegetable imaginable. There was something about being in a room full of life, without a person in sight, that made me feel at home. My tears were soon forgotten and from that day forward, anytime I found myself in need of refuge, my feet would carry me back to that special place.

Taber's courtyard reminds me of my old sanctuary. The scenery is completely different, but the tranquility feels the same.

Watching fallen leaves flutter in the breeze, I think back on Stella's monologue from last night. Somewhere between the background context and the film breakdown, Stella's words began to feel personal. Whether that was Stella purposefully hinting at the necessity of watching these films or sheer coincidence, I don't know. What I do know is that by the end, it felt as though she had found the cord tying all my insecurities together and tugged them to the surface.

My train of thought leads me to a clump of yellow daisies sitting a few feet from the bench. Plucking one from the grass, the chain of flowers appears untouched, as though the missing one never belonged in the first place. A wave of sadness crashes over me as I stare at the plucked flower resting in my palm.

When I graduated from Brooks, my departure didn't make a single mark of an impact. Unlike the professors and students handing out heartfelt goodbyes left and right, I had no one. My only friends were the petals attached to my own stem.

When I left, there was no break in the chain. It was just me.

I want Taber to be different. *I* want to be different. I'm tired of being the girl who gets nervous about social outings, the girl who is terrified of leaving her protective bubble. The last few weeks have been better than my entire high school career, but I'm still... well, me.

Folding the daisy carefully in my palm, I look at the remaining cluster. How does one go from being the social outcast to the social butterfly? Stella and Wes make it look so easy. Heck, they make it *feel* so easy. I swear the only time I don't second guess myself is when I'm around those two. Somehow, they make me feel as if every misshapen piece of me fits perfectly.

I stand up and throw the stray flower back onto the grass. The lone daisy instantly gets swallowed by the wave of yellow, its return completely indifferent to the patch. I turn and start walking back to my dorm, making a silent vow to myself along the way.

When it comes time to leave Taber, I'm breaking the chain on my way out.

Wes

"If you boys don't tighten up those passes, Silverwood is going to kick our ass next weekend."

We're all lined up on the field, getting ripped into for the second time today. Cody slowly walks past each player, holding each of us accountable. He pauses when he gets to Hunter.

"Show up late to practice again and you're off the team. Got it?" Hunter nods sullenly, his shaggy hair flopping to one side.

"Well? Did you hear what I said or not. Use your words, rookie."

"I got it, Cap. I won't be late again."

"Good." With a dismissive nod, Cody lets us go.

Hunter grabs his gear and boots it off the field like his ass is on fire. I almost feel bad for the guy. Hunter showed up late during our training camp when he got lost trying to find the practice field. Today, he rolled in ten minutes late, completely missing warm-up and making us all do a field lap as punishment. Hence the almost sympathy.

Honestly, it's not Hunter's fault Cody is in a pissy mood. Not only is our season opener less than seven days from now, but it's also against Taber's biggest rival, the Silverwood Sabers. Next weekend will be Cody's first official game as team captain, and if the school's undefeated status wasn't pressure enough, rumour is Mighty Mo might make an appearance. Add in the fact Cody's still butt sore from Hunter tonguing his freshman crush and you've got yourself one uptight captain.

"Think Stella's still giving him the silent treatment?" Nico murmurs the question as I help him pack up the nets. I check to make sure Cody isn't within ear range before responding. I'd rather not be put on his terminal list before the season opener.

"Last I heard, she's been spreading the nickname Caveman Cody among gym regulars."

Nico grins and I mentally applaud the update Trip texted me about the other day. We don't message very often but when we do, it's of the highest importance.

This particular update, or The Cody Highlight as I like to call it, came in a few nights ago, while I was having wing night with the boys.

TRIP: I've got tea.

ME: I'll bring the crumpets.

TRIP: Why are you like this?

Excusing myself from the table, I got up and wandered over to the men's restroom. I could feel the grin forming on my face and didn't want Nico to call me out in front of the team.

ME: Like what? Crumpets are a perfectly respectable tea treat. Ask the queen.

TRIP: Forget the tea and crumpets. Stella has started a revenge rumour among gym regulars.

I smirked to myself, leaning against a nearby wall. She didn't have to tell me who the revenge strike was against.

ME: If my captain finds out I know about this scheme, he'll make me run field laps until I die. SPILL.

TRIP: You sure you want to sacrifice yourself for this?

ME: Never been more certain of anything.

I stared impatiently at my screen, watching typing bubbles pop up only to disappear. I knew Trip was doing it on purpose but damn if it didn't get under my skin.

ME: Speed it up, honey. My life is on the line here.

Two painful minutes dragged on until finally her response came through.

TRIP: Caveman Cody earned himself a new title.

ME: Worth the sacrifice.

My thoughts snap back to present at the sound of Nico's voice, "Does this mean we get to call him *Captain* Caveman Cody?"

I burst out laughing, "That sounds like a bad pornstar name."

Swinging the equipment bag over my shoulder, I drop my voice to a low octave.

"Caveman Cody hungry. He see woman. He want woman."

Chuckling, Nico shakes his head at my spot-on impression, "I'll always be surprised you didn't become a drama major."

"Dude. How many drama majors do you know get laid?"

"Good point." We start walking towards the locker room when Cody comes running up behind us.

"Wes, can I talk to you for a moment?"

Shit. I hope he didn't overhear my imitation of his pre-historic self.

"Sure." I slow down, already praying the punishment won't be more than five laps. There's got to be points for imagination, right?

"What are you doing tonight?" The question takes me by surprise, and it takes me a moment not to blurt out *Wes party. Wes meet woman. Wes want woman.*

"Well, a girl in my finance class was throwing a party that I was thinking of... I mean, it was a pretty loose invitation, so if you want to hang tonight, I'm cool."

Cody does not realize the sacrifice I just made. The party is being hosted by a bombshell blonde with the nicest ass. She already told me where I could meet her for the private party, if you know what I mean. But hey, if my captain is feeling lonely, then I am happy to keep the guy company.

"Er, thank you for the offer but I was going to ask if you were attending the Punk Rockers event tonight."

Huh. So, not the lonely vibes I thought.

"Punk Rockers event. You mean like a club?" My earlier caveman impression has come back to haunt me. My brain feels dense as a rock.

No wonder Darwin's theory worked so well.

"Ya, the club Punk Rockers is hosting their first event tonight. I'm not a member but both Stella and Trip are going, so I was just thinking if you were going as well, then I would be happy to keep you company."

My neurons are starting to fire again, and I'm detecting a strategic conversation technique going on here. My captain needs a wingman but he doesn't want to ask out loud.

"Cap, I got you. You don't need to worry about anything, okay? I'll be right by your side the *whole* time." I throw him a wink Will Ferrell style, so he knows I'm on his radar.

Giving me a confused look, Cody nods, "Right. I'll let Stella know you agreed to tag along then."

Feeling like a proud dad, I clap my hand on his shoulder.

"This is going to be great, Cap. I can *feel* it."

CHAPTER 12

Lou

The only thing worse than letting Stella pick out my outfit? Letting Stella pick out my costume.

That's right. Costume. As in material worn to resemble someone else. As in showing up to the first club event looking like a rocker chick from the eighties. I don't even want to know where Stella found our matching leather pantsuits. Or how much hair spray is currently holding my 'fro in place.

The one thing I do know is I'm going to need scissors to get these pants off by the end of the night. Oh, and about a pound of conditioner if I ever want to think about brushing my hair again.

"Oh my gosh, they went all out!"

Stella's excited squeal cuts through my thoughts as we approach the bar hosting the club opener. Banners have been hung outside the entrance, loudly blaring PUNK ROCKERS WELCOME! on either side of the door. Students stream into the building, all wearing various degrees of costume. Most are sporting a leather jacket or a vintage concert shirt of some kind, while others are in full rockstar mode with big hair, tight pants, and lots of eyeliner.

For a minute I forget I am one of the wannabe rockers until the bouncer compliments Stella's leather-clad efforts.

"Not many people can pull off matching pantsuits, but you ladies do it well."

He passes back our IDs and Stella grabs them with a wink. I would guess he's around our age, but the dark sunglasses make it hard to tell. Anywhere between twenty and forty is probably a safe bet.

"Is it legal for bouncers to hit on patrons?" I muse the question out loud as we walk into the crowded bar.

"The better question is, who here is hot enough to make *you* commit a felony tonight?" Before I have a chance to respond, Stella gasps and pulls me to a halt, "Do you think that's where we karaoke?!"

Sucking in breath to prepare myself, I follow her pointed finger to a stage with smoke machines whirling and *The Killers* blasting over massive speakers. A lone microphone stands in the middle of the raised platform with a single spotlight beaming directly on to it. I look back at Stella, her eyes glowing with excitement, and swallow the bile rising in my throat.

"I certainly hope not. Those smoke machines are definitely a health hazard." Stella laughs and pulls me to a nearby table.

Thankfully, the table is empty because I don't feel ready to start socializing just yet. Between the costumes, the stage, and the crowd piling into the room, saying I feel overwhelmed would be an understatement.

Puffing the permed hair out of my eyes, I stare down at the table and focus on taking deep breaths. Karaoke doesn't start for another hour, and worse comes to worst, no one is going to recognize me in this getup.

A small hand slides across the table and grasps my fingers. Jumping in surprise, I look up to see Stella smiling reassuringly at me.

"You're doing great, Lou. I am so proud of you."

Continuing to breath past the panic gripping my throat, I give her hand a squeeze, "What did I do to deserve you?"

She grins, nodding playfully towards my outfit, "You willingly put on a leather pantsuit. I've had a wedgie for the last hour, but I think I've played it cool."

I burst out laughing. As far as comfort goes, Stella's costume choice is severely lacking. Not only is the leather tight, it's also shockingly hot. And as more students pile into the tight quarters, the temperature inside *and* outside my pants continues to increase.

Suddenly, Stella shifts uneasily in her seat, her gravity-defying hair still managing to hit her low back, "I should probably tell you-

Her words get cut off when an Axl Rose impersonator walks on stage. Cheers erupt from the crowd and despite the nerves cursing through my system, I feel a zing of excitement.

"Well, isn't this a good-looking crowd!" More cheers break out. Unsurprisingly, the rowdiest section appears to be coming from the bar.

"First off, I want to thank all of you for coming to Punk Rockers' first official club event. We love having you here and we hope you love being here. And what better way to kick off the season than with some friendly competition?"

Whoops and shouts scatter across the crowd. I sneak a glance at Stella and see her attention is wholly invested on stage. As soon as the word competition was dropped, I should have known we'd be in for the long haul.

Chuckling to himself, the MC shakes his head, "Keep this energy up folks and we'll be in for a fun night. Alright, first up we got a little punk trivia, top three winners will win prizes, after that we got our costume contest – phew, even from here I can see some fierce contenders." He pauses, sweeping his eyes purposefully over the crowd, "And as always, we will finish the night with the fan favourite... dance karaoke!"

I look at my roommate in horror as the room erupts into applause for the fifth time in the last five minutes.

"*Dance* karaoke?" I squeak out the words as Stella vibrates in her seat in anticipation.

"We *got* this, Lou. Three for three, no problem." My friend's competitive nature has already taken over her mind and left me stranded. Guess it's time to sink or swim.

"Alright, trivia is first, so we need to find the sheets..." Stella's sentence trails off, her mouth dropping open. I whirl in my seat, searching for the object that's left my talkative roommate speechless.

"What? What is it?"

Stella finally closes her mouth and gulps visibly, "Not what, Lou. *Who.*"

My gaze scans the nearby tables, trying to not laugh at the ridiculous amount of eyeliner both men and women are currently rocking.

As a familiar blonde fauxhawk comes into view, I have to bite my lip to keep from smiling. Stella is ogling none other than her sworn nemesis, Mr. Caveman Cody. The lacrosse captain appears to be wearing a biker jacket of some sort, the black leather stretching tight against his broad shoulders and trailing into a pair of worn-out jeans.

He looks like he should be on the cover of a Ducati magazine.

"I think you've found your partner in crime." My reference to her earlier comment has Stella sticking her tongue out at me.

"I didn't invite Cody for me, silly."

I wrinkle my nose in confusion, "What are you talking about? I thought you were still giving Caveman the silent treatment."

Stella turns her attention to her nails, purposefully avoiding my gaze, "Right. Well, that kind of ended a couple days ago when I asked Cody if he could get Wes to come tonight."

I stare at her incredulously, "And why would you want Wes to come tonight?"

The thought that Stella might be into Wes crosses my mind, but I immediately shoot down the idea. After the few weeks I've gotten to know my roommate, this has her matchmaker schemes written all over it.

Stella sighs with defeat, "I wanted him to come for you! You've been spending so much time together that I thought a night out would be a fun way to get to know each other a little better. Or, you know, get absolutely wasted and play a game of tongue tag."

My brows knit together as Stella gives me a pleading look.

"Please don't be mad, Lou. Joking aside, you always seem at ease whenever Wes is around. I just thought you might enjoy tonight more if he was here. That's it, that's all."

I continue to eye her suspiciously as Cody approaches our table.

"I grabbed enough trivia forms for everyone. Are you ladies having fun so far?" Cody does a double take of our outfits, eyes fixating on Stella's leather ensemble. He lets out a low whistle, "If I'd known how fierce the costume contest was going to be, I would have agreed to twin with Wes."

Stella scoffs and tosses her mane of hair, "I doubt that would have been enough."

Cody lets out a laugh, his eyes never leaving Stella's perfectly made-up face. I stand on my tip toes, peering over the mountain of shoulders in front of me.

"Where is the all-star rookie, anyways?" I ignore the knowing look Stella trades with Cody and continue my scan of the bar.

She said so herself: Wes makes me feel comfortable. So, the fact that I am excited to see *my friend* does not warrant a silent conversation with Mr. Caveman over there. And as for the tongue tag comment, that was completely off-side, I don't know how many times I have to tell Stella there is nothing going on between...

"Words cannot say how much it warms my heart to hear you say that Trip." Stella's eyes widen as she takes in the presence behind me. I force the smile creeping over my face into a scowl and whirl around, retort ready on the tip of my tongue.

"Who said I was talking about..." My response disappears and suddenly I'm the one visibly gulping.

Wes

"Are you... are you wearing eyeliner?" The question comes from Stella, who is looking dynamite in her skin-tight pantsuit and frizzed out platinum hair, while Trip continues to gawk at me.

"Sure am. Last time I checked, Billie never performs without it." My response is directed at Trip, hoping she will catch my reference. My costume is, after all, inspired by her love of punk bands.

From the charcoal around my eyes, gelled spikes in my hair, and black dress shirt / red tie combo I was going for the lead singer of her favourite band. Well, I don't actually know if Green Day is her favourite, but given they were featured on her t-shirt the other day, I figured it would be a safe bet. Taking in the stricken expression on her face, however, I'm starting to worry I was wrong.

"Billie?"

Stella is not helping the situation. I can feel my costume confidence decreasing by the second. Next time I'm bleaching my hair and going as Machine Gun Kelly. Bet she wouldn't forget him too.

"He's the lead singer of Green Day." Saving the day, Trip breaks out of her trance and pats her roommate on the arm, "I'm afraid Green Day doesn't run in the same circles as One Direction."

Not even attempting to dissect that sentence, I feel relief rush through me. My effort was not in vain.

Stella shakes her head solemnly, "The world would be a much brighter place if everyone appreciated One Direction."

I raise my glass in toast while Trip rolls her eyes. I hide my smirk, secretly pleased I am not the only one who causes that reaction.

Suddenly remembering my duties as Cody's wingman, I quickly pull out the chair next to Trip, forcing Cody to take the one next to Stella. Not my most subtle tactic, but efficient, nonetheless. Stella instantly turns and starts talking to my captain while Trip reaches for the closest trivia sheet.

Having my own costume identity crisis averted, I shift to get a better view of Trip's fit for the night. 80s style curls bounce along her shoulders as golden highlights tease their way through Trip's otherwise dark hair. The skin-tight pantsuit appears to be identical to that of Stella's, but damn do they wear it differently. Trip's subtle curves are embraced to their fullest, the black leather stretching tight over her rack and emphasizing her slender frame. Her eyes are as heavily made-up as my own – a tragic comparison, I know – with some extra sparkly powder glittering at the corners.

She looks like every guy's leather clad dream.

Sliding the questionnaire over, Trip's eyes flick to mine, and the swirling shades of grey seem to call my name.

"Alright, rockers let's get this show on the road! Does everyone have trivia questions in front of them?" Tearing my gaze from the vision beside me, I turn my attention to the MC walking back on stage.

"To make sure everyone has a fighting chance, I am giving you two minutes to google as many answers as possible. Once those two minutes are up, it will be whichever table yells out the answers the fastest. Everyone understand?" I cheer along with the rest of the bar. "Perfect. Phones out, web browsers ready... and go!"

Everyone at our table scrambles to pick up their phones.

"Alright team, listen up. If we do this systematically, we can cover more ground." Ever the leader, Cody starts delegating questions to each of us, "Stel, you've got the first section, Trip the one after that, and Wes and I will handle the last one. Got it?" We all nod in unison, jumping into virtual action.

In a screen lit blaze of glory, my fingers fly over the keyboard, pounding question after question into my search engine. Time flies and before I know it, the buzzer sounds, putting an end to our google venture. Leaning back in my chair, I shake out my fingers, giving them a well-deserved stretch. Trip sees my cool-down exercise and raises an eyebrow.

"How many did you find?"

Giving a modest shrug, I casually throw out my number, "Five and a half. I've been told my ability to type fast is uncanny."

A second eyebrow raises to meet the other, teeth coming down to bite on her bottom lip. I narrow my eyes, completely ignoring the way her lips look in that dark red lipstick and address the reason behind her not-so-hidden smirk.

"How many did *you* find?"

Trip's attempt to hide her smug smile fails and a sly grin breaks across her face.

"Seven." I gape at her, unable to process how she managed to crush my typing reputation and vacuum all the air out of my lungs with just one smile.

"I found five." Cody's voice interrupts my spiralling thoughts while Stella cackles with glee.

"Eight for me. I win, losers." Chuckling, Cody shakes his head while Trip leans over to give her roommate a high five.

I frown good-naturally, "If we're all on the same team, doesn't that mean we all win?"

"Sure does, Billie. But now we know who's the most valuable player on the team." Stella blows me a kiss and I pretend to bat it away midair.

ele

"Down to the final two teams. Now to make this round a little more exciting, we are going to get the teams to go head-to-head. Can I get the Lavishing Leather Ladies and the Punk Ponies to the front of the stage please?"

The bar breaks into applause as our table stands up and walks towards the stage. Our rival table in the far corner gets up to join us. Throughout the trivia game, the Punk Ponies had easily kept up with our Google-searched knowledge, and sadly, some of their players were as enthusiastic as Stella. You would think Stella shouting answers from atop a bar stool would be hard to beat, but somehow the Ponies managed. We couldn't see their table from our vantage point, but I would bet someone got up on the bar to match Stella's energy.

We line up along the elevated platform, facing the opposing team. I can feel Trip twitching anxiously beside me, so I reach down and grab her hand for support. Her breath catches as I thread her fingers through my own, giving them a reassuring squeeze. She squeezes back and a warm feeling envelops my chest.

Maybe I've convinced Trip I'm not so bad after all.

The MC hops down from the stage and stalks between both teams. Up close, his blonde wig is a lot less impressive, but you've got to give the guy kudos for the Guns N' Roses tattoo covering his forearm. It shows true commitment to the cause.

"Alright rockers, who is ready for the speed round?" He throws both hands in the air and the crowd goes wild. Trip shifts nervously beside me, her hand still in mine. I look at our other teammates and see Cody fighting a smile when Stella attempts to intimidate the opponents with her miniature stature. Shoulders boxed out, head held high, the girl barely hits 5'2 in those heels yet stares down our opponents as if she's LeBron James going in for a dunk.

"I'm going to read out three questions. The team that answers two correct wins. Everyone understand?"

Everyone nods except Stella, who beats her fists against her chest warrior style. I bite back a laugh as the guy opposite her flinches. Guess he wasn't expecting to go up against a mini-King Kong.

"Alright the first question is an easy one... Where was punk rock invented?"

"NEW YORK CITY!" The girl wearing fishnet stockings yells out the answer before I have time to process the question being asked.

"And a point goes to the Punk Ponies! Lavishing Leather Ladies, you better be careful. This next one could keep you in the game or knock you out." Leaning forward, I put all my focus on the MC's next words.

"Who is the father of punk rock?"

Silence falls upon both teams as brain power kicks into overdrive. Flipping through my storage of useless information, I search for anything relating to rock. Hold on, back in high school we had to watch a documentary about...

"I got it! Joey Ramone." The Axl impersonator nods in approval and Stella runs over to give me a high five. A grin the size of Mount Everest lights up my face and Trip gives my hand a squeeze. There's nothing like the rush of competition.

"And a point for the Lavishing Leather Ladies! Well done, young man." Choosing to overlook the fact this guy can't be more than two years older than me, I take the compliment, "Both teams are at one point with one question left. Are we ready to find a champion?" The bar erupts into cheers, drunk rockers wholly invested in our performance.

"Alright, last question..." I hold my breath and feel Trip do the same, "What defines punk rock?"

My mind goes blank. Are angry teenagers a definition?

"Punk rock is often described as offensive expressions of alienation and social discomfort." The crowd goes nuts, taking me a moment to register who the response came from. The question is answered when Stella runs over and wraps her roommate in a ginormous hug.

I look over at the duo in astonishment, partly for the mauling Trip is currently undertaking, but mostly for her feat of public speaking. Just a few weeks ago I was ushering Trip away from the chaos of rush week to comfort her, and now she's bringing our team to victory in front of hundreds of people.

Meeting my eyes over Stella's bouncing shoulders, Trip gives me a heart-stopping smile and mouths, *any version I want to be.*

CHAPTER 13

Lou

If someone told me I would be describing the definition of punk rock in a packed bar, standing in front of a stage while holding hands with a smouldering Billie Joe Armstrong, I would have laughed until I died. That is something social butterflies do, not social outcasts. Yet, here I am, using my personal connection with alienation and social discomfort to successfully conquer punk trivia.

"Folks, we have a winner! Let's hear it for the Lavishing Leather Ladies!"

The bar breaks into applause once more and we head back to our table. The entire walk back, I find myself congratulated by eyeliner-wearing strangers. Feeling my cheeks heat from all the attention, I duck my head until we get back to the confines of our table. My actions might be a far cry from the invisible girl back in high school, but my internal discomfort appears to be the same.

"You did really well back there, Trip." Cody's comforting voice washes over me as we return to our seats.

"Well? She was fucking amazing." The outburst comes from Stella, who hasn't stopped vibrating since we were announced the winners.

Her comment makes me laugh, "Whoever scored the winning point was bound to be ranked amazing in Stella's books." Cody nods his head in agreement while Stella gasps in mock outrage.

"Winning isn't *everything*. It just makes everything *better*."

Shaking my head in amusement, I watch as Stella and Cody fall into a debate over who is the worse loser.

"She's right, you know." The whisper breathes into my ear, sending chills down my spine.

"Winning makes everything better?" I playfully whisper back, our proximity close enough that I can smell the minty scent of Wes' breath.

Wes laughs, the husky sound resonating through my skin, "I can't argue with that, but I meant the other one. You were fucking amazing back there."

The words send a rush of pleasure through me, bringing a deeper flush to my cheeks. Between the hand holding, the compliments, and the getup Wes is wearing tonight, I am at a complete disadvantage.

"You weren't so bad yourself." When Wes pulled out the answer for the second question, I was unbelievably shocked. He didn't strike me as a head banger type of guy, but maybe I misjudged him. That certainly seems to be the case for most things involving Wes.

He leans back in his seat, throwing me a wink. "Anything to impress the prettiest girl in the room."

I feel my grin grow wider, "It was a complete guess, wasn't it?"

Narrowing his beautiful eyes, Wes tilts his head," I don't appreciate the assumption. We have already secured my nerd status, what reason do you have to doubt me?"

I continue to smirk, waiting for the inevitable. About thirty seconds goes by until he gives in.

"Fine. I only remembered someone's name being close to Ramen. The fact Ramone ended up being punk rock may or may not have been luck on my part." I raise my fist in triumph and he pouts, "Hey, it wasn't a *complete* guess. My memory simply stored the important part."

"Like someone being named after cheap noodles."

"Exactly." We smile at each other, the buzzing bar fading into the background. Suddenly all I can see are sparkling emeralds, midnight-coloured spikes, and a loose red tie that looks like an invitation to grad a hold of.

A cough across the table drags my attention away from the fantasy sitting beside me.

"So, I was just saying the costume contest is about to start. Do you want to join me?" Stella raises her eyebrow, "Unless you're done for the night, then maybe Wes can take you home?" I can't tell if the glint in her eyes is a challenge to stay or to go.

"No way I'm missing the costume contest. We're in this together, remember?"

My heart starts to pound as I hastily trade one bad idea for another. Nothing like volunteering to walk the green mile twice in one night for the sake of friendship.

"As if I could forget. Come on, we've got to line up on stage." I gulp as Stella threads her arm through mine, pulling me out of my seat and towards the stage.

Tugging me closer, she leans in to whisper in my ear, "Not that I don't appreciate the roommate bonding, hon, but the smoldering man beside you would have been a *fun* ride home."

I sneak a glance back at the man in question, huffing a laugh when he throws me two thumbs up and a beaming smile.

"That's what I'm afraid of."

Stella leads me up the stairs to the stage, scrunching her nose up in confusion, "You're afraid Wes might put his years of experience to good use?"

My cheeks burn red as we join the lineup, "No. I mean, yes. I mean… we're good friends and I don't want to lose him."

"Okay, let's get a few things straight." Stella holds up her fingers, "First off, that man has not taken his eyes off you the entire night. And don't think I didn't see your little hand holding moment earlier."

I open my mouth to interrupt, but the second finger silences me. "*Second*, an informant told me Wes purposely chose his outfit tonight because he knew you would like it. Someone who looks like that does not wear eyeliner unless he has a purpose."

Seeing my opportunity, I interject quickly, "I'm pretty sure Wes loves dressing up, period."

A third finger pops up and wags aggressively in my line of sight, "No interrupting. And thirdly, the chemistry between you two is so strong Cody and I can barely breath." She ticks off her last finger, throwing a final comment my way, "We both know you and Wes are a lot more than friends, Lou. And if tonight is any indication, that boy is not letting you go anytime soon."

Hope flares in my chest, a weak flame flickering at the edge of my insecurities, "Do you really think so?"

"Oh, Lou. I *know* so."

Wolf whistles break over the crowd as Stella and I step forward. The winner of the costume contest is whoever receives the loudest reaction, and so far, everyone has been around the same. Naturally, my competitive roommate came up with a plan to make sure we come out on top, sadly, said plan involves active participation on my part.

Instead of taking a step forward, striking a pose, and returning to our position like all the other contestants, Stella and I march to centre stage. Stella leads the way with a fierce strut: hair bobbing, hips swaying, leg muscles flexing through skin-tight leather while I scurry alongside her, doing my best not to trip. We reach the front of the elevated platform and break into phase two. Taking my hand, Stella twirls me around the stage and drops me into a low dip, making sure the audience gets the chance to see every inch of our costumes. Pulling me off the ground, we sashay back to our original positions, finishing the performance off with two curtsies executed in perfect unison. The crowd goes wild and the smile pasted to my face melts into a real one as I catch sight of Cody and Wes cheering from across the room.

"We crushed it!" Stella's voice breaks through the roar of the mob as the announcer moves to the next contestant.

"Thanks for not dropping me on my head." When Stella originally walked me through the routine, I'd thought for sure brain damage was my future. If I was lucky, maybe a slight concussion.

"Please. As if our sisterly bond would fall victim to gravity."

I smile, deciding not to point out the hours Stella spends at the gym is most likely the reason behind our success. There's no need to ruin our sisterly moment.

"Alright folks, it looks like we have a winner. And it's one we've seen before. Let's hear it for... the Lavishing Leather Ladies!" Stella and I wave to the crowd as the bar breaks into applause once again.

Edging out of the spotlight, relief hits me as we finally make our way off the stage, "Let me be the one to say, next time Wes doesn't get to pick our team's name."

Stella chuckles, "Agreed. Although, it is rather fitting don't you think?"

CHAPTER 14

Wes

I'm in trouble.

And no, it's not because Trip has somehow become my kryptonite over the last few hours. Not to say that isn't concerning but it is baby food compared to what I'm up against: dance karaoke to music I don't listen to.

Now, normally I'm not one to shy away from the stage. Hell, if Hollywood saw my grade sixth performance of Jack Sparrow, I'd be paid to never leave the stage. But karaoke? Whole different ball game. Especially when you don't know the genre well.

You know the saying don't judge a fish on its ability to climb a tree? Well, I am that fish trying to climb that tree. Meaning I am a fish out of water. Do you know what happens to fish when they're out of water? That's right. They die.

Hence my dilemma.

If I had known the deal was the girls win a competition so the boys have to win a competition, I would have hauled my ass up onstage for the costume contest.

Wooing an audience with a smile? Easy.

Throwing in a pose or two to get them riled up? Please.

Competing against authentic punk fans in the form of karaoke? Go ahead and hold that thought.

"What do you want to sing?" The words slink out of Cody's mouth like this whole situation is not one big catastrophe.

Want to know why I don't listen to punk music? Because it's impossible to dance to. Literally not possible. Hell, I'm nowhere near as good as Nico or Stella, but when it comes to moving my body in time to the beat, I'm pretty decent. But alternative rock? *Headbanging* music? Not even the master hip shakers can pull that one off.

"Maybe... Holiday?"

I kind of, sort of, not really know the chorus to that one so I could probably fake it till I break it.

"And now, performing none other than the notorious HOLIDAY by everyone's favourite band..." A fellow Billie impersonator takes the stage and any hope of victory gets crushed under the vaguely familiar guitar intro.

"That one may be taken." Cody shoots me an amused look, unused to seeing me as anything but cocksure.

The issue here is my inability to strategize. How can I put my best self on stage, give the audience an unforgettable show, when chances are I won't even know the lyrics to the song I'm supposed to perform? And I'll have to... *headbang* to it?

Jesus, my neck feels sore already.

Call it a flash of genius because suddenly a brilliant idea strikes my consciousness. What if we didn't pick a punk rock song, what if we did...

"Uh oh. That look is never good." Cody visibly shudders when he spots the Cheshire smile stretching across my face.

"Au contraire, mon frère. This look is what's going to make our performance *really* good."

ele

"Next up, we've got the *other* half of the team that has been dominating tonight... the Lavishing Leather Ladies!" The rowdy bar gets rowdier as Cody and I take the stage. Scanning the audience, I spot Trip and blow her a kiss for luck. I don't see the returning scowl as the lights start to dim, but the shot of adrenalin filling my veins makes me believe it's there.

As planned, Cody takes the right side of the stage while I take the left. Grasping the microphone in my hand, I tilt my head towards the ground. Cody mirrors my stance from the other side and we wait for the beat to kick in.

"...You're insecure, don't know what for," I start us off and a hushed silence falls among the bar, "You're turning heads when you walk through the do-or." I pass the spotlight off to Cody who takes the lead without hesitation.

"Don't need makeup to cover up. Being the way that you are is enou-ou-ough." We swagger over to the middle of the stage, hands clapping boy band style, singing somewhat in harmony, "Everyone else in the room can see it; everyone else but you, ooh."

I hear Stella's shriek as the One Direction tribute finally sets in. Killing the dead silence in the room, the shriek startles the rockers out of their pop shock and they slowly join in on our chorus.

"Baby, you light up my world like nobody else; the way that you flip your hair gets me overwhelmed; but when you smile at the ground, it ain't hard to tell." I pretend to flip my gelled spikes while Cody holds the microphone towards the audience for some crowd participation.

As one the bar sings, "YOU DON'T KNOW, OH-OH! YOU DON'T KNOW YOU'RE BEAUTIFUL."

Fully embracing the energy of the room, Cody and I launch into motion: chucking the microphone back and forth between one another, hopping in time to the music, all the while shedding clothing layers and tossing them to the screaming crowd. Somewhere in the three and a half minutes, Cody's jacket and plain white t-shirt gets lost off-stage, while my red tie becomes a fan favourite for the group of girls screaming my stage name.

"BILLIE, WE LOVE YOU!" The chants have me slowly unbuttoning my black dress shirt, the screams getting louder as the buttons go lower.

As the last chorus comes around, Cody and I pull off one last stunt: finishing the tribute with a couple of backflips. Some form of higher power must have been shining down on us because we both manage to land them – something we've never managed to do during practice – and as the song comes to a close, we hold out our arms in triumph.

The rockers jump to their feet as Cody and I hold our positions, letting the mortals enjoy the sight of our sweat-soaked skin a little bit longer. Based on the glistening eyes in the audience, I'm ninety-nine percent sure the impromptu strip tease is cause for the standing ovation, but hey, victory is ours.

Lou

"Oh. My. God." My roommate is barely able to form coherent words as she looks from me to the stage to me and back again.

"I know."

Apparently, I'm not immune to the sight of two shirtless varsity players either. Even from across the room, I can see *six-packs* glistening under the spotlight. Actually, I'm pretty sure Cody is sporting an eight-pack, but my attention is too taken by dark hair and dimples to be sure.

The boys take a good five minutes making their way off-stage, girls and boys alike reaching out to touch the Greek sculptures passing through. My stomach unexpectedly tightens as I watch a gorgeous girl in fishnet stockings put her hand on Wes' chiseled chest, lean in, and whisper something in his ear. Given the chance, I too would use those muscles as a support structure, but the thought doesn't ease the ache inside.

Watching Wes like a hawk, I finally exhale when he responds with a smile and gently removes the stray hand from his bare chest.

"Why was that hotter than both Magic Mike movies?"

Stella's question pulls my attention away from Wes and Miss Fishnets.

"If I had to guess, it's probably because they were stripping to your favourite song."

Stella sighs with content, "Any man who takes his clothes off to the God that is Harry Styles can worship me any day."

"Even Caveman Cody?"

"Even Caveman Cody." As soon as the words slips past her lips, Stella immediately stiffens in her seat, "But if you tell a single soul I said that you will be brutally murdered in our dorm."

Laughing, I draw a cross over my chest, "I'll take it with me to the grave. Or the stone age as the case may be."

Groaning at my terrible pun, Stella flops her head on the table just as Cody and Wes materialize.

"I hope you didn't close your eyes the whole time, Stella. You would have missed a quality performance."

Stella flips Wes the bird from her resting position.

The vigorous performance left a couple of gelled spikes haphazardly sticking to Wes' forehead and his eyeliner is smeared halfway down his glistening face. Most people in this situation (re: me) would look like a sweaty raccoon but somehow Wes looks more like a rockstar than a savage animal.

It's annoying to say the least.

"Where did you find those t-shirts?" My question inspires Stella to raise her head from the table and peek at our teammates.

"I Love Guns N' Roses." Stella smirks as she reads the thick cotton material, "Bet I can guess who you got those from."

"Axl was kind enough to give us a couple of the extra shirts he brought tonight. Said something about not wanting to call the cops when the mob mauls us." Delivering the response with a straight face, Cody sets off a bout of laughter around the table.

"I'm surprised you guys didn't maul each other with those back-flips. Pretty sure I saw Cody's foot graze one of your spikes."

Wes grins at my observation, his eyes sparkling with the after-effects of his performance, "The only thing I was worried about was fully rotating. Last practice I biffed it so hard I tasted grass for the rest of the day."

Wes mimes plucking grass out of his teeth while Cody chuckles at the memory. "Easily the best rookie moment of the year. Wish we'd caught it on camera."

"Why are you guys practicing backflips for lacrosse?" Stella voices the question running through my head. The varsity players exchange conspicuous glances.

"Should we tell them?" Wes drops his voice to a dramatic stage whisper while Cody taps his chin in contemplation, "Do we think they've earned the privilege?"

Interrupting their moment, Stella scoffs, "Need I remind you that Trip won the trivia *and* the costume contest? She is ahead of both you losers."

"She's right, isn't she?" Wes says mournfully, earning a solemn nod from Cody.

"I guess we have to tell them. Wes, will you do the honours?" Motioning for us to crowd closer, Wes assembles a group huddle for the confession.

"Taber is hosting our opening game next weekend... so when it comes time for the Tiger players to be announced, we are going to set off a backflip chain."

Stella claps her hands with glee while I frown pensively, "Doesn't that risk a player getting injured before the game starts?"

Wes shoots an imaginary gun at me, "Absolutely but think of it this way: A player could just as easily get injured *walking* to the field for warm up. May as well add some excitement for the effort."

Noting the confusion on my face, Cody hurries to jump in, "What Wes has failed to mention is its tradition for the home team hosting the opener to do some sort of act or stunt before the game, so backflips are what we've decided on."

Stella nods in agreement, "Backflips are surprisingly tame compared to some of the other years. I remember one time Mo and his teammates ran through a wall of fire. Took them weeks to get the fire department to sign off on the idea."

At the mention of her brother, Cody subtly shifts away from my roommate.

"The fire department actually signed off on lacrosse players running through a wall of fire?" Disbelief floods my voice as Cody shakes his head.

"It's true. It was a year before I became a rookie and my parents took me to watch a game. The fire department built a safe zone with sand and everything around the fuel line. The fire only went up about two feet and was controlled by an officer, but the effect was still pretty cool."

Stella smiles at the memory, oblivious to the increased space Cody put between then.

"Mo got students, professors, even parents to sign the fire wall petition. Basically, the fire department had two choices: help set up the fire wall safely and have an officer overseeing the process *or* allow the chem students to set up their own combustion. Either way, the fire wall was happening. Took a while to get permission but eventually they gave in."

"Mighty Mo, doing what Mighty Mo does best." Admiration fills Wes' voice and Cody gives a rueful laugh, "Even off the field Mo always gets his way."

CHAPTER 15

Wes

"Red or black?"

Nico waves two silk shirts in my line of vision. I study the identical material save for colour, answering the question with one of my one: "fiery passion or sultry seduction?"

"You make these decisions so much harder."

I smirk, unable to help myself, "I'm sure that's not the only thing that's going to be hard tonight."

Raising my hand for a high five, Nico slaps it with a groan. No matter how terrible my jokes are, Nico never leaves me hanging. Unrecruited high fives are, after all, the very essence of an unhappy friendship.

Read more about it when you purchase my self-help book available at any Canadian bookstore.

"I think I have to go with passion. No, sultry. Fuck it, I'm feeling bold tonight." Tossing the black option back on the bed, Nico pulls the red shirt over his head.

"Sure, you don't want to join tonight?" Dousing himself in cologne that matches the colour of his shirt, Nico throws me a wink, "The boys will be crushed when they find out you're not there."

I laugh from my position on the couch, where my laptop is precariously balancing on my stomach, "I'm sure you and the boys will manage just fine."

When Nico arrived at Taber, one of the first things he did was hunt for a gay bar. Being a small town in Southern Alberta, we ended up having to drive 45 minutes to the nearest city so Nico could keep his playboy reputation going. There are plenty of gay freshmen here at the university, but my best friend likes to have lots of options when he chooses the next notch for his bedpost.

My boy is a picky eater, what can I say.

"What are you doing again tonight?"

I pull up the word document that has my entire psych paper written down and delete the last sentence. Trip said I had to finish the paper Sunday night, not start it.

"Trip is coming over to watch HSM for the first time."

Placing a hand over his heart, Nico shakes his head, "The fact she grew up without Troy Bolton hurts me on a different level." He wanders over to the bathroom, calling out from inside, "Do I need to keep a lookout for sweat socks on door handles?"

A strange sensation fills my chest.

"We're just friends, man. No sex codes will be needed tonight."

Do I find Trip attractive? Of course. Have we almost kissed a couple times? Sure. But *almost* kissing is not *actually* kissing. And it most certainly isn't sex.

Noticing my tone, Nico peeks his head out from the bathroom, "How long has it been since you've been laid?"

"Pfft, like…" I trail off, doing the math in my head. I was supposed to have a one-on-one with Miss Finance last night but then I went to the Rockers event instead. There was that redhead from wing night with the team but… I lost interest before anything happened. Serena from psych invited me over after class that one time but I ended up in the courtyard instead.

"SIMONE!" I shout out the name in relief as I recall the gorgeous dark-skinned girl from the club.

"Hmm, isn't Simone the girl you ditched to teach Trip how to dance?"

Mother fucker. He's right. That means I haven't gotten laid since the cloakroom at Cody's lacrosse party.

Three weeks ago.

"May I say something?" Nico's voice echoes from the bathroom.

Groaning, I grab a cushion and smash it against my face.

"I am going to take that as a yes. Look, it's obvious you like the girl, so why don't you just ask her out?"

I mumble unintelligently into the cushion.

"Sorry, I don't speak polyester."

Blindly flipping off my roommate, I sit up and toss the pillow to the ground, "It's complicated."

Nico struts out of the bathroom, top three buttons undone.

"Uncomplicate it then."

I huff out a laugh, tilting my head back to stare at the stained ceiling, "Smartass."

"Nope, just smart with a nice ass."

I chuckle, not taking my eyes off the discoloured patch above my head. Has it really been three weeks? I can't remember the last time I went three weeks without sex. Grade twelve? Eleven? *Ten*?

Jesus, my mind doesn't even go back that far.

I frown at the stain, feeling like I'm missing something. There's a piece of my celibacy puzzle that's in sight but just out of reach.

"Hey, when we were out at wing night last week, what happened to that redhead I was talking to?"

Shit, I can't even remember her name, but she definitely had auburn curls.

"If I remember correctly, you disappeared to use the washroom and then when you came back you didn't look at her again. It was like a switch was flicked while you were in the can."

I wave of guilt hits me, "Was she upset?"

Just because I enjoy women does not mean I enjoy hurting their feelings. It's one of the main reasons I encourage flings rather than relationships.

"Hell nah, once you turned the charm off, Hunter swooped in and kept her company for the night. I think they ended up going home together."

I sigh with relief, still perplexed about my behaviour. It's not like me to drop the hunt halfway through the chase. And I don't remember using the washroom that night... oh. *Shit.*

This time, the pun was not intended.

A rush of memories hit me as I remember leaving the table because Trip started texting me. And after that, any interest in anyone else all but disappeared. The same thing happened with Serena, after I ran to the courtyard to comfort Trip. AND I bailed on the bombshell last night to attend an event where Trip was present. Oh God.

Nico's right. I have developed my first adult crush.

I'm so wrapped up in my thoughts that I miss the knock on our door. My peripheral vision catches a flash of red as Nico saunters by to swing it open. Tearing my gaze away from the stain, I straighten my head to find the missing puzzle piece staring back at me with misty grey eyes.

Shit.

Lou

There are two things I did not expect to see when I knocked on Wes' dorm door. The first was the four inches of unnaturally smooth, tanned skin Nico is currently displaying in a shirt bright enough to be mistaken for a stop sign. The second, and most concerning, is the look of panic that crossed Wes' face when he saw me standing in his doorway.

I sneak a quick glance down to make sure I didn't spill any fries or gravy on my shirt. Stain-free faces of the All-American Rejects stare back at me. So the look isn't because of my sloppy eating habits.

"Trip! Just the girl I wanted to see. What do you think of the red?"

The doubt swirling through my mind gets put on hold as Nico does a little shimmy in my direction. I blink as the silky material assaults my vision.

"It's very... bold."

Nico flashes me an equally bright smile, "That is *exactly* what I'm going for. Wes, you better keep this one around."

Heat burns my cheeks as I quickly avert my gaze. An awkward silence descends on the room as Wes and I make eye contact. Nico looks back and forth between us.

"Well, this has been a droll but I think I'm going to go find myself a tasty treat. Adios mi amor."

Blowing a goodbye kiss to Wes and giving me a quick side hug, Nico struts out of the dorm, leaving a cloud of cologne and confidence in his wake.

"So..." I trail off and look at the remaining roommate. He hasn't said a word to me but his eyes have not left my face once. It's unnerving.

"How far along are you on the psych paper?"

We were supposed to watch a movie tonight, but given the way Wes is acting, I'm thinking it might be safer to dip after the challenge is complete. A slow grin spreads across his face and to keep his earlier weirdness at bay, I playfully pull my eyebrows together.

"You better not have finished the whole thing before I arrived." The scowl on my face only brightens his more.

"*Finish* my paper? I wouldn't dream of it." His immediate response helps to ease some of the tension from the room and a sense of normalcy re-establishes itself as I narrow my eyes in his direction.

"Prove it."

The words feel dangerous leaving my mouth and the feeling only increases when Wes pops his dimples and beckons me closer. There's an unspoken challenge in the air and as I step closer to the couch it feels as though I'm entering a competition ring.

"Take a look, darlin'." His attempt at a country drawl is beyond terrible, and I can't help but to laugh as Wes swirls his laptop around. I lean down to peer at the screen.

"You've completely finished it!" I gasp loudly, pointing an accusatory finger to the man responsible, "Liar."

Wes holds his hands up in surrender, "Whoa, easy there, partner. Take a *closer* look before you make accusations. I'm a sensitive man you know."

I roll my eyes, "I thought you were an *independent* man?"

Wes wags a finger in my direction, "A man is allowed to be both sensitive and independent; if women can do it, why not men?"

Shaking my head hopelessly, I bite back a laugh and bring the conversation back to the issue at hand.

"Whatever. Do you even have anything left to write?"

He whirls the laptop around and pats the seat cushion next to him. I plop myself down, refusing to acknowledge our close proximity. If Wes can be nonchalant about our legs touching, then so can I.

Deliberately typing as slow as possible, I watch Wes write one sentence and close the word document.

My mouth falls open, "You cheated."

"Did not."

"Did too."

"Hey, you said I had to finish my essay Sunday, so I started it this morning and you just witnessed me finishing it."

I stubbornly shake my head, "Doesn't count. You watched me write my paper from start to finish. I watched you write maybe ten words."

He shifts to face me and I hold my breath as the distance between us shrinks a little bit more, "I followed the rules fair and square. And considering I didn't spend hours watching Netflix in the library, I think it's fair to say I won."

He grins triumphantly and leans back, finally allowing breath to flow back in my lungs.

"You can't use my love of TV shows against me." I scowl at the green-eyed fool beside me, crossing my arms in defence.

"You're right, I can't."

"How can you say it's fair when... wait, what?" My argument comes to a halt as I register Wes' words. I blink a few times, trying to process the 180 that just occurred.

"You... agree?" I say it slowly, waiting for the barb headed my way. It's got to be coming, Wes never gives up an opportunity to sprout nonsense – especially when that nonsense makes me argumentative.

Wes shrugs, his shoulders almost touching mine, "You're right. It's more impressive that you not only binged Netflix *in the library* but also finished the paper the same day. Doesn't mean you won the bargain by any means, but I was impressed."

Shock and a thread of pleasure flows through my system.

Wes was impressed? By... me?

A doubtful frown starts to pull at my eyebrows, "But I was just being myself. I didn't do anything special."

That much is true. Goodness knows how many times I've had to cram ten pages in one sitting because a new anime show gets released.

"That's exactly my point." Not breaking eye contact for a single second, Wes leans forward and drops his voice to a whisper, "*You* impress me, Trip. With everything you do."

For the first time in my life, I don't overthink.

I just lean forward and kiss him.

CHAPTER 16

Wes

There is nothing hotter than a woman taking control.

Don't get me wrong, I am always happy to take the lead, but damn is it fun when someone else takes the wheel. There's that element of surprise that you just don't get when you're the one making the move. And to say I was surprised when Trip planted her lips on mine would be an understatement.

Well, maybe more of a statement.

If I'm being honest, the chances of kissing Trip were high tonight. And no, not because I plan to hang a sweat sock off my door handle – although I can't deny, that has happened in the past – but because I've realized I do, in fact, like Trip a lot more than just a friend. And yes, I am aware my life has turned into a Taylor Swift song. Moving on.

My plan for the evening was simple yet meticulous: set the stage with some Zac Efron singing his teenage heart out, followed by a deep dissection of what it means to be a high schooler, and finished off with a casual conversation drop of where Trip stands on kissing me. Subtle, smooth, and full of consent. The moment would have been screen-play perfection had Trip not jumped ship early. A shame, truly, but I suppose her soft lips pressing against mine is a good compensation.

Before the lip-to-lip contact can turn into a real kiss, Trip scrambles back and hugs her side of the couch. Can't say I've ever gotten that reaction before. Ouch.

"I-I'm so sorry. I don't know what I'm doing." Crimson red heat creeps up her neck and deepens the flush in her cheeks.

"My presence does that to most people." My attempt at a joke falls flat as disappointment settles heavily on my chest, "Is this the part where you tell me to pretend this never happened?"

I've been lucky enough to have never fallen victim to that particular cliché, but hey, I guess there is a first time for everything.

Her misty grey eyes widen in alarm as she registers my tone. Bitter has never been a good colour on me.

"No! I mean, it's not that. I meant to kiss you." Embarrassment shines in her eyes, "It's just I've never... you know. *Made out* before." She whispers the last part and ducks her head, blocking her crimson face with a golden-brown curtain of hair.

My stomach clenches painfully at the sight of Trip trying to hide from me.

"Hey." I grab her hand and give it a tug to direct her attention back to me. Turning her head, she stares at a spot on my chest, completely avoiding my gaze. Intertwining my fingers through hers, I use my other hand to gently tilt her chin up. Moving as though her eyes are weighted down, Trip's gaze rises ever-so-slowly until finally her eyes lock on mine.

"Between the two of us, we are going to get through this." A flicker of a smile tells me Trip remembers the last time I used that line as well,

"Kissing is *so* much easier than dancing, and lucky for you, you've got the best teacher there is."

The responding eye roll makes me laugh, and the sound seems to dissipate some of her tension.

"Do you have any questions?" I ask without a trace of mockery. The most important thing when working with a rookie is making sure each party is comfortable and open to communication. Feel free to quote me on that.

"Would you be able to... guide me through it?" There's a vulnerability in Trip's voice that I've never heard before. It's like the confident girl from earlier, the one who pressed her soft lips against mine, has retreated back into the shadows of anticipated rejection.

As if I could ever resist my grey-eyed siren.

"I will do so gladly, but first." I pause for dramatic effect, waiting for the impatient wrinkle to form between her brows.

Ah, there it is.

"First we are watching High School Musical."

"She left him *again*?" We have made it to the final film of the trilogy, and I am pleased to report Trip is wholly invested in Troy's wellbeing. Or lack thereof, as the case may be.

"Sharpay at least stuck by him all three movies! Sure she was a bit selfish and seriously passive aggressive-

"I think it's safe to say plain aggressive." I cheerfully interject the commentary as Trip continues her rant.

-but it sure beats the meltdowns he has to go through being with *her*." Trip glares at the couple dancing on screen, as if she is visually accusing them of displaying a toxic relationship via the Disney Channel.

I chuckle, patting her hand in understanding, "Both Troy and the audience needed those breakdown songs to grow. If no one ever made mistakes, why would we change?"

Trip grumbles under her breath as another song comes on. Grinning, I take her hand and pull her off the couch.

"What do you think you're doing." Her suspicious squint goes wide as I lightly trace my fingers from the top of her shoulder down to her fingertips. I leave a trail of goosebumps in my wake, and when I reach her hands, I flatten my palms against hers and bring them up to my shoulders.

"We're dancing." I leave her hands resting there and move my own down to her waist. Trip rests her head against my chest, and I rest my chin atop her head, the two of us swaying to Efron's heartbreak.

Destiny and fate have never been something on my radar, but in this moment, with Trip between my arms and her shampoo filling my senses, it feels like this has been the plan all along.

Shit. Maybe I should be a songwriter.

Trip pulls her head back and looks at me with a question in her eyes. Or maybe it's my own question reflecting back at me.

"Trip." The words come out huskier than I intended. My gaze gets dragged down as a smile tugs at her too-full bottom lip.

"Wes." The sound of my name leaving her mouth is enough to make me want to throw her over my shoulder and carry her back to my bedroom Caveman Cody-style.

"Would it be okay if I kiss you now?"

Lou

If I thought I was breathless before, then this must be what it's like to have an asthma attack. Wes' question falls on my pounding ears, and like any sufficient vacuum, it vacates all the oxygen from my lungs. The musical fades into the background as green eyes flick to mine, patiently waiting for permission.

The room feels thick with tension as I stare at the handsome face mere inches from mine. The lack of air currently circulating my body makes me unable to form words, so I nod instead. Releasing one hand from my waist, Wes carefully strokes my cheek before slowly bringing his mouth to mine.

His lips are surprisingly warm as they press into my own. Gently caressing my jaw, he tilts my head and teases my mouth open. His tongue skims my bottom lip and hysterics bubble up inside me.

Don't you dare laugh, don't you dare...

Wes bites down on my lip and any thoughts of laughter vanish from my mind. Pleasure bursts through me and a sound escapes my mouth. Did I just... moan? The shock has me floundering for a few moments, but it doesn't seem to hinder Wes in the slightest.

Time becomes nonexistent kissing Wes. I can't tell you how long we stand in the middle of the dorm, playing a game of tongue tag as Stella would say, but all I know is I never want it to end.

Without warning, Wes suddenly pulls away and drops his hands to my thighs. My groan of protest turns into a yelp of surprise as he hoists me off the ground. Wrapping my legs around his waist to keep me from falling, I gasp when he peppers kisses along my jaw. Appearing unfazed by my bodyweight, Wes walks backwards until we hit the couch, the grip on my waist not lessening for a second.

He sits down, my legs continuing to straddle his own, and leans us back so our chests are flush together. I run my hands through his midnight hair, the silky strands giving way for my fingers. Dragging his mouth back to mine, Wes runs his hands up my jean-clad thighs to cup my butt, tugging me closer still. It's only when I shift that I feel the hardness beneath me.

Wes groans at the sudden friction and heat shoots straight to my core. Shifting again to test the reaction, I smile as the smothered sound escapes into my mouth. The hands gripping my hips tighten as Wes rocks me forward and suddenly it's my turn to gasp.

Even with two pairs of jeans separating us, Wes has pleasure humming through my body like he's been studying it for years. Well, I'm sure he's been studying the female body for years, just not my own.

The thought triggers reality to seep into my lust-filled state. I'm kissing *Wes*. The social butterfly who's been upfront about his player status since day one. And I'm the social outcast he befriended and has taken a liking to. Wes isn't looking for a relationship, he's looking for the next good time.

I put my hand on his chest and gently push away, untangling my mouth slowly from his, "I think that's enough firsts for today."

My voice comes out in huffs, lungs still struggling to catch up with the make out session. The grip on my waist loosens so I can lean back and look at the man I'm still straddling.

Swollen lips and shining emeralds smirk back at me, "And how would you rate your first experience, mademoiselle?"

"Not terrible."

Wes barks out a laugh and I feel it vibrate through his body. Not an unpleasant sensation by any means.

"My fans will be so happy to hear you say that."

I smile weakly at the joke, his words echoing the reminder that tore me away in the first place. I slide off his lap, already planning a quick exit strategy, when Wes grabs my hand.

"Hey."

Forcing myself to meet his gaze, I note the strands of hair sticking up in every direction. I swallow an unexpected laugh. It looks as though I electrocuted him.

"You know I wouldn't have done anything you weren't ready for, right?" Genuine concern floods Wes' expression and I pause, once again taken by the player's thoughtfulness.

"I know."

I mean it, too. Wes may get around with the ladies, but when it comes to making sure his partner is comfortable and willing, there is no doubt in my mind he always pulls through. No guy who would pressure a virgin into sex would ask permission to kiss her first.

"Good. I couldn't stand the thought of you not trusting me." The edge in his voice makes the raw honesty feel more like an exposed nerve than a reassurance.

With a twinge in my heart, I realize this must not be the first time Wes has had this conversation. And given the sorrow in his tone, I don't think the past left a positive mark.

"I trust you, Wes. More than anyone else on this campus." I say the words like a conviction, leaving no room for an argument. He closes his eyes in relief and I can't help but adding, "Well, you might be tied with Stella if I'm being honest."

Wes chuckles at my admission, "Make sure Stella doesn't hear that or she'll be kicking my ass for first place."

I smile and shake my head, "You got that right."

CHAPTER 17

Wes

"WESLEY!" The piercing shriek blasts through my phone, causing me to yank the device away from my ear. After seventeen years of living with the loudest creature known to man, you would think I'd be used to my sister's noise levels by now.

"You've been at university for *a month* and this is the first time you've called me?!"

I wince against the shot of guilt, "I'm sorry Lace, juggling classes and lacrosse has been crazier than expected."

I hear my sister scoff through the phone, the familiar sound bringing a smile to my face.

"Uh huh. So your excuse for abandoning me is too much homework?"

Taking one from Trip's book, I roll my eyes at my younger sister's dramatics.

"I'm at university, Lace, I didn't abandon you. Not to mention the fact we text almost every day." I pause for good measure, "And you forgot to add varsity training as one of my excuses."

"Riiiight. So you've been hitting the books and the gym 24/7, eh?"

I sense a jab coming my way, but I continue to play along. I've missed our sibling banters.

"You got it. When I'm not cramming papers, I'm running laps around the field."

"I see. So, you haven't gone out *at all* this semester?"

I grin as my cards fold. The only person other than Nico who can see through my BS is my younger sister.

Oh, and maybe Trip.

"That depends on what you classify as going out." I pivot on my heel, changing my trajectory from the cafeteria to the courtyard. I've been meaning to send her a picture of the flowers for a while now.

"Don't be coy with me, brother. I saw you dancing on Nico's story a couple of weeks ago. What were you doing at a gay bar, anyways?"

Waving to one of my teammates in the hall, I duck into the next corridor, "I was Nico's wingman."

A laugh echoes over the phone, "We both know Nico doesn't need a wingman."

I chuckle in agreement, memories washing over me.

Being only a year apart in age, Lacey would sometimes tag along with me and Nico. Childhood adventures eventually turned into teenage parties and innocent pastimes turned into not-so-innocent drinking games. Whenever my little sister was present, my participation in such activities was always toned down – I had a big brother reputation to uphold after all – but that meant in Lacey's eyes, Nico was the troublemaker. And by troublemaker, I mean heartbreaker. In the experimental years of puberty and high school, there was no fella who *didn't* fall for my boy's charms.

Hell, I'm straight and even I'm infatuated with the guy.

"You're right, Nico is his own wingman. I go to get compliments from attractive men."

My response sends Lacey into another bout of laughter. The carefree sound loosens a breath from my diaphragm I hadn't realized I'd been holding. There was a long time when my sister didn't laugh.

There was even a time when she didn't want to live.

"I've seen enough men drool over you. And girls for that matter."

I force out a chuckle, trying not to let the scars of the past taint our conversation.

"I want to hear about you. How are you doing, Lace?" Despite my best effort, concern seeps into my voice and my sister is quick to notice the change in tone.

"Enough with the worrying, Wesley. I am perfectly fine. If anything, I'm bored. High school is the same thing day in, day out. I'm ready for a challenge. I'm ready for some fresh faces." She says the last part indifferently, but I know better.

There is one face in particular she never wants to see again. The same face who took out a restraining order on me last spring when I gave him a broken nose and two black eyes. I'm not a violent person by nature, but when I saw Lacey curled up, sobbing her heart out on the kitchen floor that day, something inside me snapped. It took Nico and half the soccer team to drag me off him.

My mother says I'm lucky he didn't press charges, but as far as I'm concerned, he's the one who is lucky to still be alive.

"Boring can be a good thing."

Jesus, I'm starting to sound like her parent.

As if reading my thoughts, Lacey's scolding tone rings in my ear, "You sound like dad. Do me a favour and don't be my big brother for a minute, be my friend. I want to hear all the wild freshmen gossip. No filters."

The words tug on my conscious, a reminder of the time I failed as her big brother, never mind her friend. With a deep breath, I push the pain aside, and launch into a hilarious recount of Cody hauling Stella, ass first, out of the club.

Before the incident, my stories used to be Lacey's universal cure. No matter how angry or upset my sister was, my larger-than-life recounts could always put a smile back on her face. And that has always been my goal: keeping a smile on my little sister's face. When her heart and trust got shattered into millions of pieces, we lost that connection. A piece of her innocence got stolen away and not even my extravagant stories could bring it back.

"Oh my God. She actually *punched* him?"

Even though my stories are no longer the magical remedy they once were, Lacey remains my favourite audience member. She always knows when to laugh, gasp, and ask rhetorical questions.

"Sure did. Four times. And not light punches either." Finally reaching the courtyard, I pause to take some photos of the blooming flora.

"Whoa. I want to meet this girl." I shudder at the thought of those two firecrackers combining forces. I'm all for girl power, but that is one duo I hope to never see.

"Her roommate's got a bit of a strange name. Trip, was it?"

I feel my smile grow wider at the mention of her name. So much for building a tolerance.

"Nah, Trip's just the nickname I gave her. She's the girl I plowed down during move-in day."

My sister had laughed until she cried over that particular story. Out of all the tales I tell, my misfortunes seem to be her favourite.

"Ooh, so she has a nickname now, does she?"

My shit eating grin won't break even though my face muscles are starting to ache.

This is what an adult crush looks like, ladies and gentlemen.

"Yep. I think you'd like her. She's an original." The words fly out of my mouth with complete ease, shocking Lacey into unnatural silence.

I give it five seconds. Four, three...

"I'm impressed, Wesley. You've finally found a girl who's kept you interested longer than 72 hours."

Nope, didn't even hit the two second mark.

"You'll understand when you meet her. Are you still driving down Saturday?"

"As if I would miss your first varsity tournament. Although with how you've abandoned me, maybe I should reconsider."

I shake my head even though she can't see me, "Such a drama queen. I'm looking forward to seeing you."

"Hmm, I'll be the judge of that. I gotta go, but take care Wesley. I'll see you bright and early Saturday morning."

I smack my lips loudly, blowing her a kiss through the phone. "Miss you, Garden Girl."

A loud raspberry is my only response before she ends the call.

If there's one thing I take credit for, it's teaching my sister how to make an exit.

Lou

"Well done, Miss Mackenzie." A corrected copy of my non-procrastinated essay lands with a slap on my desk. I look up to see a perfectly shaved goatee staring back at me.

Nodding towards the circled A on the title page of my paper, Professor Anderson attempts a smile, "I am pleased to see your writing skills are improving. You've come a long way since that first class."

The words *unexcused tardiness* lay in his undertone, but I decide to focus on the compliment instead.

"Thank you, sir. That means a lot coming from you."

I hear Wes stifle a laugh beside me. Professor Anderson gives me one last nod before continuing down our row. As soon as he's past my line of vision, I turn and slap Wes on the arm.

"Ow! What was that for?"

He rubs the point of contact while I roll my eyes, "You know exactly what that was for. The laugh?"

"I couldn't help it. *That means a lot coming from you*? We both know the only thing you were thinking about is how spectacular his goatee is looking today."

Biting back a smile, I shrug in response, "The amount of effort he puts into that patch of hair pays off."

Stroking his chin like a villain from a bad action movie, Wes muses out loud, "Maybe I should grow a goatee. Think I could pull it off?"

"Absolutely not." My response comes out louder than intended and a few students turn our way. I awkwardly duck my head but not before Professor Anderson visually reprimands me from across the room. Pretty sure my essay compliment has already been retracted.

Snickering, Wes draws my attention back to his handsome face, "Like my baby face too much, do you?"

I cough, trying and failing to contain my blush.

Our make out session happened a few days ago, but so far things have been normal with Wes. Well, as normal as things can be when you have an attractive friend who happens to be a phenomenal kisser. We haven't hung out since the HSM/kissing marathon, but so far he's acting as though nothing has changed. He still stops to talk to me in the hall, sends me the occasional meme, and saved me a seat for psych class.

I have no idea what we are – or if *we* are even a thing – but so far I have been trying to follow Wes' lead. And as of right now, that means being friends who had a little make out session. Nothing less, nothing more.

"Mm, it's okay." My offhand comment puts a mischievous gleam in Wes' vibrant eyes.

That's never a good sign.

Trying to be a competent student, I turn my attention away from the man beside me and look towards the ongoing PowerPoint presentation. I flip open my notebook with the intention to start taking notes when a pen hits my leg. I raise my eyebrows in Wes' direction but he's already halfway under the desk.

I'm almost done scribbling the first slide when a warm hand wraps around my ankle. I freeze as the hand slowly starts to snake upward. My body quickly unfreezes and starts to squirm as Wes' fingers make their way up my calf, inching their way higher and higher, while a pair of lips follows the trail with teasing kisses.

"Grab your pen and get out from under there. You're going to get us in trouble." I hiss the words quietly, trying not to draw attention to us. The person to my left is busy talking to their neighbour and thankfully there's a wall dividing the rows in front of us, so even if someone looks back, they wouldn't be able to see Wes.

"I'm testing to see how much you like me clean shaven." The words themselves are innocent enough but the green eyes peering up from between my legs are anything but.

"Fine, you win, okay? You wi –" My words turn into a sharp inhale as Wes lightly runs his fingertips from the inside of my knee up to my inner thigh. And back down again.

"I like hearing you say that." He slows the exploration to lazy circles, casually tracing patterns up and down my leg. Thank God I shaved this morning.

"Am I making you uncomfortable?" The fingers stall, patiently waiting for my response.

I should say yes. I should say... "No."

The word sounds strangled through my laboured breathing.

If I'm being honest, the thought of someone catching us is more thrilling than uncomfortable. There's something about the risk factor that makes Wes' appreciation of my leg shall we say, much more exciting. Nothing like keeping one's virgin status while losing all morals surrounding public decency.

I blame the dimples.

"Good." he presses one finger against my jean shorts, right on my centre, and I have to grip the edge of the desk as my body clenches with pleasure.

Wes chuckles under the desk and I give him a swift kick. Catching my foot and tugging me forward, he drags his tongue up to the spot where my shorts end and the sensitive skin of my thigh begins. Then he replaces his tongue with his teeth.

The arrogant prick bites me.

I can't hold back my gasp and my neighbour glances over with concern, "Everything okay?"

The sound of his voice causes both Wes and I to freeze in our respective positions. After a moment of silence, I realize Wes can't speak without exposing himself, so I hurry to respond.

"Sorry, these topics take me by surprise sometimes. The methods we're discussing are a lot more *hands on* than I'm used to."

My innuendo falls on unsuspecting ears as my friendly neighbour nods in understanding. I feel Wes shake beneath me, trying to hold in his laugh.

He fails.

The seemingly random burst of laughter coming from beneath my desk causes the guy beside me to jump. With a quizzical look, he pulls his chair back to peer under my desk.

I silently groan as Wes gives him a cheerful, "Hey there!" from between my legs.

Maybe social isolation wasn't so bad after all.

"Hey... there." My neighbour pushes his glasses back up his nose, eyes wide as he takes in the scene in front of him. Taking his cue, Wes climbs back onto his chair like a normal student and holds his pen up in triumph.

"I found it!" The announcement does nothing to ease my neighbour's horror-stricken expression.

I have a feeling I'll be getting a new neighbour next class.

CHAPTER 18

Wes

Cody barrels towards me at full speed.

Think of what would happen if a 5'10 brick house got access to Vin Diesel's personal supply of nitrous oxide. Now, throw in a set of wheels and some killer abs, and you've basically created the equivalent of Taber Tigers' finest defenseman. Also known as the obstacle standing between me and the net.

Keeping an eye on the blonde fauxhawk approaching at an alarming rate, I scan the field to assess my options. If I can deke out Cody at the last minute then I might be able to make a corner shot, although my shooting angle wouldn't be ideal.

A rapid blur hits my peripheral, so I risk life and limb to turn and see Hunter making a breakaway. Sprinting up the left side of the field, he makes the signal for me to pass. I yank my stick back and fling it as hard as I can towards the open section Hunter is sprinting to. The ball hits the ground, and Hunter swoops it up mid-bounce. Ever the die-hard defenseman, Cody changes trajectory even though it's too late. With a pivot and a beautiful arm swing, Hunter secures our win with a perfect corner shot.

Cheers erupt along the field as the ball hits the back of the net. Even my teammates wearing red jerseys walk by to smack Hunter on the back for that spectacular shot.

That's my favourite thing about rallies: no matter which side wins, a good performance is a good performance for the whole team. And given the fact this is our last practice before our showdown with Silverwood this weekend, an outstanding play was just what we needed to get one last confidence boost before game day.

"Hell of a shot, Hunter." Sweat trickles down Cody's forehead as he claps my fellow rookie on the shoulder. I watch the tension dissolve from my fellow rookie's stance.

"Thanks Cap." Hunter smiles tentatively at the compliment, no doubt waiting for the criticism that typically follows. I'm pretty sure Cody is over the whole tongue-down-Stella's-throat-situation but that doesn't change the fact the man can hold a grudge.

In other words: Caveman no like Hunter.

The funny thing is Cody's constant nagging has caused Hunter's skills to improve by leaps and bounds. He's still a little weak on the passing front, but his shooting has gone from embarrassing to semi-impressive.

Am I concerned about Hunter stealing my rookie of the year award? Hell nah. To be the best you have to beat the best. The hardest competitors are the ones you learn the most from. Not to mention, I'm never one to back down from a challenge.

Just ask Trip.

"Wes, your assist was risky, but it paid off. A safer bet would have been to throw the ball at Hunter rather than in front of him. Most forwards slow down to anticipate the catch, you assumed Hunter would keep his momentum going." Cody pauses to wipe his brow, "That was either a lucky guess or seriously impressive intuition."

"It was neither." A sole eyebrow raises, "I've watched Hunter struggle to catch long shots during practice and the common denominator is he always overruns the pass. Like you said, most players slow down to anticipate the catch and make it easier for ball handling, but for Hunter, once he gets some momentum, he can't seem to slow it down. So, I figured by overshooting the pass, it would counteract Hunter's overrunning." I finish off my spiel with a casual shrug, hoping my modesty does not go unnoticed.

"So you're saying that your assist was strategic, not risky." There's a challenge in Cody's tone as if he's testing to see if I remember who I am talking to.

Hey, if my captain can't handle strategic plays and strong opinions, then maybe I'm playing for the wrong team.

"That is exactly what I'm saying. I've taken stock of all our players' strengths and weaknesses, so if you want, I'd be happy to sit down and help you create plays for our game Saturday."

Shit, now I sound like I'm vying for the man's position.

To my relief, Cody nods thoughtfully, "I've drawn up some plans, but I would love your take on it. You've played with some of these rookies more than I have, so it would be good to get a different perspective."

Resisting the urge to pump my fist in the air, I play it cool, "Sweet. Awesome. So, ya shoot me a text when you want to meet up. I'm looking forward to it."

I promise it sounded cooler in my head.

Cody smirks at my fanboy moment and I decide now is the perfect time to help dismantle the nets.

"Have you invited Trip to watch the game?" The question stops me in my tracks, and I choose to ignore the warm feeling unfolding in my chest.

"No, but I'm thinking of asking her to hangout tomorrow, so maybe I'll invite her then."

Man, psychology class has never been so fun. I didn't take a single note last class and there's no way I'm passing this next essay, but teasing Trip was one hundred percent worth it.

The way her body clenched at my touch? Oh man. I almost ate her out right then and there – jean shorts be damned. The only downfall of Operation Desk Down Under was I couldn't see her face from my vantage point. And seeing her misty eyes roll back in pleasure is steadily creeping to the top of my bucket list.

Here's the kicker: I genuinely love hanging out with her. Not because there's a chance we might fool around – although that is a welcome bonus - but because in the last few weeks Trip has somehow become one of my favourite people.

Have you ever had that out-of-body experience where you think you're about to exhale but end up inhaling instead? No? Well, I should probably get that checked out.

My point is the action takes you by complete surprise even though your body knew it was coming all along. That's what Trip does to me. She's my inhale that's taken the place of everything else.

"Well, I'm sure she will be happy to come support you." Cody's voice snaps me out of my reverie and suddenly my Spidey senses are tingling. There is a hidden conversation going on.

"Have you invited *Stella* to watch the game?"

Boom. Who's the white Gandhi now.

Cody shoots me a quizzical look, "Why would I do that?"

"Aw, come on Cap. You're talking to your boy here."

My response gets an eyebrow raise, so I'm thinking the boy comment was a little offside. But hey, if a man recruits another man as his wingman, it is only appropriate to assume an unbreakable bond has been made. Whether Cody knows it or not, we are partners for life.

"She'll be at the game. Mo's going to be there."

Shit. I forgot the legend himself is attending this next game.

"Aren't you two pretty close?" Cody barely mentions the guy, but I remember Stella insinuating they were tight.

My comment earns a shrug, "He was a great mentor my freshman year. Taught me tricks to improve my game as well as study habits. When he nominated me captain at the end of last year, I was blown away. The fact he chose a soon-to-be sophomore instead of one of the senior players caused a huge backlash, but Mo stood by his decision."

Cody pauses, his face pensive.

"Mo always gets his way." I repeat the comment Cody made just the other night.

He nods in acknowledgment, "You don't get labelled Mighty if people can push you around."

My captain looks off in the distance, perspiration glistening along his neck, "After nominating me captain, he pulled me aside to state the one condition of my position. No matter what happens on the field, we're brothers. And as his brother, it's up to me to lookout for our sister next year."

My eyes widen at the confession, "That's a lot of pressure to put on a junior. Did you even know Stella at the time?"

Rubbing his neck, Cody barks out a laugh, "He pointed her out every game. She never missed one. But as for meeting her? Until last year's banquet, she was just a blonde silhouette in the bleachers."

"Whoa." I am at a loss for words. And trust me, that doesn't happen very often.

I am all for protecting one's younger siblings, hell, Lacey has always been my number one priority, but to pass that responsibility onto someone else? Not to mention someone who's just completed their freshman year? That's a different kind of messed up. I know for a fact that if Lace was in a jam and couldn't get a hold of me, Nico would gladly take my place. But that's his decision, not one I would make for him.

"Anyways, Stella will definitely be in the stands on Saturday."

"With Mo." I voice the unspoken thought written across Cody's face.

He huffs out a breath and gives me a weary smile, "That's right. She'll be in the stands with Mo."

Lou

"What movie is it going to be tonight?" My roommate struts into the living room waving around the remote like she's the world's shortest game show host.

"You choose."

I'm scribbling down study notes for the fifteen exams coming up next week. Okay, fifteen might be a slight exaggeration; it's more like ten. Or three.

"Always giving me the tough decisions." Stella plops herself down on the couch next to me and I shift my books to make more room.

"The question is: can I find a film that's more exciting than a certain lacrosse player *admiring* a lovely pair of legs during psychology class?"

I throw my pen at her and Stella bats it away with a laugh.

"I regret telling you that." My grumble is met with a fake pout and dark blue eyes batting my way.

"Aw, come on. It would be cruel for you to deprive me of gossip that frisky and even crueler of me to never bring it up."

I sigh, pushing my study notes away as Stella starts flipping through Netflix. No more work will be done tonight, so I may as well enjoy the roommate bonding.

"Do you think it's strange, what I'm doing with Wes?" I blush as I ask the question, feeling oddly exposed and unsure of whether I really want the answer.

"You mean the kissing or the classroom fondling?" Stella unglues her gaze from the screen to glance at me. I shift uncomfortably, face no doubt as red as a tomato.

"Er... both? We haven't gone on any dates so does that make us friends with benefits or just friends who occasionally fool around?"

Both of those options make me cringe. But asking if we are kind of, sort of, maybe a thing makes me want to cringe even more.

Stella taps her chin thoughtfully, "Unfortunately for us, your boy has not taken the traditional route. So, even though his signals seem clear, at the end of the day it is still an assumption on our part."

I nod for her to continue, choosing not to focus on how much I love hearing Wes referred to as my boy.

"What we *do* know is Wes invests his time, effort, and energy in making sure you are having the best time in every situation. Whether that means giving you a hug in the middle of rush week, dressing up like Billie Joe Armstrong because he's your favourite singer, or teaching you the miracles he can perform with his tongue, Wes is always looking out for your best interests."

Stella throws me a wink with the last item and I stick my tongue out in response.

"What we *don't* know is the exclusivity of these make out sessions and whether Wes is serious about embarking on a relationship."

I've been repeating the same thing to myself all week but hearing the words come out of Stella's mouth hits me harder than expected. Unable to hide my grimace, I do my best to shrug it off.

"Look, Lou. Everyone knows Wes is interested, hell even *Wes* knows he's interested. But the problem is boys are dumb. Say it with me: Boys. Are. Dumb."

A smile tugs my lips as we chant the anthem in our otherwise silent dorm.

"That's my girl. Now, even though we don't know what Wes' intentions are, we do know that he is a great guy. So, my advice is to move forward with caution. Keep having fun but don't put all your eggs in one basket, if you know what I mean. Well, at least not until he asks you out on an *official* date because in that case all bets are off."

She makes a crude motion with her hands and a laugh bursts out of me.

"Thank you, Stella."

Holding out my arm for a side hug, my roommate shuffles over to wrap her arms tightly around me, "Anytime, hon. Just promise me one thing." Pulling away from our embrace, I see a hint of concern shining in her pretty eyes.

"When the time comes, just make sure you're the *only* girl on his mind."

Just as I'm opening my mouth to respond, my phone buzzes with an incoming message.

WES: I've got an emergency.

Stella playfully flicks me on the nose to get my attention, "Just remember what I said, okay? I don't normally break lacrosse players twice my size, but I'll do it if I have to."

Her unshakable loyalty brings tears to my eyes. When was the last time I had someone other than my parents in my corner?

Blinking the excess emotion from my eyes, I nod, "I'll remember. I promise."

"Good." Stella jumps up from the couch, stalks into her room, and returns a few moments later with a bag of microwave popcorn.

"I'm going to get our snacks ready, so you've got exactly two minutes and thirty seconds to respond to that handsome man before I steal you away for our movie night." With a disapproving wag of her finger, she declares, "No Tommy Texters allowed."

A sheepish grin takes over my face as I hastily pull up my texting conversation thread.

ME: Do you need CPR?

WES: Only if you're offering.

If there is one thing Wes has mastered, it's the art of flirting. And maybe kissing.

ME: The only CPR course I took, I failed.

WES: Note to self: Don't go to Trip for life support.

ME: Funny. What's the non-life-threatening emergency?

I can hear Stella humming above the whirling noise of the microwave. I sneak a glance over the couch – and yup, my roommate is in the middle of swaying her hips to the sound of kernels popping. I've yet to find a situation where Stella doesn't dance.

WES: The opener is in two days, and I don't have a dress shirt.

My brows knit together in confusion.

ME: You wear a dress shirt to play the first game of the season?

WES: I wish. Sadly, the formal wear is just tradition for the team to wear on game day.

Oh. That does make more sense.

ME: I see. So what do you need me for?

The microwave beeps and my roommate yells from the kitchen, "Ten seconds, Lou!"

I shake my phone impatiently as typing bubbles appear.

WES: I need your help to pick out the perfect shirt.

ME: Talk about pressure. Wouldn't Nico be a better partner for this?

WES: Nico isn't the person I'm trying to impress.

My breath catches in my throat. Surely he can't mean me, can he? My thumbs hesitate over the keyboard as more typing bubbles appear beneath his last comment.

WES: You are.

CHAPTER 19

Wes

"You drive... *that*?"

Disbelief oozes through Trip's tone as I nod my head patiently. Unsurprisingly, her reaction is one I get often.

"Sure do. Lola's a beauty isn't she."

Trip's astounded stare turns from our mode of transportation to me and back again, "I can't tell if the fact you named your car, or the name choice itself is more horrifying."

I run a hand along the side of my baby, gently stroking the peeling beige paint.

"Shh, don't hurt her feelings. Lola's hard enough to start at the best of times."

I yank open the passenger door, bits of rust falling off the old Ford 500.

Walking tentatively towards me, Trip mutters under her breath, "I'm surprised it starts at all."

Choosing to ignore the barb, I gallantly bow and beckon towards the open door.

"Malady, your chariot awaits."

With one last look at the neon zip ties holding the bumper in place, Trip shakes her head and folds herself into the car. I smile and lean down to help her with the seatbelt. She hasn't even seen the worst of it yet.

"The trick is to pull and release three times before pulling it across your body. May I?" At her nod, I stick my head in the door and give her seatbelt the appropriate number of tugs before pulling it across her waist and clicking it in place. Amused grey eyes follow my step-by-step process.

"Lola's a bit... finicky I see." Her too-full bottom lip tugs into a smirk and I find myself tracking the movement.

Want to know the fastest way to distract a guy? Move your lips. Sounds ridiculous but it's the truth: when you bring attention to your lips, the guy you're in the midst of wooing has no choice but to think of those lips. I might even write about it in my psych paper due Monday. I even know what my title would be: *Lips: The Oral Seduction of Man*.

On second thought, maybe I'll save that one for health class.

"I like my girls to have character, what can I say."

My words have the intended effect on Trip, and a mild blush warms her cheeks. Her tongue pokes out to skim her bottom lip, leaving the pale pink glistening with temptation.

Do you see what I mean? Hook, line, and sinker.

My lips crash onto hers and her yelp of surprise gets swallowed whole. Gripping the front of my shirt, Trip pulls me closer and deepens the kiss simultaneously. Our tongues tangle together as my hands cup her jaw, fingers stroking the flushed skin underneath.

"YO, GET A ROOM!" My head hits the roof as a car honks, rudely breaking our lip lock. I grin sheepishly at her, and carefully extract myself from her side of the car.

I rub my head as I walk around to the driver's side and yank the rusted door open. Plopping myself down in the seat, I take a deep breath and immediately get hit by coconut vanilla shampoo. Shit. This is going to be a long ride.

Ignoring the semi already forming in my pants, I look at the passenger beside me and feel a spark of satisfaction at her equally glazed gaze.

"Are you ready for the ride of your life?"

I turn the key and wait for the familiar battle of Lola turning over. The screeching sound fuels the soul as the engine cranks into gear.

Ah, that's my girl.

"Show me what you've got." a playful smile touches Trip's swollen lips as I jerk the gear shifter into drive.

This is going to be a *really* long ride.

———— *ele* ————

We stutter to a grinding halt in the parking lot of Taber's only shopping mall. Large and square, the hideous brown building is home to no more than fifteen stores. Five of which are fast-food chains that make up the cafeteria. You can always count on small towns to limit your number of options.

Casually yanking the parking brake into place, I go through the usual motions of making sure Lola won't go for an unsupervised stroll: wiggling the gear shifter until I hear the click, turning my wheels so they face an empty stall, and giving Lola's steering wheel a firm love pat. It sounds ridiculous, but trust me. The last time I didn't follow through on these steps, Lola found herself bumper-to-bumper with an F150.

Hence the zip ties holding the front bumper in place.

"Welcome to Townhall, otherwise known as the shopping district of Taber."

My announcer voice is sold with the perfect cheesy grin combination. Trip unbuckles her seat belt – the material flailing wildly as it returns home – and leans forward to peer through the cracked windshield.

"It's so... ugly."

I chuckle and lean back against Lola's fabric seats. The lack of leather is not by choice, let me tell you.

"Wait until you see the inside."

Misty eyes flick to mine in alarm, "The interior has a *worse* colour choice?"

Her concern is not for nothing. Townhall somehow managed to find the exact shade of well, shit, and covered every inch of their shopping mall in it.

"Oh no, don't worry. The interior has the same colour scheme. But the inside florescent lighting does wonders for this particular shade of brown."

Trip starts to giggle, and the sound spreads warmth through my chest. On my list of favourite things, her laughter is right up there with her shampoo.

Trip turns to grab the door handle and I grab her arm to stop her. "I'll get it. Lola's a locked vault once we're inside."

A single eyebrow raises in my direction, "Are we trapped?"

Considering I just vacuumed those backseats, being locked in here wouldn't be the worst situation. I have a few ideas on how we could pass the time.

"Not as long as you know the combination." Keeping my thoughts to myself, I throw her a wink and proceed to kick the inside of my door as hard as I can.

And this fellas, is why we don't skip leg day.

A good two minutes of strenuous effort passes until finally the driver's door swings open with an ear-splitting screech. I hop out of the car, freedom greeting me at long last, and scurry over to wretch the passenger side open.

"Well, you definitely cracked the safe." Trip smirks up at me as she climbs out of the car.

I give her a modest shrug, "Lola can confirm my burglary skills are top of the line."

"I can see that. And now I know why her frame is so bent out of shape."

I gasp and rub my hands over Lola's hood, "She doesn't mean that, gorgeous. You're amazing just the way you are."

Rolling her eyes, Trip nods towards the turd-coloured building, "Come on, Bruno Mars. We've got an emergency to evade."

Lou

Ugly. *So* ugly.

And this time the visual assault is not in reference to the unfortunate brown coloured walls surrounding me. Oh no. This time it's the man in front of me who is burning my retinas to the point of no return. Want to know the worst part about the bright orange dress shirt causing permanent damage? The gigantic smile plastered on Wes' face as he admires himself in the mirror.

"It will match my jersey perfectly!"

Correction: it will give the Taber Tiger mascot a run for his money.

"Or maybe we could find a black shirt to coordinate with the stripes?" My suggestion sounds desperate but it's the best I've got without flat out insulting him. He turns from the dressing mirror, looking me dead in the eye.

"You don't like it?" I gulp, trying to remember how much honesty it takes to break a friendship.

"It's not that I *don't* like it..." I trail off, biting back the H word. I know hate is a strong word but it's the only one that appropriately describes my feelings towards this gaudy piece of clothing.

"But?" Wes' eyes twinkle with mischief, the orange overpowering the green pigment in his irises. That in itself should be a crime.

"I just think a different colour might be more flattering."

Shopping has never been more excruciating. Is this what bridesmaids feel like?

"Hmm..." He turns back to the mirror, assessing the shirt from different angles, "If you don't like it, you can just say so."

There's a tease in his voice that has me narrowing my eyes.

"Is this a test?"

The innocent look he shoots my way confirms it. Wes is a lot of things, but innocent is not one of them.

"Why would I be testing you?" Busted.

I send a scowl his way and the smirk on his face grows into a full-fledged, dimpled smile.

"Not that I'm confirming this is a test, but if it *were*, maybe I just wanted to see how far your people pleasing tendencies stray." He strikes a pose in the mirror, the orange assaulting people around the world.

"And given your natural kindness, I'm afraid we have strayed too far past acceptable." His words ring with humour yet the sentiment behind them touches something deep inside me.

When Wes describes me, it's as though I've always belonged. To him, to Taber University, and to this moment.

I clear my throat to get rid of the emotion clogging it and give the dress shirt a final once over, "It's horrible. Unless you plan on lighting it on fire as soon as we leave this building, I cannot allow you to walk out of here with it."

Amusement flickers across Wes' face as he gives me a mock salute, "Roger that, commander. Arson is not on today's agenda."

Clapping one hand over my eyes, I use the other to point towards the change rooms, "In that case, try on the next one. I can't bear to look at that orange anymore."

Wes chuckles and retreats to his stall, drawing appreciative glances from the patrons mingling in the fitting rooms. The fact he draws stares in such a hideous colour attests to some serious genetics. I catch one girl eyeing the curtain Wes ducked behind, so I quickly jump up from my stool and shuffle over to his curtain, making sure my body barricades the entrance. The blonde in question gives me the evil eye, and I try not to smirk in response.

I fail.

"Which one do you want me to try on next?" The clarity and shocking proximity of Wes' voice startles me, and I topple, off-balance and headfirst into the dressing room.

Gravity takes its toll, and I plummet to the ground like an arrow. Right before I make nose-breaking impact, a pair of strong arms scoop me up and haul me back to my feet. My mind is slow to catch up, and the vision switch from pale vinyl flooring to hard planes of muscle has my head swimming.

So much for keeping intruders out.

I squeeze my eyes shut as a deep chuckle rumbles through the broad chest inches from my face. Peeking one eye open, my stomach goes into another free fall while my feet remain firmly planted on the ground.

"If you wanted to see me naked, all you've got to do is ask." Wes' teasing voice hums in my ear and I blush from the base of my neck to the tips of my ears.

The rookie standing before me is wearing nothing but a pair of navy boxers. That fit really well. A little too well.

Gulping, I run my gaze over the athletic body standing in front of me. I saw both Wes and Cody shirtless during their dance karaoke performance, but this is different. This time the six-pack leading into the narrow waist and muscular legs is within touching distance. Within *licking* distance.

One stumble later and I'm halfway to becoming a cannibal. Stella will be so proud.

"I am so sorry, there was this girl I thought might break in, so I thought if *I* guarded the curtain, it would scare her away but then *you* scared me..." My ramble trails off as Wes' eyes take on a glint that can only be described as dangerous.

"EXCUSE ME!" A pitchy voice breaks through the thin curtain, causing Wes and I both to wince. "Only one person is allowed in a changeroom at a time. ONE PERSON."

Giving me a look that says he has been in this situation before, Wes throws the woman a thumbs up over the curtain.

"Just putting on clothes, ma'am! My friend here was just helping me with some buttons."

He quickly throws his t-shirt over his head and I bite back a sigh of disappointment as the material covers his lean frame. My eyes had just started to recover from the orange assault.

Tugging on his jeans, Wes grabs my hand. We exit the stall and find the blonde from earlier standing next to the elderly manager. Doesn't take much to guess who ratted us out.

"I thought you needed help with buttons?" The snitch has the nerve to make one last comment as we head out the door. Wes and I both look down at his shirt, noticeably lacking buttons of any sort. Crap.

"I was helping him do up his jeans." The words fly out of my mouth, shocking both the girl and me into silence. Choking back laughter, Wes throws a regal wave to our audience and tugs me out the door.

As soon as we're out of sight, Wes drops my hand and bends over laughing, "The look on blondie's face... God, Trip. You never fail to surprise me."

I am still gobsmacked from my own outburst, but the awe in his tone pulls my lips into a smile.

Straightening himself up, Wes wipes imaginary tears from his eyes, "Although I have to admit, a part of me was scared shitless when you said that."

Now there's something I don't hear every day.

My eyebrows raise skeptically, "Oh?"

Wes shudders, "For a second there, I thought Stella had taken your place."

I throw my head back and laugh, the sound resonating through the crowded mall.

"That would scare you shitless, wouldn't it?"

Still giggling, I turn to see Wes shaking his head vigorously, "There is no shit left in my body at this point."

I playfully bump his shoulder, "You *did* tell me I can be any version I want to be."

"Mm, I did say that didn't I?" He taps his chin in contemplation, "Do you want to know which version is my favourite?"

"The Lavishing Leather Pants was a good look for me, I'll admit."

In hindsight, my roommate really pulled through on that costume. I still don't know where she found those pants, let alone a pair in my size.

"Your legs looked sexy as hell that night, but that's not it."

I tilt my head, looking curiously into the green eyes sparkling my way.

"What is your favourite version of me?"

"This one." Confused, I look down at my typical baggy shirt and mom jean combo as Wes continues, "From the wicked rock concert t-shirts to your inability to carry normal amounts, my favourite version is the one where you're unapologetically yourself."

And just like that, Wes knocks down the rest of my defences

Looking for a good time. He doesn't want a relationship. Remember what you promised Stella...

Conflicting thoughts swirl through my mind as my eyes scan his face for a jokester smile or a flirty wink, anything to divulge me of the delusion that Wes would ever want to be in a relationship with me.

It's not probable, it's not possible, it's not...

"So, I was wondering if maybe you wanted to come watch me play the opener Saturday?"

My thoughts render speechless as time slows to a crawl.

What. Just. Happened.

Shifting uneasily at my abrupt silence, Wes nervously glances to the floor, "I mean, only if you want to, you don't have to by any means..."

"NO! I mean, yes. I mean, I would love to. Watch you play that is." My voice sounds as flustered as my nerves feels right now. The double whammy is very much not appreciated.

Wes' entire demeanour brightens, and he rubs his hands together in glee.

"Great! Oh, and my sister is also coming to watch so maybe you'll get the chance to meet her. Now, what should we get for lunch?"

Not giving me a minute to process the tidal wave of information, Wes spins on his heel and heads towards the sad looking food court. Mind buzzing incoherently, I speechlessly follow.

Did he say I'm meeting his sister?

Chapter 20

Wes

I look hot as fuck.

Let me just state for the record that whoever came up with the concept of modesty never wore a fitted dress suit. Because if they did, they would be apologizing for coming up with such a ridiculous concept. When you look good, you look good. There's no harm in acknowledging the effort paid off.

"Holy fuck. You're looking good, man."

Appreciation shines in Nico's eyes when I walk out of my room. See what I mean?

Fitted dress shirt. That's all I'm saying.

"Thanks. Trip picked it out." I spin so my roommate can have the whole view. Not going to deny, the back is just as good as the front.

"The girl's got good taste. I don't think I've ever seen you wear purple before."

I glance down at the plum material stretching across my chest. Never in a million years would I have considered this to be my colour, but Trip picked it out so here we are.

"This is a first for me. You should have seen the salesgirl's reaction when I tried it on."

Forget the store helper, as soon as I saw Trip's eyes darken when I walked out of the change room, I was sold.

"Uh huh. I'm sure it was the *salesgirl* who was the deciding factor." Nico smirks at me from his lounging position on the couch.

Curse that man's BS radar. Gets me every goddamn time.

Shifting the cushion beneath him to get comfortable, Nico amiably throws out the question he's been dying to ask all along, "How did it go anyway? Is she coming today?"

I nod, "She is, and yesterday went well."

Talk about understatement of the year. The more time I spend with Trip, the more I want to spend time with her. Now that I've gotten a taste, I can't seem to get enough.

When was the tolerance supposed to kick in again?

Nico quirks an eyebrow at me, "That's all I'm getting? It went *well*?"

I throw him a wink as I walk to the bathroom to do up my tie.

"Let's just say, Trip falling into my dressing room and getting us kicked out was not the worst way to spend an afternoon."

Nico bursts out laughing, "That is the worst hookup cover story I have ever heard."

My fingers are too tied up to flip him off, so I shrug instead, "It's the truth. Although I did find out Trip can be quite the firecracker when she wants to be."

I chuckle to myself, thinking about her comeback to the snarky blonde. Nico watches me silently from the couch.

"You scare me when you don't talk. What's up?"

If his penetrating stare burns a hole through my new shirt, I'm going to be pissed.

"You like her a lot." It isn't a question so much as a statement.

I do one last double-check to make sure my tie is secure, then walk over and sit on the couch opposite. Two lacrosse players are two people too many for residential furniture.

Straightening himself up to mirror my position, Nico waits for my response. Exhaling slowly, I confess the truth we have both known for a while, "I do, man. I really do."

Dark eyes scan my face, picking up on cues no one other than my best friend would know to look for. "You don't need to worry, Wes. You are a good guy. You won't ruin Trip the way Jerrell ruined Lace."

The sound of his name does nothing to ease the churning in my gut.

"I just... don't want to hurt her." My voice cracks as memories of my sister's incident come rushing back.

Lacey always struggled when it came to boys. Her tall stature and natural dramatic flair – taught by yours, truly – made it so boys were too intimidated to talk to her, let alone ask her out. That all changed the summer she turned sixteen.

Just like the flowers I buy for her birthday every year, that summer Lacey began to bloom. Her long, dangly limbs suddenly became lean and elegant, and her theatrical tendencies became perceived as confident rather than awkward. Lacey came into her own and it was only a matter of time until she brought some lucky bastard home.

When the new kid on the block – a preppy kid named Jerrell Thompson – started showing up at the local parties, we all took interest. Fresh blood doesn't come around very often, especially blood that comes from money. Jerrell became a target for every hetero girl and every homo boy – Nico included – but the new kid already had his own target picked.

My sister.

They were together for six months, two of which Nico and I took turns vetting the kid like drill sergeants until even we succumbed to his charms. Lacey seemed over the moon, and as a big brother, I couldn't ask for anything more. It wasn't until after the incident that the truth about Jerrell's harassment came out.

And by then, she'd already tried to take her own life.

I'll never forget the sight of my baby sister lying in a hospital bed, tubes coming out of her body after the doctors had to pump her stomach to get rid of the pills she took. I'll never forget the overwhelming guilt that still lingers to this day.

As a big brother, I had one job to do. And I failed.

I failed to protect my little sister.

Squeezing the bridge of my nose to counteract the burning sensation in my eyes, I feel the couch cushions dip as Nico sits himself down next to me. A warm arm wraps around my shoulders and I curse as a single tear leaks out.

"Listen to me, Wes." Nico gives my shoulders a shake, dragging my weary gaze up to his, "What happened to Lacey is an anomaly. A horrendous one at that, but still an anomaly. There were a lot of different factors that led to Lace taking those pills, factors which aren't even relevant in this thing you have with Trip."

Pausing to give me a questioning look, I nod for him to continue.

"Look man, all I'm saying is you have got to let go of the past. You can't let the illusion that you failed as a big brother barricade the road to every potential romantic partner. Pretty soon your dashing good looks will be gone, and you'll still be all alone. And who's going to want to take on your wrinkly ass then? Sure as shit not me."

I burst out laughing and the smile on Nico's face tells me that was his intent all along.

"I want you to be happy. Hell, I want you to find someone who *makes* you happy. And you can't do that unless you move on. Just because Lacey got torn apart doesn't mean you'll do the same thing to someone else. Trust yourself, man. And trust your partner."

"Thanks, Nico."

Satisfied I'm back on stable ground, Nico unwinds his arm from my shoulders and pushes himself off the couch. Ruffling my hair before he walks away, Nico finishes his speech with a line that would make any award-winning coach proud.

"Now, cheer up, Rookie. There's no crying on game day."

Lou

Game day.

Otherwise known as my first date with Wes. Well, our first official date. Stella spent the better part of last night listing all the reasons why this isn't *technically* our first romantic liaison, but the first outing asked by an interested party who happens to be one of my closest friends on campus, annoyingly attractive, and good at kissing. That's it, that's all.

I hope you caught the sarcasm.

"LOU! Can you believe the season opener is finally here?!" My roommate's enthusiastic outburst causes the students mingling around the cafeteria to pause their conversations and shoot questioning glances our way.

The tiger ears and matching tail Stella is sporting on top of her signature black tank and joggers combo might also have something to do with the stares. She managed to rope me into wearing the orange and black stripped face paint, but I put my foot down when the furry add-ons came out. Stella's school spirit may know no bounds, but mine only goes so far.

"Considering you spent half an hour painting my face this morning, yes, I can believe the opener has finally arrived."

What *is* unbelievable though, is the fact we've already reached the end of September. Feels like just yesterday I was anxiously packing all my belongings in cardboard boxes.

"Pfft," Stella bats away the comment with a wave of her hand, "I know you secretly love the tiger stripes."

Rolling my eyes with a smile, I turn to scan today's breakfast menu. I don't even bother reading the new vegan items featured on the chalkboard, my meals tend towards the carbohydrate side of the board. It's not that I don't like the nutritional section legumes fall under, it's just given the choice, bagels and fries are going to win over spinach and kale every time.

Thankfully, Taber's mandatory first-year meal plan takes all diets into consideration. From vegan options to deep fried goodness, this university is one of the rare few who genuinely cares for its students' gastronomical wellbeing. Whether you're in the mood for salty fries or a freshly made salad, Taber's cafeteria has you covered.

We slowly inch closer to the counter when Stella's phone rings.

"It's Mo. Can you order my usual?"

I nod and she excuses herself from the line. Walking a few steps from the queue, a wave of excitement radiates from my roommate as she answers the phone. I smile at the blatant display of sibling love. Something I'll never experience but always admire.

"NEXT!"

I shuffle forward, placing an order for an extra slathered Screaming Bagel and an extra-large Protein Punch. Elderly eyes asses me from behind the counter, a questioning stare that's either judging my face paint or the calorie count of those two meals combined. Given the fact she deals with university kids day-in, day-out, I'm going to go with the latter.

"NEXT!" Jumping the slightest bit, I move aside for the next person to shuffle forward. Mrs. Cafeteria may be a tad judgemental, but she's got efficiency down.

I grab our order and wander over to where Stella's standing, phone still pressed against her ear.

"... you're here now? But I thought you weren't coming until later... No, no it's fine. We'll meet you in the bleachers. See you soon." Jabbing the end button, her furry tail swishes through the air as Stella turns to face me.

"Sorry about that, Mo turned up early for once in his life." Sighing with exasperation, she grabs the protein shake I'm holding out to her, "A protein punch is just what I need right now. Thank you so much."

Pausing to take a gulp of her shake, Stella gestures towards the nearest door.

"Let's go hunt down my brother and snag good seats. We need to get a good view of the field, you've got a certain rookie to cheer for."

I groan good naturedly and link my arm through hers, "Apparently number twelve is the one to lookout for."

Stella gives a little squeal and I laugh, trying to unwrap my breakfast with one hand.

Unfortunately, the coordination required to eat food single handily is apparently above my skillset because next thing I know, cream cheese is smeared all the way down my shirt and all that's left in my hand is a depressingly plain bagel.

Handing me her napkin, Stella is barely able to keep her laughter in check, "There is a really dirty joke about cream that I am not even going to touch right now."

Eyeing my non slathered bagel from every angle, I sigh in resignation.

❧ ℓℓ

The weather is unseasonably warm for the end of September, and the sun beats down on our faces as Stella and I hike across Taber's surprisingly large sporting arena. Situated in the far-right hand corner, the lacrosse field is easily the farthest distance I've had to walk this year. The best part of going to a smaller university is not having to walk more than twenty minutes from anywhere on campus. This trek is definitely pushing the edge to that time zone, making me thankful I never considered joining a varsity team.

As we wind our way to the wooden bleachers lining the edge of the field, clusters of people begin to form. I knew lacrosse was one of Taber's more popular sports, but I hadn't realized how many students would show up to support the team. Orange and black greets me at every turn, the shirts and banners screaming school spirit are as vibrant as the crowd is loud. I even spot a few girls who have the same tiger ears as Stella, but no one else has the flaming orange tail. Stella is in a league all on her own with that one.

Among the sea of stripes, flashes of silver stand out. I've never known a school to only be represented by one colour before, but apparently Silverwood Sabers is fond of their metallic mascot.

A black poster catches my eye, and I gasp. The vibrant drawings contrast greatly with the dark paper, making it easy to understand the concept. A tiger lies bleeding out on the ground, severely wounded, with a saber stabbed through his middle. The level of detail in the fallen predator is enough to make my stomach churn.

Looking at the artist holding the poster, the unease grows. The boy looks to be in his late teens, with a pale complexion that almost looks sickly under his shocking white-blonde hair.

"Skylar Vin." Stella nods towards the poster holder, "He's been coming to watch these games as long as me. His older brother is infamous in the USport circuit."

I shudder, tearing my eyes away from the gruesome art, "What's he famous for?"

Stella grimaces, "*In*famous. Vector Vin holds the record for highest number of players he's put in the hospital. He's big, he's mean, but most of all he's angry. And that makes him unpredictable."

I whip my head around in horror, "Has he ever injured a Taber player?"

"A couple, yeah. Mo's never been hurt, thank God, but our goalie last year got messed up pretty bad. He walked away with a dislocated shoulder and two broken ribs vowing he'd never step on a lacrosse field again as long as that monster is loose."

My eyes flit back to Skylar and his sign, the gory details filling me with more dread than before.

Stella continues, "The worst part is that our goalie got off easy. A defenseman from Coaldale had to get immediate leg surgery after Vector pummelled him to the ground. The guy shouldn't be allowed to walk in public much less play a contact sport."

Bile rises in my throat as I look to the empty field. The freshly painted white sidelines suddenly look more like bars on a gladiator cage than a lacrosse field.

CHAPTER 21

Wes

"Alright boys, listen up!"

The team huddles forward as Cody puts his team leader skills into action.

"There are a lot of expectations going around. Expectations of the rookies, expectations of me, and most importantly, expectations of this team. The Tigers have brought home five consecutive championship banners ranking us as the longest undefeated team since this university was established."

Whether Cap's strategy is to add pressure before the game or lessen it is still undecided. Stay tuned.

"As soon as you put on that jersey today, you became a Tiger. You became an undefeated champion."

Annnd first strategy it is. Pressure cooker, we meet again.

"Undefeated. Champion." Placing an emphasis on each word, Cody manages to unload fifty years of school spirit onto us. Just a little extra weight to help plow down our opponents.

"It's time to get your asses out on that field and play the way I know you can play. Time to make our school proud, boys. What are we?"

"UNDEFEATED CHAMPIONS!" Chants rise up and we break the huddle with Taber Tiger's famous roar. The intimidation factor has never been higher.

We run onto the field, Cody leading the pack as the full bleachers erupts into cheers. Taber is a small university by any standard, but the show of support can't help but boost a guy's morale.

As rehearsed, the team splits into two lines, all of us turning to face the thundering bleachers. One by one, the two guys at the opposing ends set off a chain reaction of backflips, each of us finishing in a superhero landing – one knee on the ground, the other bent, head majestically bowed – and finish off with the last guys facing each other, one wearing orange and black, the other a makeshift silver jersey. The two seniors battle it out, with a not-so-subtle depiction of the metallic guy getting thrown to the ground while the Tiger stands up in victory.

The crowd goes wild.

Every Taber supporter from the age of nine to seventy-five jump to their feet, stomping and clapping their approval. The energy is so intense I can feel it vibrate through the grass and into my bent knee.

Rising to give the spectators a bow, I scan my gaze across the orange tidal wave. A particularly unpleasant sign catches my attention in the crowd – Jesus, did the guy have to add so much blood? – but even that disturbing image doesn't stop me searching for one particular person.

Like a needle in a haystack, or a pin in a tub of orange paint, the improbability of my search is almost comical. But like any great riddle solver, I know exactly how to find what I'm looking for: the irresistible pull of my magnet.

Otherwise known as my grey-eyed siren.

I know the moment Trip feels my stare because even from my field position I see a splotch of red stain her cheeks. She turns away from her conversation with Stella and sends a hesitant wave my way. Taking the wave as my cue, I respond with an outstanding air kiss. And for once my reward isn't a scowl.

It's a smile that steals my breath from three rows away.

"WESLEY!"

A grin hits my face as I turn in the direction of vocal cords that can only belong to my sister.

I spy Lacey frantically waving from the corner of the first row. Her uncoordinated arm movements nearly have her toppling out of the bleachers in an effort to capture my attention. The combination of Lacey's tall stature and lanky arms gives her a much larger flailing range, much to the delight of the nearby spectators, I'm sure.

I chuckle and wave back, spotting Nico doing the same from his position down the field. If there is one person my best friend loves more than me, it is my little sister. If Nico didn't swing for the other team, I have no doubt those two would be married right now. Because hey, the only thing better than having one dramatic Williams in your life is having two.

As the crowd starts to die down, we shuffle aside so the Sabers can have a little bit of the spotlight. Since they aren't the home team and therefore have a smaller fan section, they stick to their typical pre-game routine: running out with plastic sabers hanging off their jerseys and showing off some fancy swordplay for the crowd.

A shrill whistle pierces the air, and the teams scatter to begin warming up. I partner up with Hunter and we begin rallying with the occasional passing drill to help loosen up our muscles. Cody wanders over and pulls me aside.

"Thanks for your help the other day. The strategies we drew up may start Taber off with a win this year."

"What do you mean may? Our strategies are going to bring home the V today."

Cody laughs, "Don't ever lose your confidence, Wes."

"Wouldn't dream of it, Cap."

The easy humour fades from Cody's face as something catches his eye over my shoulder. Turning, I look to see silver jerseys moving intricately across the field, performing some sort of group running drill. Immediately, I zero in on the object of my captain's concern.

Vector Vin. The guy who single-handily put Taber's fourth year goalie in the emergency room last year. *After* the shot was made. Meaning, the lumbering forward player went back for the kill after the ball was passed off to our defence.

The dude takes lacrosse to a whole new level of contact. Not to mention sets anger management therapy back hundreds of years.

That being said, watching the white-blond hair streaking in the wind, it's hard to not be impressed. Vector has got to be at least 6'3 and closing in on 220 pounds, but he moves like a ballerina. Well, a ballerina with murderous intent.

Effortlessly catching the ball, Cody and I watch as Vector spins and passes the ball off to another player. No hesitation, no fumble.

If it weren't for his impulsive aggressiveness, the guy would be the best lacrosse player in the league. It's almost ironic that his most famous trait is the same one that's holding him back. His uncontrollable temper is a loose cannon, one that puts everyone on the field in danger and diminishes the precision of his shots. When the red haze of anger sets in, Vector's technique gets pushed to the side for raw aggression.

In other words, the more mistakes Vector makes, the more aggressive he gets. And the more aggressive he gets, the more mistakes he makes.

Picture Bruce Banner wearing a silver jersey, sporting long blonde hair, and holding a lacrosse stick. Now picture what would happen if the green monster got loose and there are no Avengers to calm him down.

Oh shit, indeed.

"Should we be worried?"

The fact I am asking about my teammates' safety and not a potential loss attests to a larger issue at hand.

"Rumour is Vector had to undergo counselling after the Coaldale incident."

I am not a squeamish guy, but the photos of *that* injury had me running for the closest bathroom. Apparently it took over a year for the player to be able to run again, let alone play lacrosse.

"Whether that's true or not, I have no idea. Don't let Vector get into your head, but make sure you keep a cautious eye out."

Easier said than done when your position's sole purpose is scoring. Even if I wanted to, chances are I'll be facing the wrong direction if Vector decides to take down one of our defensemen or goalie.

I shoot a panicked look at Nico, who is putting on the last of his protective padding. Catching my glance, Cody is quick to reassure me, "I'll watch out for him. No Saber is injuring any of my Tigers this year."

Realistically, I know one guy can't protect every player on the field, but looking at my captain right now, I feel better knowing he'll do his best to make the statement true.

Lou

"Remind me again, what's the half circle for?"

Stella sighs and leans back to let her brother explain the game for the umpteenth time.

"That's the crease. The goalie and his teammates may enter the circle, but the opposing players cannot."

"Ooh, so they have to shoot from outside the crease?"

The legendary Mighty Mo shoots me a killer smile and I feel a blush warm my face, "Exactly."

Stella's brother is not at all what I was expecting. My roommate's frame is so tiny, it only made sense to picture a taller, broader version of her. That assumption was wrong to a comical degree.

Mighty is the only word I can think to describe the legendary Mo. Tall even for a guy, with shoulders almost as wide as Cody's, Mo looks more like a warrior than an athlete. I expected his eyes to be similar to Stella's but that prediction also proved to be incorrect. Where Stella's eyes dance with dark blue undertones, Mo's irises are more like a frozen lake in the wintertime. Cold and pale. With the slightest glint of mischief.

The styled light brown hair is closer to what I was expecting. The shade matches Stella's eyebrows perfectly, so now I've uncovered the colour hidden under the platinum. Unlike his sister, however, Mo keeps his hair relatively short with the trim sides leading into a slicked wave. Both of them are perfectly maintained in drastically different ways.

Approaching Stella's brother in the bleachers was probably one of the most intimidating experiences of my life. The guy has the scariest resting bitch face I have ever seen, and if I hadn't witnessed the way Mo's demeanour changed upon seeing his younger sister, I definitely would have turned and ran. Rookie number twelve be damned.

Mo's commanding presence takes some getting used to but otherwise he's been nothing but lovely to me since we sat down. Apparently, his love for his sister extends to those she loves as well, so we were able to get by the RBF without incident.

I turn my attention back to the field and try to focus. I can't even see the ball being passed around - the only indication of its existence are the swarms of players that follow the invisible puck around.

Wait. Is there a difference between a ball and a puck?

"PLOW HIM DOWN, CODY!" Stella launches to her feet and screams the encouragement past three rows of spectators.

If I had to describe my roommate with one word, subtle would definitely be it.

Cody for his part, either has superhuman hearing or is feeling extra aggressive, because next thing I know our team captain bodychecks the incoming silver player and sends the poor guy flying, giving our team the chance to swoop up the ball and haul it back to the opposing side.

"That's my boy."

Mo nods his approval while Stella rolls her eyes, "You're his friend not his father."

I shift uncomfortably on the wooden bench as Mo's pale gaze brushes mine.

"I was Cody's mentor *and* his nominator for team captain. As far as I'm concerned, there is no distinction."

Now there's a friendship definition you don't hear every day. If Mo threw on a cape and a voice muffling mask, we could have a cinematic moment in the making:

Cody, I am your father.

Crap. Even my thoughts are starting to sound like Wes.

"God Mo, do you always have to be so condescending? Do us all a favour and pull that stick out of your ass." Stella scoffs and suddenly I'm wholly invested in the lacrosse game.

The only thing more awkward than couples bickering? Siblings fighting.

"How can I be the one with the stick up my ass when you haven't touched alcohol since mom died?"

Stella freezes beside me and I do my best to drag everyone's attention back to the field, "Oh look, it's Wes!"

My intervening comment gets ignored as Stella's stricken expression darkens, "That's different and you know it."

A shot of hurt goes through me at the realization my roommate has been holding out on me.

Mo immediately softens, "You're right Stel, I didn't mean to..."

His apology gets drowned out by the sudden cheer erupting from the bleachers around us.

In unison, we all look to the field where Wes is sprinting past silver jerseys along the left sideline. Suddenly, he pivots mid-sprint, neatly catching the ball flying overhead, and in one motion hurls it towards the net. The seconds between the ball escaping the netting of Wes' stick and its trajectory toward the net seems to go in slow motion. The ball neatly bounces off the goalie's glove and into the net and the sea of orange exhales a collective breathe.

Temporarily forgetting Stella's secret, I get swept away in the pulsing energy of the crowd as Tiger fans leap to their feet and roar their approval.

"TWELVE! TWELVE! TWELVE!" Starting from the front row and working its way back, the chant echoes from every Tiger supporter in the stands.

I have never been a girl who lusts after jocks but watching Wes rejoice with his teammates, sweat-soaked dark hair peeking out from under his helmet, I'm starting to understand why varsity athletes get all the hype. I mean, on top of the obvious six-packs.

With one shot, one goal, *everyone* is part of the team. Wes may have been the one who took the shot, but the win was for every Tiger present.

One player, one team, one school.

I think my daisy chain is finally starting to grow some roots.

CHAPTER 22

Wes

My favourite thing about sports?

No matter how well you do, how many times you score, the game always goes on. The scoreboard doesn't give a damn about an impressive goal, and as soon as the whistle blows, you're back to square one with a slight confidence boost.

It's refreshing in the most exhausting way.

Like most lacrosse games, as soon as the first goal is out of the way, everyone seems to loosen up. Whether you're the team taking the lead, or the one falling behind, as soon as the first goal is scored the floodgates open and suddenly forwards start taking as many shots as possible.

Why that is? I could not tell you.

The next quarter flies by with extraordinary shots and saves made by both teams. Nico has been on fire this whole game, throwing himself around the crease like an absolute pro, while the Saber goalie stays close behind - other than my goal in the first quarter, he hasn't let the ball slip past him once.

We hit halftime with Tigers on the board with one point, Sabers zero.

And that's when Silverwood releases the Hulk.

Hunter curses under his breath as we watch Vector run onto the field, completely fresh from sitting out the first two quarters. Anger issues aside, the guy is a fantastic player. As soon as he stepped onto the field everyone's job just got that much harder.

"Ready to play, Tigers?" Vector's nasally voice would be hilarious if it wasn't for the malicious gleam in his eyes. One of our seniors flinch, no doubt remembering their teammate being carried off the field in a stretcher last year.

"Didn't realize inanimate objects could play, *Vector*."

Cody's voice breezes past the tension dividing the field, drawing reluctant chuckles from our side. Through his face guard, I see Vector blink slowly, unsure of what to make of the unexpected power play. Seeming completely unconcerned about the threat of bodily harm, Cody blows the beast a kiss, putting a smirk on every Tiger's face and setting off some snickers on the Saber side.

Vector turns and glares at his teammates just as the ref blows his whistle.

The lingering fear seems to dissipate as everyone readies themselves into position. Say what you want about my short, stocky captain but one thing's for certain.

The guy has balls. And they're definitely made out of vibranium.

elle

"Mother fu..." Letting out a string of expletives, I watch as Vector snatches the ball out of the air not five feet from where I'm standing. Hunter overthrew the shot, and I didn't get there in time to stop the bulldozer from embracing the breakaway opportunity.

Swivelling with impossible grace, Vector does a full 180 and charges down the field back to where Nico just barely managed to save his last shot. I sprint after him, but the guy's stride and sheer power leaves me with no hope of catching up.

One of our senior defensemen attempts to block Vector's pass, but one fuelled bodycheck later, the guy goes flying. One bounce, two bounces, the defensemen comes to a crunching stop and I change my trajectory to his direction. I see Cody correct his own course of action to intervene, but it's too late. Vector flings his stick with furious intent and the ball flies right over Nico's foot and into the net.

Saber cheers go up as I rush to the fallen player's side. By the time I reach the redheaded senior he's already sitting up and waving away offers of medical assistance.

"Bro, that wasn't even close to the worst body slam I've had. The only thing hurting right now is my ego. Tell me, did the fall look sick at least?"

Relief hits me as I grin, reaching out a hand to pull the defenseman to his feet.

"Sick is the only word I would use to describe that fall."

Mason chuckles and fetches his lacrosse stick from the ground just as Cody runs over.

"Mace, you alright?" Concern fills our captain's voice as he offers a hand of assistance.

Mason slaps the hand away and gives him a reassuring laugh, "Quit with the babying, Cap. You know as well as I do our position means taking a tumble now and then."

Cody shakes his head, a smile tugging at his lips, "I'm glad you are okay. Let me know if you want to get subbed next quarter."

Snorting, Mason waves off the comment, "As if I would give Vin the satisfaction."

Together we walk back to the centre circle, where the Sabers are still celebrating the tie-up. Watching Vector rejoice with his teammates feels like watching a lacrosse-playing vampire celebrate with his blood-thirsty friends and family.

That's it. I am no longer Team Edward.

As if reading my offensive thoughts, Vector glances over to us. For a split second, I think his pale expression is about to transform into something resembling an apology, but then he ruins the moment by raising his finger and sliding it slowly along his neck. Psychopath style.

Good to see Silverwood's sportsmanship is up to standard.

"That guy's got serious issues."

Mason mumbles the comment before peeling off into position. Despite his reassurances, it's pretty obvious Mason is pretty shaken from his fumble with Vector. The guy hasn't been able to look anywhere but the white-haired vampire, as if he's waiting for the kill shot to happen at any minute.

Little did I know it wasn't Mason who should have been worried.

With a tied scoreboard and only two minutes left in the third quarter, I sneak a glance at Trip in the crowd. The sight of her paint-streaked face is enough to drop my nervous system back down into its normal stratosphere.

Breathe, Wes. Just breathe.

The whistle blows and we're off.

Lou

It happened so fast.

One second he was running up the field, the next he was crumpled on the ground. And this time, he didn't get back up.

Vector was tearing down the field like some sort of madman when Hunter stepped out in front of him, ready to steal the ball from the charging bull. I've never felt so afraid for someone else's life – and that was before Cody yanked the rookie out of the way and took the full force of Vector Vin.

Tears filled my eyes as I watched the team's beloved captain – my *friend* – get trampled like a vintage rag doll across the field. Cody's body rolls to a stop, and there's no movement in sight. The bleachers, unusually quiet, let out a collective gasp as it becomes clear Taber Tigers' captain isn't getting up anytime soon.

With a scream, Stella volts herself from our bench and hurtles down three rows of bleachers, scrambling over spectators until she hits even ground. Mo lets out a curse as we watch his sister sprint across the field to the crumpled heap of lacrosse gear. She makes it there before any of the other players or medics and drops to her knees, reaching out to cradle Cody's face in her hands.

By this point players and spectators are streaming onto the field, a chaotic muddle that makes our traverse to the injured Tiger much more difficult. When we finally reach him, the medics have arrived and are struggling to move Stella aside.

"Ma'am, we can't help him if you don't let us move him."

Tears stream down my roommate's face as she shakes her head, refusing to let go. Mo sighs and walks over to his sister, crouching down to gently peel her grip off Cody's unresponsive body.

"Stel, you gotta let go. This isn't like last time. You will see Cody again, I promise." Continuing to ease her hands away from his fallen comrade, Mo continues, "They need to take him to a hospital. Let them help him, Stel. You need to let go."

Eventually, Stella lets herself be led away from Cody. The sight of Stella's tear-stained face has my heart constricting painfully. The broken expression on her face reveals a devastation much deeper than today's events on the lacrosse field.

Forcing myself to look away, I spot Wes talking to one of the paramedics. Helmet tucked under one arm, his expression grim and tired. As I approach the two men, I can't help but overhear the end of their conversation.

"... in that case, I'd be happy to drive behind the ambulance and meet you at the hospital."

"You're not going to finish the game?" My question comes out louder than expected and Mo starts to make his way over, a deathly pale Stella in tow.

Wes jolts in surprise, "Trip! God, I'm so glad you're here."

Wrapping me up in a bone-crushing hug, my arms find their way around his sweat-soaked neck and into his dishevelled hair. He smells surprisingly good for someone who has been running around a field for the last forty minutes.

"I am so sorry you had to see this. Most games aren't like this, I promise." Wes whispers the words in my ear, his warm breath sending tingles down my neck.

"Quit being so Canadian. You couldn't have expected this would happen, and I've loved watching you play today. Are *you* okay?"

I pull back from our embrace, noting the dullness in his eyes that has taken the place of Wes' signature sparkle. He looks crushed. Defeated.

"I've been better."

A rueful smile fights its way onto his face and without thinking, I pull him down for a kiss. The instant our lips touch I feel the weight lift off his shoulders. He wraps his arms around my waist and lifts me up, pressing me tight against his chest. Lost in a language only we understand, Wes spills the stress and tension he's been holding inside and I offer him a safe place to land.

A cough pulls us apart and we both turn to see Mo standing with his arms crossed. Stella stares silently at the stretcher being carried towards Cody's unconscious form.

"Did I hear you say you're *not* finishing the game?" The accusatory tone makes me wince, but Wes appears unfazed as he gently lowers me to the ground.

"That's right. I'm heading to the hospital to wait and see what Cody's results are."

Wes' response has Mo venomously shaking his head, "You will do no such thing. Your team needs you here, and Cody's condition is not going to change whether you're at the hospital in two minutes or twenty."

My jaw drops at Mo's harsh words, "I thought you two were friends?"

Frosty blue eyes meet mine and I resist the urge to flinch.

"We are. And as his friend, I know that he would want Wes to finish the game without him." Shifting his steely gaze from me to the rookie, Mo continues, "Don't let the Tigers lose their first game in five years because of an injury. Avenge your fallen captain with a victory. Right here, right now."

"If it were me in that ambulance, Cody would be riding its ass all the way to the hospital. Undefeated champions or not."

The clench in Mo's jaw has me nervously shuffling my feet as the two men stare each other down.

"If you leave this field before the final quarter, you can kiss rookie-of-the-year goodbye."

I stare, aghast, at the unbelievably handsome yet cruel man throwing around ultimatums, "You aren't even on the team anymore. You can't make those decisions."

My voice rings out over Wes' frozen silence, the fierceness in my tone causing Mo's eyes to widen in surprise.

He opens his mouth to respond when a feeble whisper cuts him off. "She's right."

We all turn to look at Stella as she sways unsteadily on her feet. Mo takes a step towards her, but I beat him to it, rushing over to support my roommate.

Stella glares defiantly at her brother, "You aren't captain anymore, Cody is. These are *his* players, not yours. So, unless you have something to say that will help Cody's condition, backoff."

Stella sags into my arms as if the confrontation used up the last of her energy. Her furry tail and matching ears got lost along the way, and for some reason, the loss hits me harder than it should. I find myself blinking back tears as I brush aside a few stray platinum strands and pull her close.

Looking up, I see guilt and concern riddle Mo's features as he takes in his sister's exhausted state.

He sighs, running a hand down his face, "You need to rest, Stel. Why don't I take you back to my hotel."

Seconds tick by, and I find myself holding my breath as we all wait for her verdict.

"I'd rather go to the hospital with Wes." Raising her chin insolently, Stella gives her brother a pointed stare, "And after that, I'll go home with Lou."

Clenching his jaw hard enough to break molars, Mo gives us a terse nod. Spinning on his heel to return to the bleachers, Nico makes a sudden appearance, and Mo goes crashing into his tall, lanky body.

The two men fall to the ground, limbs flailing as they each try to break their fall.

"*Oof.*" The air gets expelled out of Nico's lungs as the dense lacrosse legend lands flat on top of him.

Trust me, I know the feeling.

Before anyone can offer a hand, Mo jerks away from Nico as if he's caught fire. Jumping to his feet with the agility of a gymnast, the graduated Tiger doesn't look at Nico before taking off. Nico climbs back to his feet, brushes off his pants, and stares quizzically at Mo's retreating form.

"I swear I've seen him before..." Nico shakes his head, suddenly remembering the matter at hand, "Never mind. I came to tell you the game has been postponed. There was talk about forfeiting but the refs are having none of it. Silverwood has agreed to a rematch next weekend."

Wes visibly sags in relief, "Thank God. Cap deserves to at least be present when we whip Saber's ass. We're heading to the hospital now, do you want to come?"

Nico nods towards the crowded field, "The boys and I are on equipment duty and some serious crowd control. I'll make sure Lacey is alright, you go make sure our captain is being taken care of."

With a slap on the back, Nico heads back to the field and Wes ushers us to his vehicle.

"What the hell is that?"

The horror in Stella's voice breaks a chuckle out of my chest. My worries are momentarily forgotten as my roommate eyeballs the beige rust bucket Wes has so graciously provided us.

"That, my dear Stella, is none other than a Ford 500." Wes announces the fact proudly and yanks open the passenger door. The hinges groan loudly and a chunk of the rubber seal falls to the pavement.

Wes flashes me a grin, and I add the final piece.

"Her name is Lola."

CHAPTER 23

Wes

I hate hospitals.

A cliché, I know, but these clichés exist for a reason. You are never at the hospital because it is a beautiful, sunny day and you wanted to go for a stroll. No, the only reason you willingly walk along these sterile hallways is because it's a *bad* day. For someone you love.

I lead the march to the front desk, where a frazzled looking nurse is arguing with an elderly patron.

"I'm sorry sir, the coffee machine in the waiting room is all we have. The coffee the nurses receive isn't any better, I can assure you."

The stooped man throws his hands up in exasperation, the white tuffs on his head swaying like dandelions in the breeze. Man, I can't wait until my hair looks like that.

"Then where can I find a decent coffee around here?"

I clear my throat and gently tap the man's cardigan-covered shoulder, "There's a Tim's right around the corner. Two-minute drive, ten-minute walk."

Wispy eyebrows raise as the man takes in my lacrosse getup. His gaze shifts over to Stella and Trip's smeared orange faces and he hooks a thumb in our direction, "The costume freaks understand what I'm after. You were extremely unhelpful, miss, but thank you for your time."

The old man shuffles away, leaving the nurse gritting her teeth through a plastered smile.

I slide into his place with ease, "You handled that exceedingly well. Can't be easy dealing with caffeine fiends 24/7."

The nurse breaks into a real smile and chuckles in agreement.

"Terrible coffee is everyone's breaking point. We just made a new code in case of a coffee machine breakdown. It's only happened once during my shift, and let's just say, it took the entire nursing staff and four security guards to calm everyone down."

I let out a low whistle while Trip giggles softly behind me.

"I would have needed popcorn for high-quality entertainment. Coffee expertise aside, I was hoping you could point me in the right direction for my brother, Cody Ellsworth. He came in just a few minutes ago?" I flash her my dimples, hoping they will be enough to make her forget to check my ID.

"Sure thing, hon. Let me just check what room he's in." The nurse turns and types on her keyboard while I give Trip and Stella a subtle thumbs up over my shoulder.

"Oh, could I see your ID? Just want to make sure your family."

My thumbs up must not have been so subtle after all.

I rest my elbows on the desk and motion the nurse to come closer.

"Here's the thing. I don't actually share the same parents as Cody." I pause, looking her deep in the eyes, "He's my *lacrosse* brother."

The nurse blinks back at me. I think she understands.

"You mean you... play on the same team?" I beam and gesture towards my jersey, "That's right. Go Tigers!"

The frown on her face tells me she's not a Taber supporter.

I sigh, "Look, I know there are regulations for this kind of thing, but that's my captain in there. He took a hard hit today and I just want to know if he's okay. I *need* to know he's okay." My voice breaks and I feel Trip gently rub my back. Shit.

So much for no crying on game day.

The nurse gives me a small smile, "Room 211 is the one you're looking for. It looks as though he's in stable condition, but you'll have to sit in the upper waiting room until he gets cleared for visitors. Family members get first priority."

She gives me a knowing look, "Elevator is down the hall and to the left. Go on."

"Thank you. Thank you so much." Blowing my saviour a kiss, I turn and follow Trip and Stella down the cream-coloured hallway.

The further we walk from the main entrance, the stronger the chemical smell becomes. I don't have to describe the scent because you know exactly what I'm talking about: the signature hospital aroma. Soul crushing with a dash of despair thrown in for good measure.

"I see his room!"

Stella races out of the elevator, dodging walkers and nurses at every turn. Skidding to a halt in front of the white door, Stella stands on her tip toes to peer inside the small rectangular window. Trip and I catch up just as she lets out a sob.

Trip wraps her roommate into a tight hug while I take a peek. My throat tightens as I take in the outline of my captain lying on the bed, face covered with an oxygen mask, tubes hooked up to beeping machines. I exhale through my nose, willingly myself to become the leader these girls need me to be.

I turn and face the duo, noting Stella's inability to get control of herself. Lost in Trip's embrace, she seems to be fighting and losing an inner battle as tears soak through Trip's Green Day t-shirt. I quickly make an executive decision.

"Stella, let me call your brother and get him to take you girls home. There's nothing you can do for Cody, and he wouldn't want this for you."

The platinum pixie lifts her head just enough so I can see her glare, "How do you know what Cody would want?"

I sigh, readying myself to go head-to-head with another O'Brien. Two in one day, that's pretty impressive if I do say so myself.

"You're right. I don't know what Cody would want. But I do know he would hate to see you so distressed. He would want to make sure you're taken care of, so please, Stella. Let me call your brother."

Swollen, bloodshot eyes meet mine. Stella's small frame looks so fragile in Trip's arms.

"Okay."

It takes me a second to register the agreement. Trip's misty gaze meets mine in astonishment, as if she's struggling to believe her stubborn roommate gave in so easily as well. I hold out my hand and after a moment's hesitation, Stella unwinds herself from Trip's embrace, handing me her phone.

I immediately step away in case she changes her mind and goes full attack-mode. I pull up Mo's contact and take a deep breath. This is going to be ugly.

"Stel? Hey, I know you're angry, but I just want to say-

"It's Wes." I swiftly cut him off before any sibling bonding has the chance to occur.

The pause at the end of the line tells me the message was received.

"I need you to come pick up Trip and Stella. We're at the hospital and it's not looking good. Cody's in rough shape and your sister is not doing well."

I wait for the I-told-you-so to drop. He had wanted to take his sister home to rest in the first place.

"You're at St. Catherine's?"

I nod, unable to sit still even though he can't see me.

"Yes, we are."

"I'll be there in five minutes."

Mo hangs up and I stare at the cracked screen in my hand. He didn't mention anything about being right, or our fight for that matter, his sister was top priority.

Now I know where Cody gets it from.

Lou

Silence. Tense, nail-biting silence. That sums up the car ride home.

The O'Brien siblings didn't say a single word to each other the whole drive home, so I entertained myself with the sleek interior of Mo's Cadillac Escalade. I don't know what Stella's brother does for work, but whatever it is, it must pay really well. I can practically smell the cost of theses buttery leather seats, and it's not in the single digits.

If I were to compare Wes' car to a functioning escalator, one that creaks but still performs its basic function of moving people from one place to another then Mo's vehicle would be the VIP, luxury elevator. The one that only the most prestigious can use, with its own private butler who presses the floor number button for you. Same function, different league.

Sorry, Lola.

As soon as Mo pulls to a stop, Stella leaps out of the vehicle, slamming the door in her wake. I try a more civilized approach with a mumbled thank you and hasty scramble to follow my roommate into our resident building.

Entering our dorm with a swipe of my access card, our ancient sofas and TV greet us as if nothing has changed. As if Cody isn't lying in a hospital bed with tubes coming out of him. As if Stella hasn't been hiding a secret from me this whole semester.

The latter thought hurts just as much as the former. Stella called me her sister, she told me we were family. Yet, she never once opened up about her mother, about her avoidance of alcohol, or about the fact she has trouble sleeping. I had to uncover each one for myself.

My gut clenches painfully as I think about all the times I came to Stella for advice. She always pushed for the details of my struggles, but never once offered up any of her own.

My sadness quickly turns to frustration and tears prick the back of my eyes. I duck my head to hide the emotions threatening to overspill.

"Lou, I..."

Stella's voice trails off and I raise my head to look at my roommate. Her face paint has all but smeared off, her mascara in raccoon circles around her bloodshot eyes. Her normally perfect hair is in a chaotic ball of frizz, and there seems to be a light trail of snot running from her nose to her upper lip. My heart aches in sympathy, and I find myself stomping down my own tidal wave of emotions.

"Let's get you cleaned up. We both need a good night's sleep, then we can talk in the morning, okay?"

My roommate nods and lets me lead her to the bathroom where I patiently brush the knots from her hair and clean her face.

"Thank you."

Stella whispers the words as I wipe the last of the orange from her face and some of my anger drifts away. No matter what secrets Stella is keeping from me, that doesn't change the fact she has taken care of me all semester. And as silly as it sounds, it feels nice to know my strong roommate sometimes needs me to be the supporting figure.

Wrapping my arms around the girl before me, I squeeze her tightly, "You're my sister, Stella. And family doesn't abandon family."

⸻ ele ⸻

For the first time ever, I'm up before my roommate.

Not because I set my alarm for 4:15AM, but because I didn't sleep at all. I spent the night tossing and turning, while periodically checking my phone for any updates from Wes. Other than tired selfies of him with a different nurse every few hours, he had nothing to report.

I don't even bother getting changed when I hear movement through our adjoining wall, I simply march into the living room and slump onto a sofa in my matching pyjama set. They're anime themed in case you were wondering.

I hear Stella's door creak open and watch as my roommate lightly treads to the kitchen sink. She quietly fills up her water bottle, and I take a moment to observe her. The muscular outline of Stella's shoulders slump just the slightest bit forward, making her gym bag look unbearably heavy as it hangs off her shoulder. Her long hair is pulled back in a tight bun, rebellious strands of platinum poking out from the otherwise impeccable topknot. She turns from the sink, and I feel my breath catch. Her face is completely void of makeup, and without concealer hiding the bags under her eyes, Stella's face looks drawn and weary.

As if she has lived this life one too many times.

"Good morning."

My casual conversation starter gets tossed out the window as Stella shrieks and hurls her water bottle in my direction. Brain still in zombie-mode from my restless night, I don't even flinch as the metallic bottle hurtles my way.

Thump! Stella's weapon of choice hits my knee, and I barely feel a thing. Turns out my pain receptors don't work with less than three hours of sleep. Go figure.

"Oh my God, Lou! You almost gave me a heart attack." Stella clasps a hand over her chest and takes a few deep breaths, "What are you doing up this early?"

I tug my pyjama pants up to see a red circle marking the point of contact, "I couldn't sleep. And we need to talk."

Stella sighs and drops her gym bag on the floor. Walking over to the sofa opposite mine, she takes a seat. I shift uncomfortably on my own sofa, suddenly aware my attire isn't optimal for a roommate intervention.

"I don't how to say this, so I'm just going to start with how I'm feeling. I feel betrayed, Stella. I've been honest with you about my struggles, yet I had to hear from your brother the real reason you don't drink alcohol."

Stella twitches as if she's being physically assaulted, but I push on, "You told me you don't drink because your workout regime doesn't leave room for hangovers."

Stella breaks eye contact and looks down to her fiddling hands, "That is true."

"But that's not the only reason, is it?" My direct approach causes Stella to raise her tired eyes to mine.

"No, it's not."

The anger from last night flares and words burst from my mouth, "How can we be sisters if you don't open up? I've told you *everything*. You've told me nothing. How do you think that makes me feel?"

I grit my teeth against the crash of emotions battling inside me.

"You're right, Lou." Tears well up in Stella's bloodshot eyes, making her dark eyes glisten with sadness, "I've been a horrible sister."

I stare sadly at the gym guru across from me, wondering how much she's been keeping from me.

Wiping the moisture from her eyes, Stella stands up and peels off her black tank top. The action is so unexpected that I can only stare, speechless, as a six-pack that could rival Wes' pops out over the top of her leggings. Call me sexist, but I honestly did not believe girls could have muscles that defined. Stella looks like she was carved by God himself.

Is that what happens when you don't eat fries three meals a day?

Stella raises her right arm, and I gasp. A jagged scar runs along her torso, the taught flesh marred from her waist up to the top of her ribcage. The thick white line branches off into an explosion of scar tissue across Stella's ribs, the ends of the web disappearing into the band of her pink sports bra. Covering my mouth with my hand, I can only stare in horror at the damage marking my roommate's body.

"When I was 16, my mother surprised me with a shopping trip for my birthday. We flew out to New York and had the ultimate girl's weekend."

I tear my gaze away from Stella's torso to look her in the eye. A sad smile stretches across her face.

"My mom understood me better than anyone else. Grade eleven was a hard year for me, but she knew exactly what I needed: a few days just to get away." The sad smile wobbles as Stella continues, "We paid to keep our car in the airport parking lot, so my father wouldn't have to worry about picking us up Sunday night. We were getting in late, and he had an early morning meeting the next day."

My breath catches knowing what's about to come.

"We were ten minutes away from our house when a drunk driver rear ended us. It was January, so the roads were icy, and we skidded into a concrete divider. The car flipped and sent us spinning into oncoming traffic. All I remember is my mom screaming and throwing her arm out to protect me. When I woke up, I had five broken ribs and eighteen stitches in my side. It hurt to breath but the doctors told me I was lucky, the glass shards from my window had only snagged my right side, leaving my left side completely untouched. Mo came into the room, and as soon as I saw his expressions, I knew. I knew I was never seeing my mother again."

Tears drip onto Stella's cheek as she turns so I can see her other side.

"I swore that day, I would never touch alcohol. The only thing it leads to is-

"Consequences." I finish her sentence by reading the tattoo running down her left side. Most people would have used the bolded black letters to cover up the dreadful scar, but Stella chose to keep the permanent reminder.

"Every night, I hear my mother's scream and feel her arm press against my chest. The doctors told me only one side was injured from the accident, but I lost so much more than a few inches of skin that day. It didn't feel right to only have my right side marked when my whole being was crushed with the loss of my mother. So, one year after the accident, Mo took me to get this tattoo. Father would never have approved, but Mo signed as my guardian. He understood the pain I was going through and knew I needed to channel it somewhere."

I stand up and walk over to my half-naked roommate. I raise my arms in question, and at her nod, I fold her into a tight embrace.

"I am so sorry, Stella."

The words feel less than inadequate, but it's all I can do. No matter how much you wish otherwise, there's no changing the past.

"I'm sorry I didn't tell you sooner. My defence mechanism has always been to avoid the subject, but that wasn't fair to you."

She hesitates, pulling back from our hug long enough to meet my own, tired eyes.

"Are we... still friends?"

The vulnerability in Stella's voice is so familiar it drags an unexpected laugh from me. Somewhere along the way, the lines between social butterfly and social outcast became one and the same.

"Remember who you're talking to, Stella. My answer to that ridiculous question will always be yes."

CHAPTER 24

Wes

"How do I look?"

I'm hetero through and through but hearing my captain's voice just about made me drop to my knees in proposal.

I shuffle into the room, throwing a wink to the bruised and bandaged Cody lying under the covers.

"To me, you've never been sexier."

Cody's chuckle turns into a cough, and I try not to wince. His one eye is completely swollen shut, while the other seems to have broken a blood vessel. In the span of twelve hours, my captain has become a demon cyclops. And that's being generous.

"You've always been too charming for your own good, Wes." Cody tries to shift on the bed, and I hurry over.

"And you've always been too eager for your own good. Don't try to move, let me call the nurses."

Grumbling, Cody leans back against his pillow and fixes a battered eye on me. At this rate, he could give Nick Fury a run for his money.

"Is Hunter okay?" I hit the button to summon a nurse and shake my head in exasperation. Even beaten to a pulp, Cody's top priority is making sure his team is alive and well. They don't make them like this one anymore.

"Hunter is pissed you took on Vector for him. Says you've destroyed his badass reputation."

Another chuckle echoes from the lump on the bed, "Hunter couldn't be a badass if he tried. Not with that haircut, anyways."

"Facts."

I smirk at the thought of Hunter's sheepdog bangs. Suddenly remembering everyone I promised an update, I whip out my phone and send a quick *he's awake!* text to Trip, Nico, and Mo.

"Who won?"

With my phone buzzing with happy emojis, it takes me a second to figure out what Cody is asking.

"The game? It got postponed to next weekend. Taber threatened to forfeit so the refs gave Silverwood two options: either they were the ones to forfeit or we do a rematch next weekend. Doesn't take three guesses to figure out which one they chose."

Nico stopped by late last night with Lace to check in on Cody and bring me food, so I got the latest scoop of lacrosse gossip.

"Why did Taber threaten to forfeit? You boys could have easily won the game without me." Visibly agitated, Cody shifts around on his bed, wincing at the movement.

"Cap, no one wanted to win. Hell, no one wanted to play once you were injured. You're our leader, so if you sit out, we all sit out. There was no question of continuing the game."

Something glistens in Cody's red, unswollen eye, and I'm not sure if it's appreciation or pain. Kind of hard to tell at this point.

My phone starts to buzz, so I sneak a glance down.

NICO: About damn time. Tell Cap he's late to morning practice.

MO: Keep me updated on his diagnosis.

TRIP: YAY!!!

TRIP: Is he in good enough shape for Stella to come visit??

"You're smiling."

I sheepishly look at my captain, tucking my phone back into my pocket, "Sorry, everyone is happy to hear you're conscious. I think you're more popular injured than not."

Cody laughs just as a nurse rushes into the room.

"I apologize for the delay, what can I help you with?"

Cody opens his mouth to speak but I cut him off.

"My friend here is in a lot of pain. Is there anything we can give him to make him more comfortable?"

The nurse pulls out her notebook and flips the pages until she finds the right one.

"Cody Ellsworth?"

"Yes, ma'am."

The nurse runs her finger down the page, eyes trailing in pursuit, "It looks like you are due for another dose of pain reliever. Your cracked rib and broken cheekbone will still be tender, but this should relieve some of the discomfort."

"Am I free to leave?" The nurse shakes her head, tapping a spot on the page.

"The doctors have you booked for one last MRI scan at noon today. If the swelling in your brain has gone down, you are free to leave."

Cody nods and I take the pills the nurse extracts from her scrubs.

"They're extra strength, so only take two every six hours."

I look at the bottle and bite back a snicker. It's none other than your average Advil found at any local convenience store. Hope Cody wasn't counting on the strong stuff.

"Thank you."

The nurse takes her leave and I pass two pills to Cody who swallows them dry.

"Vector did a number on you, hey?"

The demon eye turns my way and I swear I see a hint of a smile, "Nah, this is what I look like every Sunday morning."

I chuckle, shaking my head, "God help your future wife."

Cody laughs, then breaks into a painful wheeze. Giving him a second to catch his breath, I whip out my phone and text a response to Trip.

ME: He's in rough shape. I'm not sure he'd want Stella to see him like this.

TRIP: Did you ask?

Busted.

"Stella's wondering if she can come visit."

I blurt out the question before Trip can guilt me from fifteen blocks away. Something flashes in Cody's eyes at the mention of Stella's name, and I immediately feel bad for bringing it up.

"You have Stella's number?"

The sharpness in his tone brings me up short. *That's* what Cody's worried about right now? Me having his girl's number?

I wave my phone innocently towards the bed, "Trip's my messenger."

Cody's bruised face immediately softens and I feel a smirk tug my lips, "Would there be a problem if I did have Stella's number?"

Rolling his visible eye at me, the cyclops grumbles, "I change my mind. You're not charming, you're irritating."

My smirk turns into a full-fledged grin, "But you are charmed by my irritating abilities, aren't you?"

Getting a groan in return, I decide to let him off the hook.

"Just playing with you, Cap. For real though, do you feel up to having visitors?"

Closing his eye momentarily, I get a glimpse of how much agony Cody is in. From the outside, it looks as though his body has been through a ringer, and that's only a reflection of the inside damage. Considering his face looks like it got trampled by an elephant, I can only imagine what it must feel like on the inside. Even if visitors mean more suffering, knowing Cody, there's no way he would turn them away. It's not in his people-pleasing nature.

"You know what, why don't we put the visitors on hold until you're back home and able to move around. Chances are you'll be released tonight, so you'll be able to celebrate your survival with everyone soon enough."

Cody slumps against his pillow in relief, and I can tell he's already drifting off to sleep.

"Thank you, Wes. For everything."

His breathing starts to get deeper and I take my cue to leave. Reaching for the door handle, I pause as incoherent mumbling hits my ears.

"What was that, Cap?"

"Can you tell Stella..." I lean closer, straining to make out the rest of Cody's sentence, "...things will be different."

"Different how?"

Leaving my question unanswered, my battered captain falls into a deep slumber.

Lou

Stella didn't take the rejection well.

"What do you mean I'm not allowed to visit Cody? Isn't Wes with him right now?"

My tiny roommate paces our equally tiny living room in frustration.

"Wes is going to explain everything once he's back. Let's wait and find out what he has to say before you go storming into the recovery room, scaring all the patients."

Stella scowls, "There's only one patient I want to scare right now."

After our talk this morning, my roommate seems to be on more stable ground. Or maybe it was the 2-hour follow up gym session that helped her calming process. Stella's flawless makeup is back in place, and her hair is pulled into a tight ponytail that separates into miniature braids flowing past her shoulder blades. If you don't look too closely at the expertly applied concealer, Stella looks no different than any other day: confident and ready to conquer the day.

A knock on our door has her bolting for the door. Swinging it wide open, Stella grabs Wes and pulls him inside.

"Tell us everything you know."

I bite back a smile at the aggressive approach. Poor Wes looks exhausted and ready to collapse, but it's heartwarming to see Stella's fiery personality spark back to life.

"He's got one more MRI to go, and if nothing drastic comes out of that, Cody will be home in time for dinner." Still wearing his game jersey, Wes shuffles from side-to-side, "You might want to give him a few days, Stella. I've never seen him look so bad."

Stella waves her hand impatiently, "I don't care what he looks like."

"That's not what I'm saying. He's just not ready to see anyone, physically or emotionally. It's not that he *doesn't* want to see you, he just doesn't have the strength or energy right now."

Stella takes a step back as if he slapped her.

"I see." Hurt flashes through her dark blue eyes before a neutral mask takes its place, "In that case, I'll make sure not to bother him. I wouldn't want to *drain* Cody with my presence."

Stella turns and marches into her room, slamming the door behind her.

Wes turns to me with wide eyes, "Was it something I said?"

Shaking my head, I sigh, "She's had a rough 24 hours. I'll talk to her later."

Taking a step closer, I reach out a finger to smooth the worry line etched between his brows. Wes closes his eyes and rests his forehead against mine. I do my best to keep my eyes open, wanting to count how many freckles line his perfect nose, but my vision goes blurry and I find myself closing my eyes as well.

"I need a nap."

Wes' gruff voice tugs my lips into a smile, and I choose to keep my eyes closed for a moment longer.

"A shower wouldn't hurt either."

Wes chuckles and inches away, just enough so I can open my eyes without making myself dizzy. Flecks of gold sparkle through vibrant green and the mystery to Wes' sparkling eyes is finally solved.

"I'm going to go shower then nap, but maybe you could come over and I can make you dinner tonight?"

Despite my efforts to keep a straight face, a smile tugs at my lip, "You mean like a date?"

"Exactly like a date." Wes drops into a bow, holding his hand out like a Disney prince proposing a dance, "Trip, would you do me the honour of feasting with me tonight?"

Rubbing my chin in consideration, I let the lacrosse player sweat a few seconds before giving him a beaming smile.

"I would love to."

With a flash of movement, Wes has picked me up and is spinning me around the room. I squeal as my legs go flying through the air and we somehow manage to miss the old TV set and patchy sofas. He finally puts me down and kisses me briefly on the lips.

"Dinner is at seven. Wear anything you like." He moves towards the door then pauses, flashing me a set of dimples, "Or nothing at all."

The door shuts and I'm left standing in our living room, body flushed from the top of my head to the bottom of my toes. I know Wes is joking, but a part of me is intrigued.

Conflicting thoughts start to crowd my brain and my head starts to pound. For someone who's always been behind on social etiquette it's safe to say my experience in relationships lacks an equal amount, if not more.

I think it's time to call in the calvary.

"STELLA!"

My roommate's door creaks open and a platinum ponytail peeks out. Given we are not five feet away, the shout was a touch on the dramatic side.

"I need your help." My cheeks redden as a smirk creeps over Stella's face. It's pretty obvious she's been eavesdropping, yet she still raises an eyebrow in question.

"Yes?"

I gulp, gesturing helplessly towards the door through which Wes departed, "I have a date."

Stalking out of her room like a tiger on the hunt, Stella circles me slowly, "So, I heard. And what, may I ask, is the goal for tonight's date?"

Her outburst from earlier seems to be momentarily forgotten.

"Er, well, it's not that I have a *goal* per say, but theoretically speaking, if this is almost our third *official* date..." I trail off and let my flushed cheeks fill in the rest.

Waving my concerns aside, Stella responds matter-of-factly, "Sex after the third date is just a suggestion. If you do it before or after, it makes no difference whatsoever. Every couple is different, it simply depends on what you're comfortable with."

I shift nervously from side-to-side.

"So, its normal for me to want to... you know, with Wes? Even if this is only our second date?"

Placing her hands on my shoulders, Stella stops my restless fidgeting and looks me deep in the eyes.

"Lou, it's perfectly normal to feel what you're feeling. I mean come on, you've seen the man, if you *didn't* want to jump his bones, I would be concerned."

I chuckle uneasily, unsure of what to make of the hormones racing through me.

Adjusting her grip, Stella gives me a little shake, "That being said, there's no pressure to do anything tonight. Go have fun and see what happens. If it feels right, go for it, if not, don't. Wes is a good guy, he won't care either way."

Some of the pressure lifts from my shoulders and I exhale heavily.

"About what Wes said earlier, I hope you know he didn't mean anything by it. Cody doesn't have the energy for anyone right now, not just you."

I scan my roommate's face for her reaction, but Stella gives nothing away as she flicks a braided end over her shoulder, "I know."

Something in her tone tells me there's still hurt lingering below the surface, but before I can prod any further Stella raises a finger to silence me.

"No more stalling. It's time for the biggest decision of the night."

The butterflies in my stomach start to flutter, "And what's that?"

"Figuring out what you're going to wear, of course." Stella's face breaks into a grin and I burst out laughing.

When it comes to priorities, my roommate always has hers in order.

CHAPTER 25

Wes

I didn't do it on purpose.

Okay, that's a lie. I totally did.

But come on, when a golden opportunity falls into your lap, you can't just brush it off like, *oh, maybe next time*. That's how you die from a total freak accident. Like falling off a skyscraper. Or getting pulled over at airport security.

It's universally known that if you give karma the finger, you get the finger in return. Call it bad luck, bad energy, or just plain old bad vibes, the fact remains that if you disrespect the universe, she will disrespect you back.

So when Trip's knock intercepted my dash from the shower to my room I couldn't not strut over and swing the door open wide. It would have been rude to leave my guest outside and I'm not about to sign up for a lifetime of luggage searches.

Or, you know, a thousand-foot fall.

"Hola senorita." Using the worst accent possible, I fling the door open with a shit-eating grin plastered to my face. My smile falters as I register the girl on the other side.

Holy shit. I've forgotten how to breath.

"Uh, Wes?"

The vision in front of me tilts her head, making the golden-brown waves slide off her shoulder and reveal the thin black spaghetti strap of her dress.

Words, Wes. Use your words.

"Hm?"

The moan-like sound isn't quite what I had in mind, but it'll do. Trip's eyes light up with amusement, and my attention is dragged to the sparkles outlining the swirling shades of grey. Jesus, since when do I notice the makeup girls wear?

"You're wearing a towel."

The comment brings me back to reality and with a smirk, I casually lean against the doorframe. Trip's skittering gaze jumps from my chest to my abs, and back up to my face again. I'd be lying if I said I wasn't enjoying myself.

"I was in the middle of making dinner."

"In a towel?" A blush creeps its way along Trip's neck, making me wonder how far down it goes.

"You'd be surprised how productive I can be in this outfit." I throw her a wink and step aside to wave her in, "I was just about to get dressed when you knocked. Thought I'd give you a pre-show before dinner."

I try not to sniff Trip's hair as she walks by, but it's no use. Like an addict, I inhale as deeply as possible and grip my towel tighter. The thin material is not doing me any favours right now.

"Make yourself at home." I wave grandly towards the worn sofas and scurry towards my bedroom in search of clothes.

Keep it in the towel, Wes.

Keep it in the towel.

"Can I do anything to help?"

Trip's voice echoes through the crack I leave in my door and I let my towel fall to the floor.

Is it presumptuous to assume Trip will sneak a glance while I get changed? Probably. But hey, if she wants a peek, she wants a peek. I'm not about to deny my girl one of life's greatest pleasures.

"Nope, just sit back, relax, and prepare your taste buds to go to heaven."

Pulling a dark green polo shirt over my head, I run a hand through my wet hair and walk back to where Trip is trying to peek in the fridge.

"Get your hands out of there! Don't ruin the surprise."

Trip jumps back, laughing, her short black dress swishing with the motion. Smooth, slender legs distract me momentarily as I march over to protect the surprise.

"What are we having?"

I slap her prying hands away, creating a protective bubble around the fridge with my body.

"If I tell you, it won't be a surprise."

Trip sighs and looks around the room, "Always so dramatic. Do you want me to set the, uh, TV stand?" I chuckle and shake my head.

Given the mandatory meal plan for freshmen, the kitchen – if you can call it that – is more for emergency ramen than actual food. No oven, no stove, and no dining table. Taber offers first years the bare minimum with a small heating plate and a microwave. Luckily, given the meal on tonight's menu, there wasn't much need for anything more than that.

"Nope."

Gorgeous grey eyes narrow with suspicion as I carefully open the fridge and place various containers into a grocery bag. I flash her a dimpled grin and haul the bag over one shoulder.

"Now, if you would be so kind as to follow me..." Letting my voice trail off to build anticipation, I lead Trip out the door and into the hall.

Remnant beams of sunlight streak through the dimly lit corridors, giving the campus an eerie glow. Looking back to make sure Trip's still with me, I smile at the sight of her eyes fixating on the sinking sun.

"Almost there." Whispering, I slowly push open the side doors.

"Is this... are we in the courtyard?"

Delight fills Trip's voice as familiar cobblestones come into view.

"I can neither confirm nor deny."

I lead her through rows of flowers until we arrive at a makeshift table lit with candles and a checkered cloth thrown over top. Two stolen benches line either side, giving it a slight homeless vibe, but one that fits the scenery perfectly.

Trip gasps, "Oh my gosh, Wes. You did all this?"

I shrug, offering a sheepish smile, "Nico helped. If we get reported to campus security for stealing these benches though, you better come bail us out."

Those benches were fucking heavy. Nico and I aren't small guys, but it still took two of us to carry the wooden slabs off to the side. The worst part of the situation was when our struggle was witnessed by no less than five girls walking by, each one stopping to offer assistance.

Nico and I still don't talk about it.

"Deal."

Laughing, Trip settles herself on the far bench, crossing her delicate legs at the ankles. Letting my eyes roam over the extra two inches of skin revealed, I turn my attention back to the task at hand: carefully placing each container on the relatively small table and passing my guest her napkin and utensils. A plastic knife and fork fall out of Trip's napkin, and she raises her eyebrow in amusement.

"Curtesy of the cafeteria." I pass her a paper plate – also from the cafeteria – and wave a hand over the laid-out feast, "Help yourself."

Trip inches forward to peer into the closest one, a smile stretching across her face as she studies the contents, "I'm not sure what I was expecting, but this... this is perfect."

I beam at the praise and pass Trip a taco shell.

Full disclosure: I can't cook for shit. Hence the meal choice that is ninety percent cutting and ten percent cooking.

Hey, I'm not just a pretty face you know.

Grabbing a shell from the pile, I start filling one for myself, "I figured it was the least I could do after our last date ended up in the emergency room. How is Stella doing by the way?"

Trip reaches for the salsa, and I nudge it closer, "I think she's doing better, I mean it's hard to tell sometimes. Stella doesn't open up easily."

A slight frown tugs at Trip's brows.

I think back to her roommate's reaction at the hospital. Even as someone who doesn't know Stella well, it was pretty obvious there was more to the story than just Cody's injuries.

"Has she opened up to you at all?"

I bite into my taco and wince. The ground beef is a little more cooked than I thought.

"We had a good talk this morning, but it definitely stung when I found out how much she's been keeping from me." I nod in understanding, trying not to cough from the charred meat stuck in my throat.

"That... makes sense." I wheeze out the words and suck in a lungful of air. God, I didn't know ground beef could taste this bad.

"Did you tell her how you've been feeling?"

I casually move the meat container off to the side so Trip can't reach it. I hope she likes vegetables.

"Ya, I did. The conversation itself was really good, and she's still the closest friend I've ever had... but I guess I'm still a bit tender." Suddenly, Trip covers both cheeks with her hands, "I'm sorry, this isn't what we should be talking about. You don't need to hear about this."

Now it's my turn to frown, "Hey, I want to hear about this. Life isn't always sunshine and rainbows, most of the time it drop kicks you in the face and leaves you bleeding in the gutter."

Trip blinks at me, her lips pulling into a wry smile, "That is quite the visual."

I lean forward to rest my elbows on the table, "It's true though. Life is a trainwreck with short intervals of smooth sailing sprinkled in between. But here's the thing, Trip. I want to be in your life, and that means being a part of the good, the bad, and the ugly. Excuse the cliché."

I dab my mouth with a paper napkin as though I'm wiping off the residue of the overused phrase.

"No matter how crazy amazing or utterly horrible your day is going, I want to hear about it. I want to be a part of it."

I abruptly finish my monologue and lean back on my bench, suddenly aware my rush of verbal diarrhea may have my date running scared.

Looking across the candlelit table, I see tears glistening in Trip's eyes. The sight makes me want to scoop her up in a hug, but I hold back, knowing she probably wants some space from the creeper who just dumped eighteen years of devotion onto her.

"Wes, I..." Trip swallows thickly, voice dropping just below a whisper, "I want to be part of your life too."

Relief floods my veins and a smile stretches across my face.

"In that case, cheers."

I raise an imaginary glass – another thing I forgot to bring – and tilt in her direction.

"Cheers to going on a terrible yet never boring ride together."

She pretends to knock her glass against mine and I grab her hand, bringing it to my lips for a kiss.

Those rare, perfect moments I was just talking about? Pretty sure I'm in the middle of one right now.

Lou

If you asked me two months ago, whether I was a romantic, my answer would have been a nonchalant shrug. Neither here, nor there, just doing my best to keep my head down and get through life as socially pain-free as possible.

But now, if you asked me that same question, I am not sure what my answer would be. The feelings stirring up inside me as I look at the guy across the table feels too genuine to throw a label as cheesy as romance on it. But maybe that's just it. Maybe you spend your whole life seeing the world through one perspective that when a new one comes along, when a new *person* comes along, suddenly all the labels you applied to yourself, and to the world around you, suddenly become transformed to the point where you can't remember where they stemmed from in the first place.

Oh God. I am starting to sound like Professor Anderson.

"I really am sorry about the meat. I swear I only had it on high for like two minutes."

It only took about ten minutes for Wes to confess his lack of cooking skills, and by that time he had already warned me to stay away from the burnt taco meat.

I raise an eyebrow in his direction, and he sighs, "Fine. It was probably more like twenty minutes. Or thirty."

I giggle and gesture towards the rest of the empty containers.

"At least the vegetables were impressively chopped. And I must say, the salsa was outstanding."

Wes barks out a laugh, shaking his head in agreement.

"The store-bought salsa was the highlight of the meal. Next time I'll take you to a proper restaurant, so we can eat meat without indigestion. Promise."

"I'll hold you to that." Smiling, I look around the table and clear my throat, "We should probably clean up, it's getting pretty late."

Wes gasps in horror, "But we haven't had dessert yet!"

I sneak a look at the empty grocery bag tucked beneath his bench, "I don't see any more food hiding in that bag, Wes."

He wags a finger at me, "You gotta start having more faith in me, gorgeous."

I feel my cheeks grow warm from the endearment.

"Well then, what's for dessert?"

Wes' gaze flicks to my lips before returning to my eyes. A slow smile spreads across his handsome face and I have to stop myself from sighing.

"Let me quickly run back to my dorm to get it. I'm afraid this option on the menu had to stay refrigerated." He stands up and starts stacking the containers back into the grocery bag. "You stay here, I'll be back in a flash." He throws me a wink but before he can go anywhere, I jump up and snag his arm.

"Or maybe we could have dessert back at your dorm?" My heart thunders in my ears as the words slip past my lips. Seeing Wes' eyes widen with surprise, I find myself adding, "It's getting a little chilly."

Green eyes trail down my arms, raising goosebumps on exposed skin that has nothing to do with the cool night air. Hastily removing the candles from the table, Wes bends down to gently drape the checkered cloth around my shoulders.

"Is that better?"

I nod and hug the tablecloth tighter around me. Grabbing the grocery bag with one hand, Wes nods towards the path from which we came, and together we make our way back to his dorm.

❧❧

"Aren't you going to guess what it is?"

Wes' voice echoes from where the top half of his body has disappeared into the refrigerator. I lean against the back of the couch, admiring the way his jeans hug the round curve of his butt. Wes definitely doesn't skip leg day.

"Ice cream?"

A muffled scoff echoes from the kitchen.

"Please, I deserve more credit than that."

Tussled black hair and a cheeky smile come into view as Wes straightens from behind the open door. The polo shirt Wes is wearing stretches tight across his shoulders, outlining the hard planes of his chest.

I swallow, remembering the towel from the pre-show earlier, and try to focus on the green eyes that seem to glow brighter against the dark forest colour of his shirt.

"Chocolate ice cream?" I offer the suggestion with an eyebrow wiggle as Wes struts over with a single glass bowl.

"Not even close. Close your eyes."

Sighing, I clap my hands over my eyes. The couch cushions dip as Wes sits down beside me. My body naturally tilts towards his with the movement and I feel his arm reach out to steady me.

"Okay... open them." Wes' warm breath tickles my ear, and despite the warmth radiating from his body, a shiver runs down my spine.

I slowly remove my hands, holding my breath as I take in the non-existent space between us. My bare thigh presses against Wes' jeans, his arm wrapped around my waist to keep me steady. My gaze travels up to the glass dish being pressed against my side and I gasp, "I was right!"

Wes chuckles, the sound vibrating through me, "Technically, the ice cream is just an addition. What do you think?"

A grin splits my face as I take in the delicious smell of the cafeteria's dessert poutine, complete with cinnamon sugar and chocolate sauce.

"I think dessert may very well beat our meatless tacos."

Wes smiles as he holds up two spoons, metal this time.

"Bon appetite."

Before Wes can finish his career as a waiter, I grab a spoon and the dish from his hands, dashing from the couch to make a breakaway. Given the four feet of space, I make it two steps from the sofa before Wes grabs me by the waist and wrestles me onto his lap.

"That was mine!" I squeal with outrage as he takes my spoon and steals the first bite, moaning loudly when the sweet blend melts on his tongue. I push against his chest to steal back my spoon, but Wes leans back and holds it just out of my reach.

"That's what you get for not wanting to share. Didn't your mother tell you sharing is caring?"

I scowl at his handsome face, the furrow of my brows deepening the divots of his dimples.

"You're annoying."

Wes clucks his tongue, scooping another large bite, "Maybe if you ask nicely, I'll let you have some."

I narrow my eyes at him, watching him slowly chew another bite of the poutine.

Fine, two can play at that game.

"Kind sir." Looking at him from beneath my lashes makes me see double but desperate times and all that.

"May I pretty please have some of *my* dessert?"

I flutter my lashes for extra effect and Wes laughs, "Don't appreciate the sarcasm, but I'll take it."

Beaming in triumph, I watch Wes scoop the perfect fry to ice cream ratio and offer it to me. Keeping my eyes trained on his, I lean forward and take the spoon in my mouth.

Sighing with content, I pull back and lick my lips, enjoying the way Wes' eyes track the movement. Gently removing the spoon from his hand, I dip it back into the dessert and hold it up to his mouth. He opens without hesitation, and I watch breathlessly as he skims his tongue along the bottom of the spoon before taking a bite.

Whoa. Does this qualify as foreplay?

Caught in an emerald stare, I feel my breath catch as Wes raises his finger to lightly trace my bottom lip. His finger runs past my jaw, gently tapping the soft skin of my throat as I swallow. Wes leans forward and I meet him halfway, our lips crashing together in a tangle of tongues and teeth.

Any slow burn from earlier falls away as a fiery need sweeps its way across the room. I grip the front of Wes' polo shirt tightly as he hoists my hips higher on his own. My dress creeps up until it's just the thin lining of my panties against the hard ridge of his jeans.

I gasp at the sensation and the sound seems to trigger something inside Wes, making him abruptly pull away. Our heavy breathing fills the room, and Wes' gaze scans across my flushed face.

"Maybe we should slow down. Unless you're ready, I mean..."

He curses, trying to shift my hips so they aren't pressing against the bulge in his pants. I bite back a smile at his fumbling.

"Not that I'm expecting anything, I just... shit. This is coming out all wrong, and I can't think when you're looking at me like that." Shaking his head, Wes squeezes his eyes shut, sexual energy radiating from his every pore.

Shifting so my body position is less of a distraction, I softly tap his chest.

"Wes?"

Peeling his eyes ever-so-slowly open, I can tell from Wes' heavy breathing that he's feeling out of control right now. He shifts beneath me, an uncertain expression on his face. I reach out to brush the dark, midnight strands from his forehead, and smile at the overconfident rookie who seems to have lost his confidence.

"Will you have sex with me tonight?"

CHAPTER 26

Wes

Any rational thought leaves my brain as I process the words leaving Trip's luscious lips.

Remember who said the famous line, consent is sexy? That's right, this guy. My motto is looking pretty damn good to all you lonely fellas out there, isn't it.

Snapping back to the situation at hand, I can't help the uncomfortable clench forming in the base of my stomach. And no, it has nothing to do with the fact Trip's golden-brown waves are close enough to touch. Well, not completely.

Although Trip's question implies that she is on board with the whole getting-it-on-tonight, I'm pretty sure she's still a virgin. Don't get me wrong, that doesn't bother me in the slightest, but it might change things for her.

Some girls want their first time to be special. Hell, *I* want Trip's first time to be special, but most of all, I don't want her to feel pressured. I don't want her to wake up in the morning with regrets, and I especially don't want her to get scarred halfway through and feel like she can't say something. That was one of the pieces that broke Lace and I'll be damned if it happens to Trip as well.

I take a deep breath and look at the gorgeous girl perched on my lap.

"That depends." My eyes flick from one grey iris to the other, noting every micro expression that passes through, "Do you trust me?"

Surprise flickers across Trip's features, her head tilting the slightest bit in response.

"Of course, I do."

The certainty in her tone causes my chest to loosen by the smallest degree.

"Okay, then I need you to promise me something."

Dark memories tug at my conscious, images of Lacey curled up on the kitchen floor flashing through my head.

"If at any point you want to stop or feel uncomfortable, you have to promise me you'll say it. No matter how awkward or embarrassing it might feel, promise me you'll say something."

Trip blinks in surprise, taking a second to let my words sink in.

Finally, she nods. "I promise."

Giving her a beaming smile, I exhale the weight of the past off my shoulders, "In that case, I would love to have sex with you tonight."

She laughs and two spots of pink stain her cheeks.

"Is there anything I can do to make tonight special?" Pulling her close, I murmur the question against her neck, using my teeth to nip the sensitive skin below her ear. She shudders in response.

"You've already made it special."

Grinning like a fool, I swoop her up in my arms and carry her like a newlywed to my room. I kick the door shut behind us and place her carefully on the bed, sitting back on my heels to wait for her permission to continue.

Hey, I wasn't messing around. The ball is in Trip's court tonight.

Smiling coyly, Trip runs her fingers down to the edge of her dress and pulls it off with one tug, leaving her wearing a non-existent pair of lacy underwear. My mouth goes dry as I take in the view, round breasts and slim waist begging to be touched. But still, I wait, letting my eyes feast on the delicate skin as Trip settles herself down on my blue comforter.

Only once she beckons me closer, I move from my position, letting my body stretch along the length of hers, soft skin pressing against my clothed frame.

Small hands tug impatiently at my shirt, and with a grin, I pull it over my head and drop it to the floor. The sight of my bare chest has Trip gasping with delight.

"So many bumps!"

I chuckle, pressing a soft kiss against her collarbone, "Most people call those muscles, but bumps work too."

My voice goes hoarse as Trip's hands tease their way up my torso, virgin hands exploring undiscovered territory.

She winds her hands through my hair and tugs me down for a kiss. I oblige, letting Trip set the pace. I am a gentleman, after all.

Her nails run down my back, the sting making my hips thrust involuntarily. She moans at the friction of my jeans, and I take the cue to head south. Running my tongue down her neck to her collarbone, her arched back is all the encouragement I need to keep going until I hit pert nipples.

Checkmate.

Teasing the left bud with my lips, I glance up to make sure my girl is still on board. Amused eyes look back at me.

"If I want to stop, I'll say something. I promised."

Her words snap the last of my restraint and I turn my attention back to the mission at hand: seeing her misty grey eyes roll back with pleasure.

Sucking her nipple into my mouth, Trip gasps and arches against me, giving me better access to slide my hand down between her legs. Keeping my mouth fused on her breast, I gently stroke the thin material, making Trip squirm beneath me. Switching to her other side to keep things equal, I resume stroking until I can feel Trip's wetness soak through the lace.

"WES!"

Trip's shout pulls my mouth off her nipple with a pop and I snatch my hand away from her centre.

"What? What's wrong?"

I shift so my weight isn't on top of her, and Trip slaps me upside the head.

"I didn't tell you to stop! Get back down there and finish what you started."

Relief collapses onto me, and the furious expression on her face has me laughing out loud.

"I meant no disrespect, madame. I was just making sure you were okay. You're new to this... aren't you?"

Trip rolls her eyes and the familiar reaction has me smiling from ear-to-ear.

"Yes, I'm a virgin, but quit worrying about me. I'm not going to break, okay?"

Her words hit a nerve and suddenly there's a lump in my throat that wasn't there before.

Jesus, you would think this is *my* first time.

Coughing to get rid of the emotion clogging my airway, I ask her one last time, "So, just to be clear... you want me to continue?"

The scowl Trip sends my way sums up our relationship perfectly.

Holy shit, I'm in a relationship.

"I don't know why you are still talking when you have other business to attend to." She huffs and crosses her arms, snapping my attention back to the body that is mine for the taking. A smirk creeps its way across my face, and I do the only thing I can do.

Head down to finish the business I started.

And in case you were wondering, pun intended.

Lou

Holy mother of...

I cry out as an orgasm hits me, Wes' face buried deep between my legs. Limbs trembling from the climax, I watch as Wes resurfaces from the edge of the bed and crawls his way back up towards me.

The sight of his glistening lips sends a flush of heat to my face, a forbidden awareness of what he just did sending pleasure rushing through my body.

Planting his lips back on mine, Wes settles himself between my legs, and I moan at the bulge pressing against my bare core. Somewhere in the time of me losing my panties and Wes doing dirty things with his mouth, the situation in his jeans seems to have gotten bigger.

A lot bigger.

I wiggle my hips against the ridge, causing Wes to tense on top of me. His eyes scan my face, silently asking the question that's been bothering him all evening.

Do I trust him? Ever since the first week at Taber, there hasn't been anyone I have trusted more. Whenever I needed an escape, whenever I needed a hug, it's always been Wes who was there.

My heart expands knowing even now, when Wes has *bigger* issues to think about, he still puts me first. My comfort is his number one priority, even when his own desires have the potential to be front and centre.

"I think it's time you took those off."

I whisper the words, giving the permission he's been hunting for this entire night. Stripping off his jeans with lightning speed, I giggle as his boxers go flying across the room.

Rejoining me on the bed in all his naked glory, my breathing turns shallow as his hard shaft presses into me. Unsure of what to do, I freeze in panic, my body stiffening on the bed. Immediately noticing my discomfort, Wes takes my palm and gently guides my hand down, letting me explore his length at my own leisure.

Wrapping my hand around the smooth skin, I experiment this way and that, watching his reaction range from groans to miniature thrusts against my hand. My initial discomfort wears off as Wes continues to give me free reign, his own fingers tracing random patterns up and down my body.

Finally, after what seems like forever, Wes reaches over to grab a condom from the rickety nightstand. Shifting so he can crawl between my legs, I watch him roll the rubber on and carefully place himself at my entrance.

"This might hurt."

His words serves as a warning but all I see is the tender emotion shining in his eyes. Gripping his shoulders with my hands, I give him a terse nod.

"Ready."

Trailing his hands down to lift my legs higher on his waist, Wes starts to sink into me. The sensation is foreign, the pressure almost overbearing as Wes inches his way inside. It doesn't hurt per se, but my grip on his shoulders doesn't ease until he stops moving.

"Okay?"

Wes' voice comes out gruffer then usual, the control he's struggling to hold on to visibly straining through the tendons on his neck. Unclasping my hands from his shoulders, I give him two thumbs up.

With a laugh, Wes starts to move and my hands fly to the firm cords of muscle running down his back. Given the chance, Wes' body would make a great climbing wall.

My legs grip his hips tightly as his movements become faster, the earlier pressure transforming from uncomfortable to pleasurable. The friction between us grows and soon I find myself on the verge of yet another climax. Digging my nails into Wes' back, I hold on as he takes us on a ride, climbing higher and higher until finally his fingers find their way back to my centre and pushes me right over the edge.

Body exploding for the second time this evening, I feel my eyes roll back in my head as pleasure overwhelms my senses. Finishing with a few jerky movements, Wes flops down beside me, the sound of our heavy breathing echoing off the stained walls of his dorm room.

"That was fun."

I roll to my side, giving the man beside me a little nudge, "Any chance we could do that again?"

Chuckling with his eyes closed, Wes reaches over and pulls me close.

"We can do that all night, every night if you want."

"Really?" Excitement weaves its way into my voice as I wiggle closer, reaching up to brush the damp strands of hair from his forehead.

"Really."

Feeling sedated and content, I place my palm over his chest and watch it rise and fall to the rhythm of his breathing.

"Who hurt you?"

The question blurts out of my mouth before I can think about shoving it back in. Nothing like ruining a nice moment with curiosity.

"Hm?" One green eye blinks at me, sleep and confusion mingling together.

"Who made you so paranoid about virgins?"

I've already asked the question, so I may as well see it through.

Wes sighs and rolls onto his back, keeping one arm wrapped around me.

"Remember when you asked why my sister was my prom date?"

I nod, eyes flicking to the grainy photo taped above his desk.

"She'd been dumped by her first serious boyfriend about a month prior. We found out after they broke up that the punk not only spent months verbally abusing her but he gave her an ultimatum the night they broke up: have sex with him or they were done."

I fall silent, hearing the pain seep into Wes' voice.

"She gave him her virginity, but it still wasn't enough. He ended things that same night, and I found Lacey bawling her eyes out on the kitchen floor. Five days later she tried to take her own life."

I gasp quietly, looking at the picture of the playful girl executing a curtesy. So full of life, yet so much sorrow hidden just below the surface.

My mind flashes to my roommate, and the scars lining her torso. It's easy to forget the marks on the outside are nothing compared to the ones on the inside.

"I'm sorry."

I wrap my arms around the rookie to make up for everything my words fail to do. Wes leans into the embrace, as if the past is a burden he doesn't want to carry any longer.

"The worst part? No one saw it coming. *I* didn't see it coming."

An angry glint shines in his eyes, and I wish I had the power to make it go away.

"It wasn't your fault, Wes. I'm sure you did everything in your power to support Lacey in the aftermath, but you couldn't force Lacey to leave a toxic relationship. Even if you did know what was going on, chances are you wouldn't have been able to convince her to leave, especially if she's any bit as stubborn as you."

A rueful smile plays on Wes' mouth, and I know I've hit the nail on the head.

"You know, this guy once told me that here at Taber you can be anybody you want to be. Maybe it's time to try the version of yourself that forgives the past."

I fall silent, hoping my words didn't overstep.

"You're right." Wes shifts so we're lying facing each other, nose-to-nose, on the bed, "I need to let go of the past. Nico's been saying the same thing for a while."

He exhales heavily, dark lashes fluttering against his pale skin. Why do guys have the nicest eyelashes?

"But if I were to say this new version of myself wants to be in a semi-stable relationship with a girl who can't carry boxes to save her life, what would you say to that?"

My heart slows to a stop as emeralds sparkle back at me.

"I would say she needs a guy who isn't afraid to bulldoze his way to her mother's phone number."

Laughter rumbles from Wes' large frame, and I find myself smiling to the point of aching cheeks.

"Well then, Miss One Trip. What do you say about being my girl-friend?"

I tap my chin in consideration, "I suppose that doesn't sound too bad."

Moving with the speed of a predator, I swing my leg over Wes' waist and shift until I'm straddling him. Rubbing myself shamelessly on his hardened length, I shoot him a wicked grin.

"Contingent, of course, on your next performance."

EPILOGUE

Stella

You didn't think you would read this whole book without my POV, did you?

I'm disappointed. Really.

Everyone knows the side characters are the ones who make novels interesting. They are the key to the protagonist's success – just look at Frodo. His best buddy Sam had to *literally* carry that hobbit's ass up the side of a volcano. If that's not MVP material, then I don't know what is.

"I think I see them!"

I follow Lou's pointed finger to the ugly beige car making its way towards Taber's parking lot. Black fumes cough out the rear, and I can't hold back my grimace.

"Your boyfriend might be the definition of sex appeal, but Lola couldn't win a beauty contest if her life depended on it."

My remark draws a smile from my roommate as she reaches up to fiddle with her new necklace. One week after their official status, Wes went out and bought Lou her first present – a silver necklace with a small T pendant hanging off the end.

Yup, he totally stole the idea from HSM, swapping out the name Troy for Trip, but you know what? The cuteness level is high enough that I'll give him a pass. The yellow daisy sparkling on the chain is a nice addition.

The rust bucket rattles to a stop and the passenger door swings open. My stomach drops as a pair of black Nike hit the ground, but the nerves instantly vanish as the lean frame of Wes' friend Nico comes into view. Rust goes flying as the driver's door swings open and Wes struggles to unlatch himself from the manic grip of his vehicle.

After a few minutes of comic struggle, Wes finally manages to unfold himself from the car, and we watch him scurry over to help Nico extract the third passenger from the backseat.

Cheers break over the crowd as a blonde fauxhawk comes into view. Face swollen with varying degrees of bruising, Cody smiles and slowly makes his way towards the varsity dorms – where Lou, me, and the entire lacrosse team are waiting. Each step looks more painful than the last, but Hunter lets out a wolf whistle all the same. Laughter rings out over the crowd and the battered captain gives everyone a cheerful wave.

The MRI scan came back to show the internal swelling needed to be monitored a few more days before his release. There was no talk of visitors, but I'm pretty sure Wes and Nico made a couple of food trips to the hospital. Wes never once mentioned Cody asking for me, so as far as I'm concerned, my presence was neither missed or needed.

My roommate sniffles beside me, and I look over to see tears streaming down her face. Lou isn't the only one crying, looking around, I spy a few glassy eyes among the lacrosse team.

"Can we count on you for morning practice, Cap?"

A redhead steps forward – Mason, I think his name is – and folds Cody into a hug.

"Hell, someone's got to whip your sorry asses into shape."

Chuckles ring out as Wes steers his captain in our direction.

Lou sighs, "Here we go."

I shoot her a glare. Roommate backup is always needed but not always welcome.

The green and yellow bruising on Cody's face makes his molten brown eyes look even darker in the sunlight. Stamping down the urge to squeal and throw my arms around him, I offer Cody a cool nod as he lumbers by.

See? I can be subtle when I want to be.

Choosing to ignore my attempts at nonchalance, the bruised defenseman walks right up and wraps his arms around me. Cursing my suddenly active tear ducts, I feel my eyes well up for the first time since game day as he presses me into his soft hoodie.

I'm probably allergic to his fabric softener.

"Missed me, Stel?"

Even with his short stature, Cody has to bend to whisper the words in my ear. Between the two of us, I'd be hard pressed to say who has the worst case of little man syndrome.

"Didn't even notice you were gone." I whisper the words back and Cody laughs, shaking his head as he pulls away.

Wes somehow found his way back to Lou, and the two of them look sickeningly adorable together. Cody and I exchange bemused glances as the once-promiscuous rookie plants a sloppy kiss on Lou's forehead.

"You're the worst."

Grumbling, Lou wipes the slobber off with her sleeve. Wes chuckles and whispers something in her ear, making my roommate blush from the base of her neck to the tips of her ears.

Feeling like I'm intruding on a private moment, I clear my throat to remind the two lovebirds of my presence and turn to see Cody studying me.

"What?"

I mentally wince at the sharp edge to my tone. There's something about Cody that brings out my belligerent side like no one else. Actually, I know exactly what rubs me the wrong way about Taber's all-star defenseman, and it has nothing to do with his annoying habit to work out at the same time as me.

"Did Wes pass along my message?"

My eyes narrow as they flick from my gym buddy to the guy currently performing way too much PDA on my roommate.

"What message?"

Something flickers across Cody's face, but before he can respond, a shadow falls across us.

"Good to see you up and moving, Ellsworth."

Instantly taking a step away from me, Cody increases the space between us as the deep voice draws near.

And there it is. There's the divider that will always remain between me and Taber's lacrosse captain.

"Thanks for stopping by old man. It's good to see you too."

My brother grins at the response, his all-mighty presence shoving my own to the edge of existence. With a gentle clap on the back, Mo steers Cody towards the rest of his welcome party, no doubt eager to bask in the rookies' adoration. He is, after all, a legend here at Taber.

I sigh, turning to my roommate whose lips are swollen from the mauling they just underwent.

"Ready to go, Lou?"

Untangling herself from Wes, Lou gives him one last kiss before linking her arm through mine.

"Where are we headed?"

I shrug, "Anywhere but here."

Accepting my sullen mood without question, Lou starts humming as we walk away from the two men who make my life infinitely more complicated. Her tone is so off-key that it takes me a couple of seconds to realize what song she's singing.

"Lou?"

"Yes, Stella?"

A wide smile breaks across my face, "Is that One Direction I'm hearing?"

"Sure is. They are my new favourite punk rock band."

I burst out laughing, sneaking a glance at her All-American Rejects concert t-shirt. The baggy top hangs past her ripped mom jeans, doing absolutely nothing for her figure, but the smile on Lou's face shows a girl finally comfortable in her own skin.

And it's got to be the most beautiful thing I have ever seen.

Acknowledgments

I wrote this book for my beloved Granny, Louise MacNeil, but the truth is this book would not have been written without her. She was the first person to encourage my love of writing, telling me long before this novel that she could not wait to see my name in print. Thank you for the endless support, Granny. You are as much of this book as I am. Love you to the moon and back.

She's already been mentioned, but Mara Tepavac was my personal cheerleader from the moment I confessed I was writing a novel. She managed to find something positive in every single piece of writing I sent over, and let me tell you, some of that writing did not deserve to be supported. Without her endless enthusiasm, I honestly would not have had the confidence to finish the story she was determined to read. Thank you for everything, Mara. I hope you're ready for the next novel to fill your inbox.

A huge thank you goes to my family, who didn't end up with a varsity swimmer but a writer. Logan, you set a high sibling standard, but I wouldn't have it any other way. Dad, thank you for teaching me that through hard work comes results. I would not have accomplished half of what I've achieved in my few years without that mentality. Mom, thank you for refusing to read my novel until it was complete. I lost a good twenty years off my life waiting for your verdict but it was worth it. Your love and guidance keeps this family afloat, and we all appreciate you more than we say.

To my Grandad, Maurice Fielder, whose wry humour is the stuff of legend. I hope you get a kick out of seeing your name in print. Miss and love you.

To Michelle Baseden, who remains to be my favourite boss, workout partner, and role model to anyone who meets her. Thank you for letting me write during working hours. I would blame my phone skills on the distraction, but we both know that isn't true.

To Sharon Barr, who will always be my coach and mentor. You didn't know I was writing a book this summer but attending your conditioning swims was easily the highlight. I hope you enjoy this one.

To Elizabeth Feddema, who always has my back. We had a rough summer but we made it through. Can't say the future will be any easier, but at least we have each other. Thank you for all the love and support.

To Taylor Platt and Christine Stipanov, who are always down to hit the dance floor. Thank you for the encouragement you both showed me along this journey.

To Karena Peterson, who would have happily joined the CanDoobies Club. Thank you for promising to love this book. Chaz would have been lucky to have you.

To Mrs. Basra, who introduced me to the joys of English back in high school. Sorry for always trying to ditch class early.

To Riley Woods, who said he would read my book then did. Thank you for putting the research articles aside for a couple of days. I hope it was worth it.

To everyone who had a hand in making my own freshman experience memorable, you know who you are. Studio Thursdays, Lime Saturdays, and its best if I don't mention the rest.

To anyone who opened this book and made it to the end. Thank you for choosing to spend your time reading Wes and Lou's story.

Last but not least, celebrity shoutout to Elle Kennedy, who introduced me to the New Adult genre with *The Deal*. Thanks for showing me the type of book I would love to write.

ABOUT AUTHOR

Jade Everhart writes heart-warming romances with flawed characters and laugh-out-loud banter. When she's not using her own terrible meet-cutes as inspiration for her next novel, Jade spends her time listening to loud music and tearing up dance floors from the prairies of Southern Alberta to the glistening beaches of Miami.

Jade loves to hear from readers – connect with her on Instagram @authorjade_everhart.

Printed by Amazon Italia Logistica S.r.l.
Torrazza Piemonte (TO), Italy